THE FOURTH LEVEL

MASQUERADE

BOOK THIRTEEN

NICHOLAS HUNTLEY

First Edition, May 2020

WHITEWOLF PUBLISHING

Paperback ISBN 978-1-988765-36-5

Digital ISBN 978-1-988765-37-2

The text of this book is set in Times New Roman.

"Yea, though I walk through the valley of the shadow of death, I will fear no evil, for thou art with me; thy rod and they staff, they comfort me."

– St. David, the Prophet

Act 1, Scene 1

The aroma of freshly cut grass permeated around the field behind Lord Phoenix Secondary School. The sprinklers flickered as they hydrated the perimeter of the field and maintained the healthy green that lively grass carried. Before the school, the blossomed tulips pink and yellow tulips danced in the light breeze that flew in from the east where the sun had risen from on this summer morning. The sun brought with it a heavy heat that weighed down on the county from above. The vast blue sky was free of clouds, but no more blue as the light blue balloons that floated up at the top of the steps of the front doors from the small weights on the ground.

Above the main doors of the school entrance was a banner that read out, 'Congratulation Class of 2020,' and below the front doors of the school were open to reveal the polished tiled floors and each locker with its door open and inside cleaned out. The immediate classroom on the left had every desk pushed against the side of the wall with the chalkboard and through the other door, entering the south corridor, one could look into the cafeteria where the white lunch tables were spotless. The second-floor windows looking down into the cafeteria were opened and a custodian gently washed them from the other side with a cloth to leave them to be perfectly clear.

The second-floor corridor was quiet with no students in sight. The floors were equally flawless as below, but from here there was a distinct tranquility from the loneliness on this late-June day. The library doors were open, and behind the main counter the surfaces were clear and every detail organized. Each table was clear, chairs pushed in, and fans above them spinning gently. The bookshelves were packed with books, organized and ready for the next year. The computers at the back table shut off for this year as the ones in the computer lab.

Atop of the front desk of the library, several newspapers were stacked upon each other from the recent weeks, one detailing of the global turmoil as the world slipped into an economic depression, another of the crisis that has faced Zimmerman Corporation since the disappearance of its owner, and another describing the hostile situation in the Caribbean where indigenous children have been vanishing from their villages.

From within the halls, there was a gentle echo of an orchestra in the distance. From the staircase, returning down to the main hall, one could view the biographies of the small graduating class of this small high school posted on a wide corkboard in the hallway. Towards the rear corridor, there was a mess of equipment pushed against one wall, desks pushed against another wall with mirrors placed before them, and small group of graduates in blue gowns, mostly females, readying themselves like performers about to perform. Around the other corridor enroute to the gym, there was a red carpet with a sign that greeted parents as they reached the gymnasium where the doors were wide open and music poured from.

At the back of the gym, behind two large groups divided by a central aisle of foldable chairs, the school band played at full breadth, chiming the tropical tune of *Brejeiro* at its peak as they faced the stage on the other side where a podium was positioned at the center, and behind it, a foldable table decorated in a red table cloth with diplomas sat above.

To the left of the stage, at the set of concrete stairs that went down to the change rooms, the basement was quiet, but the door to the male locker room open. Inside, before the sinks and mirror, Diana, dressed in a cobalt blue dress, fixed the tie of

Tristan in a white dress shirt and dark green trousers as he looked down upon her lovingly. Behind the couple, hooked onto the walls of the toilet stalls, were two graduation gowns. Tristan continued to look at Diana as she fixed Tristan's appearance, brushing the side of his temples gently with her hands and then bringing down her hand over his cheek. Diana's dark brown hair had been straightened as she typically does it for a formal event. Tristan's hair was trimmed with no guard at the sides, a minor fade to the top where it was less than an inch tall – this appearance gave his hair an orange appeal.

Tristan carried with him tired eyes, but he shared a warm smile with Diana as the two looked at each other and she patted her hands on his chest to rid the front lapel of lint.

"I think that's fine," Tristan remarked to her. "I'll be wearing a gown over it anyways."

Diana stopped and looked back at him.

"But people will still be able to see the tie and your collar," Diana replied, scanning him. "I think you're right though."

"Are you going to fix my tie every day before I go to work in the future?" Tristan asked.

"For sure," Diana answered, "at least… for the first couple of weeks."

Tristan raised his smile and tilted his face down. He then looked back at Diana, looking into her royal blue eyes.

"Who am I that is so lucky to have you?" Tristan flirted.

Diana raised her smile and lowered her own head as she blushed.

"The one that I can't imagine myself without anymore," Diana simply said.

Tristan's phone vibrated. He took it out of his pocket and looked at the lock screen.

"Looks like they're here," Tristan plainly said.

"Good," Diana replied, going around Tristan to pick up their graduation gowns. "The ceremony is about to begin."

Tristan lowered his smile and carried a plain face as Diana turned behind him. His tone completely shifted and his face carried a serious overtone. He turned around and raised his emotion again as Diana handed him his gown.

· · · ·

Charlemagne stepped out of his sedan and looked out at Lord Phoenix Secondary from the curb. He was dressed in a dark grey suit, blue tie with a camera hoisted around his neck, but hung around the side. Charlemagne was clean-shaven aside from his moustache. He too had tired eyes, and his blue eyes were slightly faded to be a slightly steel color. Next to him, exiting from the back passenger seat, Charlemagne looked at his sister, Allodia de la Cabernet, who was dressed in a white gown. She carried with her a matching white purse. From the drivers' seat, Lacplesis exited, dressed in a suit, and from the seat behind him, Mavis Quinn, dressed in a black polka-dot dress. Charlemagne looked at the old school and then walked with the family and his protection towards the front steps where various parents were gathered.

Inside the school, Charlemagne quickly met with Richard and Jacqueline Huxley, Richard dressed in a moderate beige suit and yellow dress shirt. Jacqueline in a regal white gown with her hair tied back as it usually was. They were with their son, Peter Huxley, who was about as tall as his father if not an inch taller. He was handsome with his long medium-brown hair. Each of them shook Charlemagne's gloved right-hand and then Allodia's.

"Good to see you, Charles," Richard remarked. "Congratulations to both your children.

"Congratulations to your second," Charlemagne replied.

"Hello, Allodia," Richard greeted. "I haven't seen you in close to a year…"

"Yes, that's me," Allodia said with a smile. "Busy, busy, busy."

Charlemagne looked to the side and saw a man in a wheelchair, Mayor Cole Phillips, who was dressed in a black suit and with his wife and two daughters, Lila and Emilie. The family was conversing with the Graysons – Theodore and Grace Grayson who were also with their tall son, Alex Grayson. Charlemagne looked at the mayor with pity and then looked back to Richard who was conversing with Allodia.

"Anyways, why don't we all head in and sit together," Richard remarked. "It's almost nine o'clock."

"Certainly," Charlemagne replied, looking at his watch as the three of them proceeded to walk down the corridor to the gymnasium. "We wouldn't want to hold them up…"

"Are you and your family coming to the reception later this evening?" Allodia questioned as they walked.

"I'm afraid not," Richard replied. "I've hosting the Phillips and Graysons for a barbecue at my place instead."

"Oh…" Allodia quietly replied before turning to look forward as they entered the gym.

Charlemagne, Allodia and the Huxley couple took seats to the right-side of the gym. Charlemagne led them towards the company of some of his friends from town, including Kristoffer Kristoffersen who greeted him with a great hug and pat on the back, and Miklos and Tanya Horvath with their young boy.

Diana stood in front of the queue of the five graduating students at the rear corridor, looking into the gym. She glanced from the school band at the back of the room to the parents and guests, seeing Charlemagne with the Huxley couple, but Peter Huxley sitting apart from them and with the Graysons and Phillips. In total, there appeared to be less than twenty adults in the room, not including some faculty members and Mrs. Phillips who was in a black dress that contrasted her extremely fair skin. Behind her, Maia and Vivian conversed until Mr. Hughes returned and hushed them. The teacher received an okay from Mrs. Phillips at the front, and then he signaled Mr. Chopping, who was conducting the band students, to start playing music once the visitors had settled.

"Okay, Diana," Mr. Hughes stated. "You're on in, three, two, one…"

Diana walked in and proceeded from the door to the aisle between the two groups of seats. She held her head up high as she walked and came to the front of the right-side where there were five seats reserved at the front for the Class of 2020. Not too far behind her, Maia and then Vivian walked, followed by Tristan and then Aaron. Once the class was seated, the music settled down and Mrs. Phillips walked to the podium.

"Please rise for the national anthem," Mrs. Phillips remarked before walking to the side.

The ceremony proceeded with a signing of the Canadian national anthem, and once that was complete, the audience and graduating class sat down, and Mrs. Phillips returned to the podium. She held a smile as she looked at the audience.

"Well, here we are," Mrs. Phillips said, "all five of you made it. In all honesty, this class may be one of the smallest I've had the pleasure of seeing off, but they could really make quite a noise in the school, particularly Ms. Huxley and Ms. Grayson, but in my opinion (and this is not bias), they are a special group of students who will be dearly missed. In comparison to the

Class of 2021, there are more than triple of them in that class than with us here now. At one point, there were seven of you, and I know all of us in this room wish the best to the two students who had left us in the last years, but let this be a testament to the fact of life, which you now fully step into once you leave this property, and that in life, there are changes from how it was in the beginning to how it ends, including in yourselves than just those around you. However, I don't want to lament or reminisce in the last couple of years, but instead celebrate your triumphs as this is a commencement ceremony, a time to celebrate the start of something new."

Tristan tilted his head slightly down as he listened to the rest of the school principal's speech. He held a solemn face and appeared to be focused, but not on her words. His attention shifted as there was applause. Tristan raised his head and spirit, and aimlessly clapped with the others.

"I would like to now invite my son, who was selected among his peers last April to represent them as valedictorian, and deliver his own speech. Please come up, Aaron."

The audience and graduating class continued to clap as Aaron Phillips stood up from his seat next to Tristan and walked up to the podium to deliver his valedictorian speech. The applause settled as he stood behind the podium.

"On behalf of the five of us, I would like to express my gratitude towards both the faculty of Lord Phoenix Secondary School and to our family and friends, especially our parents, who have been with us on this journey of the last five years. All of us can express that this journey had not been an easy one, but on behalf of my fellow graduates, I say that we wouldn't exchange the time we spent in these halls where we learned more than just the curriculum set out by the provincial government, but were shaped to become ideal citizens of this town by the virtues and expectations set upon us. For that reason, I cannot express how thankful I am for those people in our lives who both taught us in the classroom, but also taught us in our homes.

"And from here ends our time in these halls and begins our time in the outer world where we will continue to grow, learn, and understand as our parents and teachers had once done, in keeping with an important cycle that sows the fabric of our community. However, this fabric is not just any fabric, but a hand-woven wool that has been gently and carefully put together with love and kindness. In the last five years, we have learned to not only to be kind, but also communicative, honest, pro-active, and courteous in all that we do. We have learned to love each other, to help each other, and the benefits of cooperation over conflict. However, we have also been taught not to be confident, strong, as well as humble and disciplined. All these virtues and more, my fellow graduates, we should seek to express wherever it is we go, even if it is far beyond the county or right here in our home realm, not simply because we are citizens of Allabrese and our actions are reflective of those around us, but because that is who we are, collectively, and for those of us who will remain here, it is these qualities that give us the place we call home the comfort we enjoy. All of us have our individual characteristics, but we are more than just them, and vice-versa. We are both ourselves and a collective group. We have been taught to do good whether it be for our family, community, or people – in the end, they are one and the same, and as my father taught me, it is this goodness that is like a light in a darker world. Allabrese is a bright, warm town because all of us exert this goodness. We are lucky to be from here… Today, some of us leave and some of us stay, but ultimately, our lives change and we graduate not only as students, but adolescents. Today, we begin our lives in this greater world as young adults and by our inherited virtues, even when we are alone, our virtues will see us shine like a light in a dark place, and it is this darkness that we should hope to flush out wherever it creeps its head, wherever we are..."

Tristan zoned out again. By the time the audience and his classmates were clapping, Tristan focused around him and clapped with them. Aaron returned to his seat next to Tristan while Mrs. Phillips continued to clap as she took the podium. She looked to the band and they started to play a soft-beat. Tristan paid attention.

"And now, we begin the receiving of the diplomas," Mrs. Phillips remarked, moving to the table behind her.

Mrs. Phillips stood in front of the podium with a diploma certificate in a crisp blue envelope with an engraved golden frame.

"Diana Anne Cambridge," Mrs. Rivers projected over the gymnasium.

Diana stood up and proceeded to walk up the steps at the side of the stage.

"Diana has been accepted into Declan Walham University in Harlech, British Columbia, where she intends to receive a Bachelor of Science," Mrs. Rivers expressed.

Diana took her diploma from Mrs. Phillips who smiled to her. The two shook hands and Charlemagne took a photograph while the audience clapped. Once Diana had received her diploma, she walked off the same way she came.

"Maia Celine Grayson," Mrs. Rivers said next, prompting her to rise from her seat as Diana had. "Maia has been accepted into the University of Alberta in Edmonton where she intends to receive a Bachelor of Arts with aims of becoming a psychologist."

Maia received her certificate and posed with Mrs. Phillips. She then came off the stage and returned to her seat.

"Vivian Clara Huxley," Mrs. Rivers said next, prompting her to rise from her seat. "Vivian intends to take a gap year and remain in Allabrese, where she hopes to help the community, especially here in Lord Phoenix Secondary School."

Vivian received her certificate and posed with Mrs. Phillips. She then came off the stage and returned to her seat.

"Tristan Luke Merrick," Mrs. Rivers said next, prompting him to rise from his seat and go receive his diploma. "Tristan has been accepted into the University of Harlech where he intends to receive a Bachelor of Science in Cellular, Anatomical, and Physiological Sciences before applying to medical school with aims of becoming a doctor."

Tristan approached Mrs. Phillips and received his diploma from her. She smiled to him and posed for Charlemagne to take a picture while the audience applauded. Diana looked at the meek smile that Tristan held as he posed. The two then shook hands and Tristan returned to his seat.

"Aaron Edgar Phillips," Mrs. Rivers finally said, prompting him to rise and go up the stage and receive his diploma from his mom. "Aaron intends to apply for the Nattau County Police to become a police member with the municipal police force."

Aaron took the diploma and received a hug from his mom. A camera flashed behind Tristan and the two then posed as the others had posed. Another flash was felt from behind Tristan. Tristan proceeded to zone out again between the flashes and loud claps. He gently shook his head as Aaron returned to his seat.

"Graduating class, please rise," Mrs. Rivers remarked.

Tristan stood up and the claps intensified. The audience stood up and gave them a standing ovation while the kids turned to them.

"Congratulations, Class of 2020," Mrs. Rivers projected over them.

Act 1, Scene 2

Once the graduation ceremony had ended, Diana and Tristan returned their blue robes and exited to join Charlemagne, Allodia, Mavis, and Lacplesis at the entrance of the school.

"Congratulations," Allodia expressed, taking Diana into her arms for a friendly hug. "To the both of you."

Allodia extended her reach to attempt to include Tristan, but Tristan was too large. She looked at him with a bit of surprise.

"You really have grown, haven't you?" Allodia expressed to him. "Look at you."

Tristan held a timid smile.

"Oh, both of you have grown," Allodia remarked, looking at Diana. "I'm sorry it's been so long since I was last able to see you – it's been almost a year and half now, hasn't it? You look nothing like the kids I met in Russia or went to the arctic with."

"Some might say that they aren't kids anymore," Charlemagne politely commented, looking to them with a proud smile. "Not after all they've been through…"

Tristan lowered his eyes for a moment before looking back at Allodia.

"Ho ho ho," Kristoffer laughed from behind. "Congratulations, you two!"

Tristan received a slap in the back from behind, causing him to tense his reflexes before receiving a great big hug from Kristoffer. Unlike with Allodia, Kristoffer's sheer mass allowed him to hug the both of them.

"Thank you, Kristoff," Diana replied, giving a warm smile and closing her eyes as he hugged the jolly old king.

The two broke off from him. Tristan held a slightly embarrassed smile, but his attention shifted as he saw the

Grayson, Phillips, and Huxley families all huddled together not too far away.

"Who's hungry?" Charlemagne chimed. "I have reservations for us at the Great Range Bistro, and I believe Miklos, Tanya, and Kristoffer will meet us there."

"Good idea," Allodia replied. "Boy, you sure had a small graduating class, but for sure that ceremony went on and on... It's almost noon!"

"Yes, I'll see you there then," Kristoffer remarked.

Diana gave off her own timid smile as she walked with her aunt, or rather, her distant cousin, and her boyfriend alongside Mavis to return to the car where Lacplesis waited. Kristoffer walked off with Holger and Hardrada who took them to a black sedan parked on the curb. Diana and Tristan stopped as they reached Charlemagne's vehicle, holding onto Tristan's arm as he held his hands in his pocket.

"I suppose I'll meet you at the restaurant," Charlemagne remarked, looking at his watch. "Drive carefully – don't dent the new truck, please."

"I'll be careful," Tristan replied in a simple tone.

"Good," Charlemagne nodded, opening the front passenger seat door.

Allodia looked at the couple briefly, eyeing their linked arms. She simply gave a pleasant, but confused smile as she opened her own car door and stepped inside before the two turned around and walked off. Tristan gave off a sigh as they went down the sidewalk and went to the parking lot. Allodia said nothing to Charlemagne.

"I can't believe we won't ever return to this school again," Tristan remarked, turning around to look at the place.

"Never say never," Diana replied.

"What do you mean?"

"Well, I'm sure Charlemagne, or actually, Allodia, had the same mentality, and yet here she was today to see us off," Diana said. "Who knows... maybe in the future, here we'll be again because of our own kids."

Tristan did not respond and simply looked at her. The two parted for a moment as they reached the brand new grey pickup truck in the parking lot.

"You'd raise our kids in Allabrese?" Tristan questioned.

"I don't see any better place to raise them," Diana answered. "As much as I love Harlech because it's my hometown, I would never raise our children in a place like that. Tristan, Allabrese has become our home – and I understand the pain that St. Nazaire brings to you for you to not want to return there ever again. At the same time, St. Nazaire never really was your hometown..."

Tristan looked at her plainly. Diana brought a hand up to his cheek. She looked at him and through his eyes. At first, she looked at him lovingly, but then her head tilted and she looked at him with a slightly confused expression. The look slightly intimidated Tristan as he looked back at her into her eyes. Tristan took Diana's hand at his cheek and tried to part from her.

Diana grabbed his hand and kept him near. She quickly embraced him. Tristan panted slightly, holding a mildly shocked face, but accepted Diana in his arms, tilting his head down as she held the left-side of her face against his chest. He rested his arms around her upper back.

"Home is wherever I am with you, but it is also where the people we care about live," Diana quietly said.

"They don't care about us."

"Don't be so presumptuous to assume what they think," Diana replied. "You're not omniscient."

"I would rather live somewhere else..."

"You want to live in utopia, but that doesn't exist..." Diana responded. "Not in this physical world. A town like Allabrese is as good as it gets. If we're alienated, it's because of what we've done."

Diana gave a light laugh.

"We're truly of the Cabernet household then," Diana stated. "Eccentric and estranged."

Diana parted from Tristan. He looked down at her with a neutral expression.

"We should head out," Tristan remarked. "I don't want Charlemagne asking what took us so long."

"Okay..." Diana quietly replied. "Let's go."

$$\bullet \ \bullet \ \bullet \ \bullet$$

Diana and Tristan met with Charlemagne, Allodia, and Mavis at the base of the stairs that went up to the Great Range Bistro. Lacplesis held the door for them as they entered and then walked behind Tristan as they went up. At the top of the stairs, they were received by a hostess and taken to a group of tables where there were balloons and Miklos with Tanya and their son alongside Lukas, his wife, and several other members of Charlemagne's private guard, including Holger and Hardrada who were with Kristoffer. Diana and Tristan were welcomed with an applause from all of them before they went to thank them.

Charlemagne and Allodia sat down with Mavis as the kids went to each of them, shaking their hands. Miklos shook Tristan's hand with a firm grip and Tanya hugged them. The couple gifted Tristan a military-style dagger, while to Diana they gave her a Romanian novel known in English as *The Forbidden*

Forest, in excellent condition as it was an early edition from 1978.

"Thank you," Diana expressed to them.

"The Forbidden Forest is a classic from my homeland," Tanya remarked. "We read it in school, and I'm sure you will enjoy it. I was surprised to find this copy in the local bookstore – I couldn't find it online."

"Wow," Diana replied. "I'll get to reading it as soon as I finish my current novel!"

"Here," Kristoffer said, handing Tristan a brown package. "Go on, open it!" he boasted with a hearted laugh, placing a hand on Tristan's shoulder.

Tristan opened the package, which revealed a small box. Inside the box, there was a brown leather watch.

"Oh, thanks…" Tristan said.

Kristoffer took the box and picked up the watch.

"Handcrafted, far superior than any you might find in these so-called department stores, and what not," Kristoffer stated. "Enjoy!"

Tristan took the watch into his hands.

"My old watch broke, so this is really handy," Tristan said, looking at the analog watch and each of the three complications. "What are the small circles within the clock?"

"A chronograph and a thermometer, and that there is a calendar," Kristoffer stated, taking a seat. "Did you know that you can determine north and south by the position of the sun with a watch?"

"No…" Tristan responded.

"Let me teach you…!"

Charlemagne looked on as he sat down at the opposite-side and corner of the table. He held a hand around a cold glass of beer and was comfortably leaning back in his chair with his left ankle above his knee.

"So," Allodia remarked, setting her glass of wine on the table and turning to her brother. "What's new with you?"

"Well, I've mostly been cooped up in Allabrese, given the global situation," Charlemagne replied. "I was contracted by the United Nations to travel to Japan and Asia over the pandemic, and after that, I stayed here to rest. I've been imputing some feedback on the development of our new laboratories in Harlech – Dr. Lambert, Barry, my old friend, has been overseeing that and since we're on a strict schedule, he had to miss the – Diana and Tristan's graduation."

"I see," Allodia replied, picking up her glass and taking a sip. "Tell me about the kids."

"Oh, they're kids no more," Charlemagne said with a sigh, taking a drink. "I suppose it has been three-years since I adopted them…"

Charlemagne leaned over and set his feet on the ground.

"I've offered them all I could hope to offer them," Charlemagne remarked. "Sometimes I wonder if it has been too much, but…"

Charlemagne looked at the couple as they held smiles as they were with Kristoffer. He didn't finish his sentence.

"Anyways," Charlemagne said, clearing his throat and looking to his sister. "What have you been up to other than the project in England? Plans to return to the Arctic? I'm sure Kristoffer would be keen to join – perhaps even the kids. The north is far more beautiful in the summer than when we went."

"Oh no," Allodia replied, shaking her head. "I mean, there is a trip planned, but I won't be going… No, I'm off to *Isla Paraiso* in the Caribbean."

"Isla Paraiso?" Charlemagne questioned with concern. "Isn't that where those islander children have gone missing?"

"Yes," Allodia confirmed. "Several indigenous children have been disappearing from the villages there, but that isn't the primary reason for my visitation. Instead, I'm diverting some of our resources to support a relief mission sponsored by our very own parents. I'm going to go see and help them."

Charlemagne scoffed, shaking his head, and replied, "Help? When has our father ever asked for help?"

"Mom has asked for help, and I'm going to deliver," Allodia argued. "They're trying to help the locals, especially since they've become the victims to some deforestation in addition to the disappearances. She's worried about dad, and I offered to send some security to help keep the peace, but the presence of firearms wouldn't sit well with him. Instead, I'm going to head own down and lend a hand – on my own time."

Charlemagne didn't respond as he looked forward.

"You know, some are blaming Cabernet Industries for the disappearances," Allodia remarked. "At least, that's what I've heard from Gilbert."

"Gilbert does like to exaggerate," Charlemagne responded.

"And then others are blaming this forestry company – Obelisk. There's a conspiracy that they are the ones behind the disappearances to try and get the indigenous population to sign a treaty with the local government, but that won't happen. I'm don't believe it since it doesn't make sense and there's no proof."

"What does our father make of it all?" Charlemagne questioned.

"He believes that the youth are leaving the villages and going into the main town in search of work – dangerous work that might get themselves in trouble or even killed."

Charlemagne didn't respond again as he looked forward.

"The subject of the disappearances, although tragic, is really none of my concern though," Allodia stated. "My flight to Isla Paraiso leaves tomorrow and I'll be there for the entire summer."

Allodia paused as she looked at her brother, resting her elbow on the table and her head with her hand.

"You know, the island is extremely beautiful, although very humid and hot this time of year," Allodia said. "And due to travel restrictions, it'll be quieter. My flight is one of the only permitted through due to our charitable intentions. If you want to treat the kids to a nice, peaceful summer vacation, this might be it... You could also see mom and dad. When's the last time you've seen them?"

Charlemagne looked forward again and shook his head.

"The last time I saw either of them, it was before they left the manor for the last time," Charlemagne answered. "That was the same day that our father resigned as chairman of Cabernet Industries... we argued that day. I haven't talked to him since... him that is. I've been in regular contact with mum, and she had told me about this little project around last month when I returned from Asia. We exchange letters in the post."

Allodia looked at her brother.

"Come and see them," Allodia asked. "Not even for the kids, but for yourself, Charles. The pair of them aren't going to get any younger... this could be the last chance you get before they pass on."

Charlemagne tilted his head. He looked at his gloved hand.

"I'll have to think about it," Charlemagne responded. "It would be nice to see mum in the least, even though I never wanted to see that miserable nutter."

Allodia sighed.

"Please think about it," Allodia replied. "And soon, because my flight leaves from the airfield tomorrow – it's a private charter, so if the three of you, or even just you want to come with me, it shouldn't be any trouble. Although, if you don't want to come, perhaps let the kids travel with me? The island is beautiful, that's why the Portuguese explorers named it 'Paradise Island.'"

Charlemagne sighed.

"Yes, we'll see," Charlemagne expressed, finishing his beer. "We'll just have to see."

Act 1, Scene 3

At the end of the party, Charlemagne and Allodia were driven back to the manor with Lacplesis and Mavis. Not too soon afterwards, Diana and Tristan arrived and rejoined their guardian and his sister on the patio as it was now late afternoon. Charlemagne walked out from the trophy room. The French window doors were wide-open and he held a bottle of champagne in his hands. Diana wore the same dress, which worked well outside, while Tristan had rolled up his sleeves. Charlemagne had taken off his blazer, but kept his gloves on as he had his sleeves down.

"Ah, here we are," Charlemagne remarked, stopping at the circular glass table where four flutes were positioned.

Charlemagne popped the cap. Diana stepped back as it went off and Tristan flinched. Foam poured out and touched onto the patio floor as Charlemagne brought the liquid into each glass and then sat the bottle down.

"Now, although I'm not one to agree with laws," Charlemagne remarked with a smile to the kids, "underage drinking, and even then, excessive drinking, is not the sort of decadence I'm prepared to tolerate in this home – that being said, today is the day the pair of you have left high school, so an exception to that rule, as well as the fact that the pair of you are to turn eighteen in the next half of the year, I believe I can permit one celebratory glass of *mousseux*."

Charlemagne took a glass, followed by Allodia, and then Diana and Tristan.

"Cheers," Charlemagne toasted. "Let the next year be one of fortune and perseverance!"

The four of them touched glasses and then drank the sparkling wine. Diana slightly shook her head with distaste upon taking a sip of the wine. Tristan drank almost half of the champagne without reaction, similar to the adults. The four of them laughed as Diana reacted to the bitter taste of alcohol for the first time.

"What an awful taste," Diana stated. "How does anyone enjoy this?"

"I don't see what the problem is," Tristan replied, holding his glass before finishing the wine.

"Oh yeah?" Diana questioned. "You better not get too used to that taste, because I *hate* alcohol."

Tristan gave a nervous laugh, and quickly evaded eye contact with her as he sat down at the table. Both of them set their flutes before them, while Charlemagne poured some more wine for both himself and Allodia before he returned inside with the bottle.

"So, tell me about each other," Allodia remarked, crossing her legs. "How long have the pair of you been like this?"

"Like what?" Diana questioned.

"Our two-year anniversary was last April," Tristan remarked. "April 29th to be exact."

"Oh, that…" Diana replied with an embarrassed laugh, looking back at Allodia. "Sorry, it's just that, being with Tristan has become such a part of my life that questioning the fact or concept of us being in a relationship is strange for me. For me, we're just together, and that's how it's always going to be."

Tristan gave a warm smile to her and started to blush. Allodia laughed.

"What a lovely way to word your relationship," Allodia commended. "You see, Diana, I told you, didn't I? I knew that there was something special between you two by the way either of you looked at each other. You were in love before you even knew it…"

Diana began to blush. She looked at Tristan lovingly and took his hand for a brief moment until Charlemagne returned.

"Alright, you two," Charlemagne remarked, holding two bags in either hand, one larger than the other. "Come and open your presents from me to you."

Tristan and Diana stood up and went to Charlemagne.

"Diana, this is for you," Charlemagne said, giving her the smaller bag, "and Tristan, this one is for you."

Tristan took the present and brought it to another table near the patio door. Diana joined him and Charlemagne stood nearby as he watched them open the gifts.

"You shouldn't have gone all out for this," Diana remarked with a smile. "I'm overwhelmed."

"Nonsense," Charlemagne replied with a laugh.

"You only graduate from high school once," Allodia noted.

Diana opened her present and looked at the small box for an expensive smartphone.

"Oh, wow…" Diana reacted. "Charles, you really shouldn't have…"

Diana continued to smile and then went to hug Charlemagne.

"I know how you feel about smartphones, but if you're to return to the city this autumn, you may as well have one so that we can keep in touch," Charlemagne stated, looking over to Tristan as he had finished opening his present.

Tristan looked at the reinforced case before him. He had his hands atop of it and looked at it in a strict face.

"Tristan, please don't take you present with you into the city… or even university," Charlemagne remarked. "I thought that if we had time, we could go into the forests and do some hunting – either way, a man ought to have a rifle."

Diana looked up from her gift and over to Tristan and his. Her face swapped to one of mild concern.

"Tristan?" Diana questioned. "Are you alright?"

Tristan looked back at her and shifted his expression. He gave a light smile.

"Yeah, I'm fine," Tristan replied, looking at her and then Charlemagne. "Thanks a lot, Charles. I simply don't know what else to say – this is phenomenal."

Allodia took a picture with her smartphone.

"Well, it certainly beats what I gave them..." Allodia remarked from the table with a smile. "In my defense, I was in a hurry, putting those cards together on the plane over..."

"Your card and the money with it was more than you should have given us," Diana remarked, walking over with her present to sit with her. "Thank you, both."

"Never a problem, Diana," Charlemagne replied, placing a hand on Tristan's shoulder. "Come on, open it up and give it a gander."

Tristan opened the reinforced-case and took out what appeared to be almost like a sniper rifle. The body of the rifle was a dark tan color, while the scope and other minor details were black. He picked it up by the handle and forestock. Tristan examined the bolt and then detached the empty cartridge.

"It's beautiful," Tristan simply said, placing the cartridge back in and securing the bolt. "I don't have a license for this, though."

"Oh, not to worry – not to worry," Charlemagne replied, patting him on the back. "We'll sort that out no problem. I'll have the paperwork completed and such – for the both of you. No sense if Diana didn't also have a firearm license."

"So, tell me," Allodia said, looking to Diana, "what else have you been up to since I last saw you? How was your trip to Asia?"

Diana looked away from Tristan and Charlemagne. She looked at Allodia with a mildly anxious face.

"Japan was beautiful – I didn't get to see much of China though."

"Weren't you in Beijing? Charlemagne told me that you spent some time in Tokyo and Beijing."

Charlemagne looked over and looked to Diana with concern she hesitated to answer.

"We spent most of our time in Japan – didn't get to see much of Beijing," Diana lied. "What about you? How has England been?"

"You mean my work with the national park? It's been steady… we've made a lot of progress, but there is lots to be done and we're under-funded," Allodia remarked.

Tristan's ears poked at the mention of the national park. He looked over to Allodia.

"A lot of the forest was reduced to a crisp, but the ecologists go on and on with saying that this is good, or that 'the fires were actually good for the forest because now it can restart,' but I'm not sure I believe that. For me, I simply want all the wildlife to return to what surely must have been a beautiful space of nature."

"Yeah," Tristan replied out of the blue with a mild smile. "A beautiful space of nature, among an entirely urbanized country."

Charlemagne looked at Tristan. Diana looked at him too. He simply stood awkwardly before turning his back to continue examining the rifle by himself.

"You're right, Tristan," Allodia remarked with a smile before looking back to Diana and Charlemagne. "The experts say that it'll be years and years before it can grow to how it was though – what more, I received a rather somber email not too long ago about how the development officers had retrieved the corpse of an unknown person who had perished in the fires near Kielder Lake."

Tristan spun around and looked at Allodia. Diana dropped her smile and Charlemagne cleared his throat.

"Yes, I heard about that," Charlemagne replied, looking down.

"Were they able to identify the body?" Tristan questioned.

"I'm not sure," Allodia responded. "I wasn't given any more details. I suppose they assumed it was either Mr. Cunningham or his son, both of whom went missing during the wildfires."

Charlemagne turned to Tristan and then cleared his throat again.

"Yes, anyways," Charlemagne remarked. "To change the tune, I forgot to tell you, Allodia, that Manon sends her regards to you, as does her father."

"Manon? Manon Dumas?" Allodia questioned. "Your ex-girlfriend?"

"Yes," Charlemagne replied with a hearted laugh.

Charlemagne went on to tell Allodia about how he had reunited with her in France, how the two of them had a minor adventure, and how the two are now in semi-regular contact with each other. Diana watched Tristan as he had turned around to quietly fiddle with the rifle on his own. She caught a glimpse of his somber face and gave a sigh. Charlemagne went on to talk with his sister, but the two of them more or less tuned out until they heard the word 'Huntsman.'

"Yes, they've been disbanded," Charlemagne told Allodia. "After all this time, and for what I assume to be a lack of leadership, they've either disbanded or gone into hiding. I assume the former, because for one, I knew they were no more than crooks, and two, they were outlaws pursued by the Russian government."

"Good riddance," Allodia said with a sigh of relief. "After all the trouble we went through – you and the kids went through because of those people and Dmitri – I'm happy they're at least gone."

"Not just them, but their ringleader, Audric Zimmerman, who had been a thorn in my side for the past couple of years. Ever since he's disappeared, I've been a lot more stress-free..." Charlemagne remarked.

"How so?" Allodia questioned.

"Oh..." Charlemagne replied, stuttering to answer. "He's a devilish competitor, that Zimmerman. He had spies in my company, been using his position as a board director to befriend me and keep an eye on me, etcetera."

"Well, that's good..." Allodia simply said, standing up and stretching her arms. "My, it's so good to be back at the manor."

Allodia walked around the pool and went to stand behind the balustrades that looked out to the garden. She then looked beyond and to the fields behind it that stretched out to the edges of a forest where Scruton Creek was. Allodia looked on with nostalgic eyes.

Tristan put his rifle away and closed the container. Meanwhile, Charlemagne went to look out with his sister. Tristan walked over to join Diana at the table, but she stood up, looked at him with a warm smile, and then the two walked to the balustrades to join Allodia and Charlemagne.

"The garden looks as beautiful as ever," Allodia commented. "Whoever is maintaining the garden is doing a fabulous job."

"That'd be ol' Mavis," Charlemagne replied. "She loves to spend her time in the gardens. Sometimes Diana will lend a hand, and by extension, force Tristan to help out," he also said, looking to them.

"And from time to time, I see you out there too," Diana said with a smile.

Charlemagne gave an almost shameful smile.

"I've spent more of my time at the easel – painting,"
Charlemagne responded. "We have certainly been blessed with
flawless weather this month."

"Mum used to love spending her time in the gardens,"
Allodia remarked to her brother. "Don't you remember?"

"Yes," Charlemagne answered. "Her favorite pass-time."

"What a treat to be here again," Allodia stated. "I spend so
much time either out of the country, or in the penthouse, that I
forget what it's like to be back where I was born. Here. I
remembered that when I was in England at that national park."

"Well, perhaps you should return to Allabrese more often,"
Charlemagne replied. "We have the spare room for you to come
in and out whenever you please."

"Maybe," Allodia remarked, sighing. "I wouldn't mind
returning to Allabrese to retire to – Harlech has become a
horrible place to live in. It really depresses me sometimes to be
there, which in itself encourages me to travel out. And then, the
rest of the world appears to follow suit with what is going on in
Harlech," she said with another sigh. "You know, that classmate
of yours, the valedictorian, was more right than I believe he
knew himself to be. To be in Allabrese, is to be in almost an
entirely different world, because there is so much beauty and
goodness here, which Harlech and the rest of the urban world
lack. All that's in these parts of the world is corruption and greed
– evil men, and women too. Evil. I'm terrified of what the world
has become, and I'm terrified to think of what is to come. Take
for example the Harlech Syndicate – I'm sure a lot of the crime
in the city has to do with them, which is ironic given that Oswald
Montgomery owns a security-firm that is meant to prevent
crime. I don't understand why people like him can't be
prosecuted… it's the same everywhere in the world. Charles
tells me of what is going on in Europe, the rape and murders

against people there, and in the United States too, and these people are practically given a slap on the wrist."

Allodia turned around, shook her head, and rested her elbows atop of the balustrades.

"A lot of it has to do with the system," Charlemagne replied to her. "Eventually, all of this poison and corruption will fall upon itself though. Yes, the situation has worsened, but at the base of all this evil is both the media and the politicians, and I would blame the media more than the politicians even with my bias, and even then..." he said with a pause. "I don't want to dredge on about politics... the entire thing is more complicated than I can express in words. Our grandfather understood.... What I'll say instead is that you don't do a service to yourself to be depressed, or even fearful, of the world situation, Allodia. You do marvelous charitable work through Cabernet Foundation, and the lives you have changed and saved are numerous. You, as the young Phillips boy expressed, have expressed the kindness and warm-heart of the people of Allabrese. You should be honored for that."

Allodia gave a warm smile, sighed and then looked over to the French window as Mavis walked out with a tray that held a strawberry pie. Charlemagne looked over and proceeded to walk over.

"Oh, Mavis, love," Charlemagne expressed, "that pie looks exquisite."

Allodia and the couple walked over to join Charlemagne in some desert. Afterwards, the family remained outside, in light conversation, for the rest of the evening.

Act 1, Scene 4

Charlemagne retired to his study as the sun began to set. He closed the door behind him and then proceeded to remove the thin gloves at his hands to reveal his wrinkled hands, especially his right hand which had been marked with a dark plaque that extended over the top of his hand and reached towards his fingers before coming down the left of his palm. Charlemagne sighed at his hand and then walked over to his desk to sit down. Upon sitting down, Charlemagne looked over to the door as he heard a knock.

"Come in," Charlemagne said, hiding his hands at the arm rest of his chair.

The door opened and Diana entered.

"Ah, Diana," Charlemagne responded. "What can I do for you?"

Diana closed the door behind her and walked over to Charlemagne's desk to stand at the side of it.

"What is it?" Charlemagne asked again.

"Do you think it was a good idea to give Tristan a rifle?" Diana questioned. "Especially so soon after what happened to him?"

Charlemagne sighed and turned to face Diana.

"I don't want to be rude – I know you when give us a gift, it's because there was genuine thought towards them, but Tristan isn't open with you like he used to be, but he's open with me. You're not aware of his mental health as I am – not that he talks to me so openly either, but... recently I've been having some weird moments with him where sometimes I'll look at him, and without speaking, the two of us seem to communicate and I understand what he's feeling. I don't know if this is because we've been together for a long-time, or what, but he's in deep pain. What happened to him with the Huntsman has hurt him as much as losing his mother, his father, and Finn over course of the last year. I'm… I'm worried he might use that rifle to hurt himself or others…"

Diana closed her eyes and turned around. She sighed.

"I hate to say that," Diana confessed. "I know he'd hate me if I said that to him, or if he heard us speak in that tone…. He has such a large ego…. I don't want to think that he would hurt someone, nor do I believe that he would, but it's a possibility."

Diana turned back around. Her eyes dropped to Charlemagne's right hand for a moment, which caused him to quickly raise his hand and tuck it into his waistcoat out of sight.

"Thank you for addressing these concerns to me," Charlemagne replied with a sigh. "Tristan has not been forward with me since we returned from China, or even England, but I knew that he would be with you. All I've been told from his experiences with the Huntsman was that they had 'brainwashed' him. The means of which they achieved that, I shudder to think. If his psyche were dire, I would have hoped you'd come to me."

"They… they tortured him…" Diana confessed. "He told me all about it, and I hate thinking about it… The worst part is that…" she said, choking up as she started to cry, "is that he was so calm when he told me about it."

Diana turned to the side as she proceeded to cry and cover her eyes with her hands. Charlemagne stood up and went to pat her on the back.

"Easy there," Charlemagne remarked. "Take it easy."

"He was like that with his adoptive-parents too!" Diana cried out. "I don't understand that aspect of Tristan and feel like I never will – it scares me. The lack of emotion; the indifference."

Charlemagne continued to comfort Diana as she settled down. She wiped tears from her eyes and then moved back from Charlemagne.

"At least..." Diana expressed, taking a breath, "at least he was open to me about this experience. You wouldn't believe the time I had trying to get him to open up about Finn... it took me months."

Diana took a deep breath.

"You know I had a hard upbringing, but ever since I came here, my life has been better and I'm so grateful for that – the peace in this county and manor – I've considered it a blessing of the Lord, but with Tristan..." Diana said, closing her eyes. "He had such a peaceful life before his parents died – all because of that cruel assassin too! A death that could have been avoided, and here he is now, suffering... I wish it were me who was taking what he's going through, because I could take it."

"Come and sit down," Charlemagne replied to her, bringing her to the armchair before his desk.

Diana sat down and kept her head down. Charlemagne sat at the edge of his desk as he looked to her. Diana took a tissue from a box that Charlemagne presented to her from his desk.

"Sorry about this," Diana expressed. "I didn't mean to come here and unload on you."

"It's fine," Charlemagne responded, crossing his arms to hide his hand. "although the sufferings may be Tristan's, they reverberate onto you and it is good that you can talk about them. I would rather you come to me than to go to Allabrese General and speak to one of them psychiatrists..."

Diana didn't respond and instead blew her nose.

"Are you afraid that the two of you may part?" Charlemagne asked.

"I was," Diana confided. "For the last year, it was a more real situation than ever before, but ever since I had my experiences in Japan, my opinion has changed. I love Tristan, and I don't ever want to let him go, but if I do need to let him go, I feel like I'd be capable. For now, at least, he needs me. I hate to say that too, because I hate to have an idea that either of us need each other..."

"You know," Charlemagne expressed, straightening up and going around to the other side of his desk, "although I don't believe Tristan and I to be quite similar, there is an aspect of him that I have reflected on since our voyage to China, and that is that Tristan enjoys his independence. I won't claim to be an expert on Tristan's inner psyche, what is going on in his head, especially since the traumas he has endured in the last year are so foreign to me, aside from I suppose the torture... I couldn't possibly know what he is going through. However, if Tristan senses that he needs you, he will come to reject that because Tristan is a man who avoids problems unlike you or me, who tackle them because otherwise, we will feel anxious. And to be dependent on another person is something that Tristan will consider to be a problem in his life – it'll damage, as you expressed, his 'large ego' and he might even avoid you or resent you. Be careful that you don't exert yourself too much on him..."

"All I want is for all of this hurt and pain to leave him..." Diana expressed. "He doesn't deserve any of it – I hate when people suffer for reasons they don't deserve."

"Such is life," Charlemagne expressed with a sigh, "as the Lord said to Job, look at Behemoth and Leviathan, and see that they are good and a part of the natural world..."

Charlemagne clenched a fist into his desk as he looked out to his bookshelf.

"… such a strange ending to a book on suffering, isn't it?" Charlemagne questioned. "What I've come to take from that story is that we live in a natural world that is larger than our own ego. Tristan's sufferings are simply a part of nature, but only if he does not dishonor the name of God and turn to evil, will his sufferings produce double of what he has lost…"

"I'm scared of that," Diana confessed as well. "I'm scared of him and this suffering having an effect on him that could damn him."

Charlemagne sighed.

"How about we go on a vacation?" Charlemagne asked in a shift of tone. "The last couple of trips we've taken have been nothing but chaos, and Allodia invited us to join her on a trip to the Caribbean Sea, to the tropical island of Isla Paraiso. What all of us need is a chance to relax and experience an authentic holiday free of assassins, or the Huntsman, or any of that nonsense. I believe a voyage like that could be beneficial for all of us."

"Okay," Diana simply replied in a soft tone.

Diana stood up.

"In regard to Tristan," Charlemagne said, causing her to stop and turn around, "the rifle will remain in the manor while we are abroad, and I expect us to stay in Isla Paraiso for the whole summer break if all goes well. Afterwards, the pair of you will be in Harlech, and the rifle will remain here. Until then, Tristan has no ammunition to possibly hurt himself. Believe me, when I knew something was off with Tristan, I was sure to secure all the firearms in this home. He shouldn't be able to get his hands on a single cartridge. Nonetheless, please continue to be there for him because although you have the comfort to know that we are blood, Tristan has no one but you. He won't come to me. I've tried to go to him. You're all that there is for him – don't let him know that though (provided he doesn't already know it). And if you feel overwhelmed, please reach out to me too. I'm always here for you, Diana."

Diana nodded to him and then left. She closed the door behind her and left Charlemagne alone. He let out a sigh and then went to his desk to return to work. Within a couple of minutes of typing emails, Charlemagne was met with another knock at the door.

"Yes? Come in," Charlemagne greeted to whomever was at the door.

The door opened and Tristan entered.

"Tristan, come in," Charlemagne ushered. "Sit down."

Tristan walked in with tired eyes and walked closer towards Charlemagne, crossing his arms. He looked at him with a bored face.

"What were you and Diana talking about?" Tristan questioned.

Charlemagne stopped typing for a moment and then continued without looking at Tristan.

"What do you mean?"

"She looked like she had been crying.... Is everything okay?"

"Oh, yes..." Charlemagne responded, moving his hands from the keyboard and sitting back in his chair. "She was a bit emotional a moment ago because we had a personal conversation between the two of us, our families and that... You see, I've made a decision about what we would be doing this summer, and have decided that we'll be going to Isla Paraiso in the Caribbean with Allodia to aid in the Cabernet Foundation project there. However, the compromise," he said, looking forward, "is that I will have to see my parents, because they are the ones that have requested Allodia's aid – not to mention, they won't expect either myself or you two to show up. I was telling Diana an anecdote of my childhood, she went on about hers, and I'm afraid that's when we became rather tearful… Poor Diana… never you think to abandon that woman, Tristan. She has a delicate heart and loves you greatly."

Tristan lowered his crossed arms and dropped his plain expression to show remorse.

"Yeah," Tristan confessed. "I know."

Charlemagne returned to type at his computer. Tristan looked at Charlemagne's right hand.

"So, we're going to meet your parents?" Tristan asked.

"Yes," Charlemagne affirmed with a sigh. "I haven't seen either of them in years and years, so I'm… anxious. My mother, I'm quite eager to see because I love her dearly, but my father…"

Charlemagne sighed again.

"The last time we spoke to each other, I had been in this chair and we had argued in this room," Charlemagne explained, looking forward. "To this date, I don't think either of us could forgive each other for what we said to each other."

Act 1, Scene 5

Charlemagne looked forward, across the study, standing straight in the brown leather office chair with either hand down on the surface of the desk. Both his hands were lively and fair, dried around the knuckles. Charlemagne was dressed in a sweater, collared-shirt and jeans. His hair was light-blonde and cut-short. Across his face, he had a moustache under his nose, but it was not white, but instead colored like his hair. The white around his blue eyes were not strained, but pure and healthy. Charlemagne looked fit, but held a brooding expression over his face as he looked forward.

The door into the study opened and a man walked in dressed in a trench coat. He held a hat in his right hand, which exposed his balding head with a receding line of light-blonde hair, and a briefcase in his left hand. Unlike Charlemagne, this man did not have any facial hair and was instead clean-shaven. He had similar light blue eyes and perhaps a stockier shape than his son who looked towards him while he looked back in surprise from the door.

"Charles, what the hell are you doing in my study?" Everest questioned in his Cascadian accent. "How did you unlock the door?"

"Hardly your study anymore, is it?" Charlemagne bitterly responded in his East Anglian accent.

"How dare you," Everest replied, walking towards him. "I'm not dead yet! The manor is still mine until I set it for sale! You don't live here anymore! Get out and go live in the penthouse for all I care – it's yours now!"

Charlemagne pushed himself back from the desk and stood up as his father got close.

"Since the manor was constructed on company property, it belongs to the company and is not yours to sell," Charlemagne rebuked. "All of this land belongs to Cabernet Industries... not you, because when grandfather built our home, he did it on a plot of land that was marked as industrial zone by the county... a fact that was never changed and has largely been forgotten. It was your shortcoming to have never have transferred the property into your possession as chairman and owner of Cabernet Industries. That being said, this property belongs to myself, Allodia, and Salmar – not you, since we're the majority shareholders of the company now. You are trespassing on our home."

Everest scowled at him and then shook his head.

"What damn do I give about this manor? It was never my home..." Everest remarked, opening a drawer in the desk and rummaging through for a key. "I'm done."

"You've quit as Chairman of Cabernet Industries, and now you hope to quit as the head of the household? As the patriarch of the Cabernet name?" Charlemagne questioned. "That's certainly laughable since you've never acted as either."

Charlemagne stepped back, flinching as his father passed him to open a safe under a cabinet next to the desk. Everest ignored his son's remarks.

"I was only going to sell the property, but I have my fortune and all the money I'll need to live out the last years of my life with your mother, alone and in peace, doing better than some fascist corporation could ever achieve."

"I find your contempt for our family legacy to be tiresome," Charlemagne responded, looking down at his father as he opened the safe.

Everest stood up and pointed a finger at his son.

"I find *you* to be tiresome, you spoiled little brat," Everest insulted before kneeling before the safe. "Always undermining me... always critical of me... but one day you'll understand. You live in a fantasy, Charles. Ever since you were little, you've lived on a cushion, but look around the greater world and see that others don't have it so easy and worse of, that Cabernet Industries, our 'family's legacy' as you put it, is an abettor in all that. 'Our family's legacy...'" he repeated, "what a joke. It's a statement like that, which kills me inside. If it wasn't for the law, I'd have sold all my shares and redistributed my wealth – leaving you penniless as you ought to be."

Everest shoveled

"How demoralized are you? Our forefathers had painstakingly made sacrifices to land us where we are now, and you dismiss all of it out of your own self-righteousness?"

"My God, how you have become like your grandfather," Everest complained, bringing his hands to his face. "How could I have raised a son to be as uptight as that old man?!"

Charlemagne's scowl towards his father deepened.

"You never raised me," Charlemagne refuted, "and in the past, I lamented the fact, but now, how I am eternally grateful for your negligence that forced that 'old man' to raise me instead of you. You're nothing more than a pitiful and spiteful shell of a man with the spirit of a child.... Always sorry about himself and at the same time, always unsure. I have come to detest and loath people like you.... My grandfather was a man of action, and I'll always love him more than I love you."

Everest closed the briefcase and stood up.

"Let me tell you, Charles, that you worship a monster," Everest argued. "You were not his son – *I was his son*... I was the one that was stuck with that callous deadbeat from the day he returned from the war until the day he shoved me into a private school in Harlech. You never knew Derby for his alcoholism, or his depravity, his maleficence... You never received the belt when you were late returning home from school, or a sock when you were out of line, because if you had... God only knows you wouldn't be kissing the ground he walked on if he was as harsh with you as he was with me...."

"You're a liar," Charlemagne simply responded. "You disrespect the memory of that great man for the pitiful sake that you'll never amount even close to him."

Everest looked back at his son.

"You know nothing about him, Charles. You were eight-years old when he died..." Everest replied, looking at his son with pity. "Hopefully, by the time we meet again, you'll understand and maybe then, I can look at you without shame or regret. Goodbye, Charles."

"Goodbye?" Charlemagne questioned. "Where are you going?"

"Far from here," Everest answered. "To the furthest reaches of civilization to help the less fortunate with your mother..."

"Where are you taking her?" Charlemagne questioned with slight anger. "Leave her out of your self-pity!"

"Your mother and I function as one," Everest answered. "She's not following me anywhere – we're going together. Goodbye."

Charlemagne followed Everest towards the exit of the study.

"Where are you taking her?! Where are you taking my mother?!" Charlemagne shouted.

Everest ignored his son and continued to walk out of the manor. Charlemagne reached the front entrance and stopped atop of the steps as Everest went to a taxi waiting at the front. The skies were grey and there was a drizzle of rain. Everest entered the vehicle.

"Dammit, you coward! Where are you taking her! You leave my mother alone! I'd better see you in hell than let you take her from me! Father!"

Everest closed the car door and the taxi drove off. Charlemagne watched and his eyes watered. The taxi turned right and proceeded away from the manor, leaving Charlemagne alone at the family home.

• • • •

Charlemagne looked away from the exit of his study and back to Tristan who was sat before him.

"And I haven't seen him since," Charlemagne stated. "I was content to never see him again, given my last words, but now… my mind has not changed about him or his views, but I've changed," he said with a sigh. "There's a trend in this family where every Cabernet is destined to be hated by his first-born son. My grandfather, Derby, had a feud with his own father, Pepin, but Salmar… he and my father got along easily and rather well, and I believe Salmar loved and cared for my father. My father was very much 'Anti-Derby' as much as I suppose I was 'Anti-Everest,' and with that and recent times, I've come to think whether Finn would have been 'Anti-Charlemagne.'"

"Finn was a lot like you," Tristan said. "He may have never have even heard of you, but the genetic influence was there… You and him were certainly father and son. I don't think he'd have hated you."

Charlemagne maintained a frown as he looked away from Tristan and forward.

"I would have hated me," Charlemagne confessed. "If I was Finn, in all the suffering I had endured at the hands of an oaf like Aidan Cunningham, I would have resented to know my biological father had abandoned me for some 'hussy' in Switzerland, leaving my biological mother in Paris, alone for the rest of her life. A different life, it seems, would have extended towards Finn…"

"You can't know that for certain…" Tristan replied. "Every day I imagine what my life could have been like if the assassin hadn't killed my aunt and uncle, or if my mother hadn't given me up and instead kept me as she intended to reunite with my father. For a start, I know I wouldn't be here and with Diana…"

"Well, we can certainly never know…" Charlemagne admitted, looking back at Tristan and standing up. "Anyways, I suppose that'll do. I have some work I need to complete before we leave tomorrow. Prepare your bags and set your clock for an early rise tomorrow morning… Instead of seeing Allodia off, we'll be travelling with her to Isla Paraiso."

"Sure," Tristan replied, standing up. "Goodnight."

"Night, Tristan."

Act 2, Scene 1

Allodia's private jet, which was similar in design to Charlemagne's and belonged to the Cabernet Foundation, flew over the Lesser Antilles in the Caribbean and began to make its approach to Isla Paraiso not too far from the coast of South America. The jet passed the island and made a U-turn, lowering itself as it homed in on the airfield beside the main city of Isla Paraiso, Villa Paraiso, which appeared from the skies to be a medium-sized seaside town of tan-brick structures with terracotta rooftops in a grid-like pattern that concentrated around a small bay where a port had been built. The beaches on the coast were made of a fine, pure and light beige sand, and the water of the ocean was a very light blue. Here and there, a bit of green could be seen in rows of grass and various parks with lively green deciduous trees. At the beaches, palm trees could be seen. The island did not appear to be as large as Tristan imagined it would be, as the main town, which was the only town, sat on the northside of the island and around it was a display of farmland that then blended into a dense and dark green jungle. The town and countryside was at least one-fifth of the entire area of the island, and the island was perhaps a quarter of the size of Puerto Rico, which was approximately the average size of some of the islands they had seen.

Tristan observed Villa Paraiso as the jet touched down, adjusted his watch given to him by Kristoffer to read the local time of approximately five o'clock in the afternoon from the time in Allabrese at the moment of around two o'clock. Diana put her latest read, *Brave New World* by Aldous Huxley, away and then moved with Tristan to leave the plane with the others. The four of them went through the usual procedure with customs until they stood at the front of the airport and could see the town close up. The heat in the town was immense and the humidity was almost as insufferable as it could have felt. The architecture of the town was distinctly Spanish Colonial with white and light-tan brick structures. The streets were not paved with asphalt, but instead consisted of a chiseled-stone, and the sidewalks were not paved in concrete, but instead made of a similar set of stone. The traffic on the street before the airport was extremely light, and the cars were not modern models of your ordinary cars, but mostly vintage cars that must have been as old as Charlemagne. Tristan took in the sight of the town and then looked over to Charlemagne as he went towards a taxi parked on the curb.

Charlemagne was dressed in a tan-suit with white leather gloves. Diana wore a white summer dress, while Allodia wore white capris trousers, high-heels, a pink blouse, and sunglasses. Tristan wore a navy blue polo and dark-tan shorts with sneakers. He followed the others as they moved their luggage into the trunk of the taxi sedan with the help of the chauffer, who appeared to be of a fair-skin, dark brown hair and brown eyes, but was relatively distinct in appearance compared to most people that Tristan had met. His appearance was Iberian, or more specifically, Basque-like, which was shared with Welsh people, and entailed fair skin at an olive hue. Tristan noticed that a lot of the residents in the town that he could see as the taxi drove to their hotel shared this appearance, which was unlike other Hispanics that ranged from being Amerindian, mixed, or mestizo, to castizo with a predominantly Andalusian appearance, or Turkish/Arabic/Persian-like appearance. At the same time, Villa Paraiso and Isla Paraiso was not a former Spanish colony, but a Portuguese colony, but that did not make a difference as the Spanish and Portuguese were both Iberian. Charlemagne looked out his window from the front passenger seat while the others sat quietly.

The taxi took them through the town and stopped at the front of what appeared to be like a palace, but was the main structure of the Windsor International Resort they'd be staying at. The family took their luggage with them inside the hotel lobby while Charlemagne went to check-in. The interior of the lobby was large with a tall ceiling and the floor consisted of wide caramel-colored tiles. The walls and arches consisted of a tan-colored brick. At the sides of the main lobby there were arcades that led to corridors that sprouted to the rest of the hotel, which were lit by modern incandescent chandeliers that gave them a warm appearance. In the open space of the lobby, light filtered through from overhanging windows above. In terracotta pots there were palm trees and shrubs positioned about. In the center of the foyer there was a square carpet with squared-beige loveseats around a birch wood glass coffee table. Behind the check-in desk there was a waterfall fountain wall that like some of the lights and decorations, blended the old architecture with the new. The space around them was moderately quiet, but there were other guests, which Tristan observed with curiosity and ambience of talking in Portuguese met with the clashing of porcelain plates and chimes from a windchime.

Diana, Tristan, and Allodia waited at some couches until Charlemagne returned with their hotel room keys. A bellhop in a black suit assisted them with their luggage and then led them down the left corridor where they came outside to a quiet courtyard. In the center of this plaza was a fountain and in the center of the fountain, atop of a small platform, was a black cube on its corner. Within the arcades of this courtyard there was a restaurant, some shops, and other venues. The bellhop took them through the courtyard, down a short corridor that took them out of the palace, and onto a stone path with mowed grass and shrubbery of tropical flora and palm trees. Behind all this greenery, there was a large pool in a curved design with lounge chairs and bars that connected with the pool. The bellhop continued down the left and past this pool to continue along where there were mowed lawns up to some black iron fences with apartment-like complexes on the other side. Some paths led to gates, which then led to the front entrances of these buildings. The structures had tanned stucco exterior walls and balconies with railings made of the same black iron. At an intersection, the family continued on the left where they passed a golf course on approach to another to a larger structure where they continued on the left to enter the complex, which had a modern interior with dark wooden floors. Diana took a deep breath as they entered the air-conditioned lobby of the hotel complex where they waited for an elevator.

Once the elevator arrived, Diana, Tristan, Allodia, and Charlemagne were taken to the third-floor of the complex, down a corridor, and to their suite, which included a kitchen, dining room, living room, and four bedrooms in a modernist design; smooth and plain surfaces, simple, solid colors, and cuboidal shapes. At the rear of the living room, the suite led out to a veranda at the corners of the structure, which looked out towards the ocean, the private beachfront in front of the hotel with its fine sand, and a small plaza with a bar and some tables next to a pool. On the right and middle of the hotel complex, which was U-shaped, was another pool with lounge chairs and tables spread about. Behind this area, on the ground floor of the hotel and raised from the pool, was an outdoor restaurant. From the veranda, Diana felt a warm breeze as she looked around with Tristan.

"Four bedrooms," Charlemagne stated to the couple. "That's a room for each of us. I've booked this suite until September, so make yourselves at home. Allodia, why don't you take the left-side with Diana? It'll surely be quieter at nights if I expect there to be ruffians below as is typically the case in these resorts."

Diana and Tristan split up and went to their separate rooms at opposite-sides of the suite. Diana brought her luggage into her room and sat it down on the ottoman in front of her queen-sized bed. The bedrooms were set on the sides of the main suite, two bedrooms each, one with access to the veranda. The two bedrooms were connected to each other by a sliding door as the bedroom that did not have access to the veranda had the bathroom on the opposite-side instead. Diana closed the sliding door between her room and Allodia's and then continued to look around her bedroom. After Diana had settled into her room, she went into Tristan's room, which was opposite from hers, and began to look out his window that looked to the pool.

"Why don't we go out to the pool?" Diana questioned.

"Already?" Tristan replied, moving some of his clothes from his suitcase and into a closet. "We just got here."

"You don't want to go to the pool?"

"No, I mean," Tristan responded, hesitating for a moment, "I'm just trying to get all my stuff sorted."

Diana observed as Tristan continued to hang his shirts in the closet. She then looked over to Charlemagne in the other room who had been observing them. He walked over and stood in the opening between his bedroom and Tristan's.

"Don't feel the need to rush," Charlemagne remarked. "We don't set off for the encampment where my parents are for a couple of days. According to Allodia, a cargo plane with supplies is touching down tomorrow and we have to organize transport for these supplies, which'll be the majority of our work, Allodia and me. In the meantime, you'll have plenty of time to acquaint yourselves with the villa."

. . . .

Later in the same evening, Charlemagne and Allodia met with Diana and Tristan in the restaurant downstairs when twilight was upon them and the sun more or less under the horizon. The couple came up the steps from the pool, Diana had changed out of her dress and into a swim dress, while Tristan wore board shorts and an open Hawaiian floral shirt. He also had his sunglasses over his eyes as they came under the cover of the restaurant to meet with the others. The four of them sat at the side of the restaurant by the iron fence that looked out to the patio below and beach ahead.

"How was the pool?" Charlemagne asked.

"We didn't do any swimming," Diana answered. "We just lounged at the side when we realized we were both too tired to swim around. It's a lot cooler now that the sun has set."

"Hm," Charlemagne responded in an optimistic sense. "Allodia and I went back to the hotel lobby and we saw that the hotel has a promotion for surfing lessons if the pair of you are interested. There's also going to be a fire performance at around nine o'clock that would be worth to see. They also have scuba diving, and…"

"Charles," Allodia said, stopping him.

"I'm sorry," Charlemagne apologized. "We're on vacation. Perhaps I'm too enthusiastic over the fact."

"I think I want to watch the fire performers," Diana answered, "and surfing sounds fun too. Right, Tristan?"

"Sure," Tristan responded. "I'm in, if you're in."

"Good," Charlemagne responded, looking pleased. "Thank you."

A waiter brought a bottle of wine, which Allodia and Charlemagne split. Afterwards, Allodia began to look around the restaurant at the other patrons who appeared to be mostly fair-skinned people speaking in English.

"You know, for an island that's supposed to be isolating itself from the rest of the world, I see a lot more people than I'd think to see.

"Well, Isla Paraiso is a U.S. territory, so the only people who would be allowed in or out would be Americans," Charlemagne answered. "At the same time, there is not much demand for air travel or luxurious retreats… A lot of paranoia and germaphobia remains in the public, I believe."

"Wait, if this is a U.S. territory, then why around your parents of all people helping the locals? Technically, we're not in a third-world country, or even a country. It's U.S. territory, even if they are semi-autonomous," Tristan stated.

"Precisely that, Tristan," Charlemagne replied. "They are semi-autonomous and only partially funded by the U.S. government, and the parts that are in strife are their own autonomous areas because they are part of a reservation with no ties to the U.S. government other than the fact that they are on an island claimed by the Americans."

Diana moved close to the table and looked to Charlemagne.

"If we are technically in the United States, don't you think it's a little risky that we came here without the Protection Squad?" Diana asked.

"I'm not too worried," Charlemagne responded. "Between the pair of you, it appears that you are more than capable of handling yourselves…"

"But what about you?" Diana questioned. "And Allodia?"

Charlemagne crossed his arms.

"Well, given the travel restrictions on the island, my father's stubbornness, and also some false intel that Heavner will spread about me, I'm technically not here at the moment. The hotel suite is not in my name, but in an alias of mine. The only people who know we are here other than us are my parents, Heavner and Miklos. Should anyone ask, I'm at Cabernet Manor this summer with the pair of you."

Allodia remained silent. Charlemagne uncrossed his arms and extended a gloved hand to his wine glass.

"Besides, from what I've heard from Heavner, it appears that ever since Zimmerman's disappearance, our security risk has been low. When Zimmerman disappeared, almost all of our problems went with him."

Diana looked unconvinced, but hid her face as she looked out to the beach.

"I'm not too fresh on the history of this island, but I know that places like the Philippines and Puerto Rico landed in the pockets of the Americans out of the Spanish-American War, but how did a Portuguese colony land in their pockets when they've never been at war?" Tristan questioned.

"A good question," Charlemagne replied, setting his wine glass down. "The simple answer is to backtrack, because before the island was an American 'territory' it was a British colony. The British had pawned the island off the Brazil Empire so that they would help negotiate peace between Brazil and Uruguay, setting up a naval base here, and before that, it was simply a port-town owned by the Portuguese for their activities in the New World, similar to Santo Domingo for the Spanish."

Upon Charlemagne finishing to explain the island's history, their waiter returned with their dinner, so they ate.

Act 2, Scene 2

Afterwards, Diana and Tristan accompanied Charlemagne and his sister to the large pool they had seen near the hotel plaza. There, there was an outdoor bar with various small round glass tables with lit candles in the center and seats that looked to a stage surrounded by a part of the pool with its back facing a two-story annex that extended from the main palace. The wall of the palace thus acted like a stage background with entrances left and right that went inside. The four of them found a seat by the pool, which was more or less vacant apart from several people at the far-side. Most people, although not many, were at seats like the family or at the bar itself. There was a mild rowdiness that came from the bar from some patrons that were loud with their laughter and talking. Diana mostly ignored them, but Tristan couldn't help but look over to them every time they wound up.

Tristan observed them with their drinks with a frown. By now, a mild summer chill had fallen over the island as the sun had set, so he buttoned up his shirt. His attention then returned to the stage where there was an ongoing comedy act that was finishing up. Tristan's eyes wandered to the other tables as he looked at what other sort of people were present, and it appeared to be mostly adults. He looked back at the comedian and observed him. He appeared to be like most islanders he had seen so far with the olive skin-tone, but this man had thin curly brown hair and a sort of wide, pointed nose. His eyes and eyebrows made him appear to be more castizo than the others, but at the same time, he did not look to be castizo nor Iberian. Tristan looked at him with an unsure face.

The comedian bowed and waved goodbye to the audience at the end of his act, receiving an applause as he left the microphone on the stand and then wandered off backstage. A young male in his twenties, dressed like a lifeguard with red swim shorts, a white t-shirt, and flip-flops came around from the side and took the microphone. This man appeared to be castizo, or like your typical Hispanic male, with a light cinnamon skin-tone, black hair and Middle Eastern appearance.

"Thank you," the male remarked in the microphone in a Hispanic accent. "Hadad Perez, everyone."

The audience gave another light applause.

"Next, we have a special performance from the island's very own Kathunoaco of the Arawak people, a traditional dance of fire that was performed by the indigenous people to ward of demons. Enjoy."

The male took with him the microphone to the left back entrance from the stage, while from the right a group of four indigenous men in traditional garb rushed out. The local indigenous people appeared typical for Amerindians, if not darker due to the climate. The dancers wore flamboyant costumes with a headpiece that had strands of a very thin metallic-like gold material that was very shiny and about three-feet long. At the end of these strands were white balls of cotton. The whole headpiece stuck out like a giant shrub. The dancers were led by a male who had a larger headpiece that wrapped around his jaw like a helmet. In addition, the 'shrub' at the top appeared to be like a sort of mohawk on the median plane, while for the females, it stuck out at the opposite angle, from the coronal plane. The male was a muscular, fit Kathunoacan man who carried a small pot of fire. Behind him were four females in a similar costume, but with a chest-piece. The chest-piece of the costume wrapped over the torso like a poncho, but was scale-like and made of type of glistening stone. The whole of the costume apart from the headpiece was made of these colored stones, giving it a gold and turquoise appearance. The lead dancer did not wear a chest-piece as instead, his bare chest was exposed to the elements. From the waist, the costume wrapped around the pelvis, exposing the legs as the arms, and a rectangular-piece dangled over the groins to droop down to the ankles. For the women, the chest-piece blended with the lower portion like a dress, hiding it. At the ankles and wrists, bands were worn in the same material. At the back, the dancers wore a cape that went to the ankles too. They also wore sandals. The females took position at the sides of the stage, shaking a type of maraca in their hands while a drum beat from the speakers and the male brought the pot of fire and sat it down in the center of the stage.

The lead dancer then shouted on in a deep voice, speaking in the native tongue of the Kathunoacan people as the dancers turned to the side and proceeded to kick their right leg forward and back. The male brought a hand up and continued to shout a war cry and then stamped his foot down over the fire, not even singeing his foot. The females proceeded to twirl from where they stood. The headpieces ruffled like the shrubs they appeared to be with their movement. The females stopped and faced the audience from the opposite-side, kicking forward and back their left legs while the fire from the pot spat upwards and the man stepped back to join the others. The beat of the drum kept up with the pace of the dance, which was fast. With a shout from the dancers, they proceeded to twirl in place before kicking each leg forward. The lead dancer maintained himself in the center of the group, especially as they began to move from left to right, maintaining the exact same distance between each other as they twisted their torsos left and right, swinging their arms up and down, and then kicking their legs up as they moved with a ferocity. The lead deviated from the others as he began to spin about, side jumping around the fire as he kept his head down and was hunched over.

The dancers then paused on their knees and shouted out, causing the lead dancer to stop before the fire and shout even louder as he looked up to the sky. The beat then settled down. The dancer kept with a groove as he jumped small steps around the fire before kneeling before it on both knees. He raised his arms up before the fire and shouted out. The females around him emulated his movement. The man then looked down at the small pot of fire. He picked it up and raised it up. The women bowed. He brought the pot down and stood up, maintaining himself hunched as he swung his arms and kicked back. He moved to the side and proceeded to stamp down over the fire, exposing his thigh to the flames. The man continued to stomp, but when he stopped, he shifted to twist his torso and arms while his leg cooked over the flame. He twisted his body forward, bringing his torso to the flames. He then stood up and moved behind the fire again. The other dancers remained where they were, but had gotten down onto their knees, maintaining their upper bodies straight as they shook the maraca-like instruments in their hands, arms abducted apart.

The lead dancer took a small piece of burning kindling from the fire and shouted out as he showed it to the audience. He then took the burning piece of wood and placed it on his chest as he pulled himself back. The man then took the piece and stood up on one knee, bringing the piece to his mouth and then breathing out a huge flame that dissipated upwards. Once the fireball had flown up, the man stomped into the pit and extinguished the rest of the flames. The other dancers stood up and continued to dance in the tempo previously danced to while the man smothered his sandal into the pit. He then jumped back and joined the dancers, twirling around on the spot with his left leg raised up, but not extended out. The lead dancer stopped and knelt down on a knee as the fire reignited in the pot.

The other dancers spread out around him and began to side flip back and forth. The male picked up the pit and walked towards the edge of the stage, towards the audience and raised the pit of fire up to them. The other dancers proceeded to dance off and return behind the stage as he continued to hold the pit. Once they had left, he took a step back and with the pit still in his hand, he left while the audience began to applaud, walking with his chest puffed out. The performances went on after that for another thirty minutes, but were not as grand as the first.

When the performance was over, Diana and Tristan returned to the hotel suite with Charlemagne and Allodia. Diana took Tristan to the balcony while the adults went to their separate rooms to prepare to go to bed. The couple looked out to the sea. Diana held onto Tristan's arm and tilted her head onto his shoulder.

"Isn't this nice?" Diana questioned with a sigh.

"It really is like a paradise here, I suppose," Tristan replied in a plain tone.

"A utopia?"

"I've been told they don't exist."

Diana let go of Tristan's arm and gave him a sly look. Their attention then shifted down to the patio bar by the pool where there were some males enjoying some drinks loudly near a hot tub. They had begun to scream at each other before bursting out laughing.

"Well, I suppose we have that to look forward to tonight," Diana remarked with a sigh. "Charlemagne was right."

Tristan looked at the young men and then at Diana.

"Hey, you weren't serious about 'hating' me if I ever had alcohol, were you?" Tristan asked. "I'm only curious."

Diana looked at him with surprise.

"I mean, I understand the rationale – your father was a drunk, but you're not going to bar me from enjoying a drink or two in the future simply out of that?"

"Gosh," Diana replied with another sigh. "I suppose you're right, but I don't know how you process liquor, Tristan. You don't even know if you like liquor since the only times you've ever had a drink was in France at Manon's brother's home and then yesterday."

Tristan evaded Diana's glance as he looked out to the sea.

"I was only curious if you were serious or not," Tristan repeated.

Diana did not immediately respond. The drunks below began to get into a fight.

"It's behavior like that, which feeds into my aversion of alcohol," Diana finally replied. "I don't like it."

Tristan sighed.

"I'm sorry I brought it up," Tristan responded.

"I don't know why you brought it up – you're not even eighteen yet, Tristan, and we're going to Harlech where the age to drink is nineteen. You're another year from even being able to slip into that…" Diana remarked with a sigh. "I'm sorry."

Diana hugged Tristan's arm.

"It's okay," Tristan replied, bringing his other hand behind her back "I understand."

Diana embraced all of Tristan.

"You know, this couldn't be a utopia if I couldn't end my nights with you. I miss sleeping with you," Diana stated. "A lot."

"Not even possible to risk with those screens dividing our rooms," Tristan replied. "It definitely sucks."

The couple jumped at the sound of glass shattering below. Diana looked down with a disgusting expression on her face.

"Come on, let's go back inside," Diana remarked. "I've heard enough of this racket."

Act 2, Scene 3

The next day, Allodia and Charlemagne took a taxi cab from the hotel and were taken to Ricardo Plaza, which was a beautiful square in town surrounded by the traditional colonialist architecture. At the corner of the plaza there were enclosures of shrubbery and tall palm trees. In the center of the plaza there was a statue of David Ricardo, the economist, and behind that was a temple-like structure made of a stucco foundation and red bricks. The roof was sort of arched and above the main doors there was a hexagram. This structure overlooked the plaza, statue, and on the opposite-side there was a series of shops and businesses, from a grocer at one corner, to a pizzeria, and a Planned Parenthood clinic. Allodia and Charlemagne entered the last of these venues, which was a vehicle rental shop.

"I'm glad that you decided to join me after all," Allodia said as they walked down the street. "You've halved the workload for me by volunteering to help."

Charlemagne turned his glance from towards the plaza and the temple on the other side and looked to his sister with a quaint smile.

"I'm always happy to help – keeps me out of mischief," Charlemagne stated.

The siblings entered the rental shop where their entrance was announced with a ring of bells. Allodia went to the front-desk.

"Hello," Allodia greeted. "I have two trucks reserved under the name Allodia Cabernet for the Cabernet Foundation.

Charlemagne watched as the desk clerk left for a moment. Allodia turned to him.

"How come you never told me about Diana and Tristan?" Allodia questioned.

Charlemagne's face fell in a sort of shock over the question.

"Well," Charlemagne responded, "I… I never really learned about their relationship until the end of last year, and even then, it was never my first instinct to announce it to the world. It came from them rather delicately, and in all honesty, I don't make it my business to intrude on their relationship."

"Is that why you split them up to sleep in separate rooms?" Allodia questioned.

"Diana is a practicing Catholic – Even then, what kind of a role model would I be to either of them if I permitted them to sleep together?" Charlemagne responded. "The pair of them may be together and in love, and it may very well be that one day the two of them will be the first couple to get married at the manor since Salmar, and in that case, the first couple of this millennium, but even then, I have a duty to uphold as their guardian, even as feeble and weak as I may appear at times."

The clerk returned and presented two keys to Allodia. She signed a book and then they were led out and behind the business to a small impound where there were various vehicles parked. A lot of the vehicles ranged from the older models more commonly seen on the streets to newer models of cars. The trucks that Allodia had rented were not by any means modern, but appeared to be old army trucks with backs covered in tarpaulin. Even at the sides of the truck, the old white army star had been painted over, but could still be made out.

"Will that be enough?" Charlemagne questioned. "How much are we expected to transport to the camp?"

Allodia took out her phone.

"I think this'll be enough. Dad said that two volunteers will meet us at the airport to give us a hand," Allodia stated.

"How considerate of him…"

"Do you have the directions to the airport?" Allodia questioned.

"I can make my way there," Charlemagne replied.

"Good, then I'll meet you over there."

Allodia tossed a set of keys to Charlemagne. He then climbed aboard the cabin of one of the trucks and ignited the engine. Once he was set, he drove out of the impound and proceeded to make his way to the airport where he was permitted onto the tarmac where he saw the cargo plane ahead with its rear-ramp down and a forklift moving palettes of supplies off. Allodia parked her truck near the plane alongside Charlemagne, and then the two exited to meet with the volunteers and airplane crew.

The skids were taken out from the rear of the cargo plane and then raised into the back of the trucks. Once the skids were placed within the truck, the volunteers helped pull them back to make room for the next. Three skids barely managed to fit in the back of one truck, which left half of the supplies in the cargo plane.

Allodia flipped through a manifest and then handed it back to the supervisor of the cargo plane.

"That's alright," Allodia said. "Have the rest of these taken to the Arctic, if not back to Harlech."

"Yes, ma'am."

The forklift drove back into the rear of the cargo plane. Charlemagne wiped sweat from atop of his forehead as Allodia walked to him.

"I suppose that's as good as we can do for now," Allodia remarked. "They'll return on Sunday for us to take another round of supplies with us when we meet dad for lunch then."

"Very well," Charlemagne responded.

The siblings split up, each to a truck, and were taken off the airfield and dropped off in front of the airport as the volunteers drove the trucks onwards to the base camp at the other side of the island.

"Have a safe trip," Allodia regarded to the volunteer as she hopped off. "Send my regards to Everest, will you?"

Allodia closed the door and then walked over to meet up with Charlemagne.

"Well, what now?" Charlemagne asked, looking at his watch. "I thought that'd take all day, but it only got us to noon."

The pair of them proceeded to walk down the sidewalk.

"Well, like I said, you halved the amount of work I had to do," Allodia remarked. "Let's go and have lunch then. I'm starving."

Charlemagne and Allodia continued to walk through the town. Charlemagne admired the local architecture as they quietly walked from the airport and back into the heart of town.

"When was the last time you saw them? Our parents, I mean," Charlemagne remarked to her all of the sudden.

"Not too long ago," Allodia replied. "We met last Christmas in Africa and spent it together."

"How are they?"

"You'll see," Allodia remarked to her brother. "Why?"

"I'm anxious," Charlemagne confessed. "I don't know what he's going to be like most of all."

"He'll be as he always has been with you – respectful, and I expect the same from you. I invited you to relax and unwind, and help out. I didn't invite you to fight with him."

"I don't intend to have an argument with him," Charlemagne affirmed with a sigh. "All I want between us is peace, but I'm not guaranteed peace, am I?"

"Dad is a peaceful person, Charles, and he's also a lot older. Even with all this work, he doesn't have the energy that he used to have, and he's also going partially deaf in one ear. Between that, you shouldn't have much to worry about. I'm sure they'll be both surprised and pleased to see you."

"Surprised?" Charlemagne questioned. "Do they not know that I'm here?"

"No," Allodia replied. "I wrote to him that I was travelling to assist through the Cabernet Foundation, and that was it. I never planned to invite you here with Diana and Tristan either. When we meet on Sunday, it'll be a surprise for him to see you and the pair of them for the first time."

Charlemagne didn't respond.

"Dad was never one for surprises…" Charlemagne replied with a slight grumble. "Him and nan."

Allodia rolled her eyes. The two continued to walk until they found a small restaurant to dine at and rest for the afternoon.

Act 2, Scene 4

Meanwhile, as Charlemagne and Allodia were in town and finished off, Diana and Tristan were left alone at the hotel suite. At about noon, the couple left the hotel and walked into town to attend the surfing lessons by the main beach in town, Praia Icaria. The beachfront consisted of two-miles of delicate and fine sand like that behind the hotel, but with an addition of a waterfront park that included a path and shops that overlooked the beach. The couple checked into a surf shop where they each purchased attire appropriate for surfing.

Tristan bought and changed out of the shirt he was wearing, another Hawaiian shirt, and pulled down a long-sleeved sun shirt that covered his torso, while Diana bought a one-piece long-sleeve surf suit, which she changed into. The piece covered her torso, but only had a six-inch instream at the legs, allowing her legs to breath. The couple left their belongings in a rented locker at the surf shop and then walked out to choose a surfboard and begin the lessons. Tristan observed down the side of the waterfront at how busy the beach was in comparison to the rest of the town, seeing dozens of people.

Diana picked a cyan-colored surfboard, while Tristan chose a white one that was slightly longer, as recommended due to his weight of over two-hundred pounds. Afterwards, the couple met with their instructor, a young Iberian man named Vinicius, or Vini, who appeared to be at most twenty-four years old. Vini had straight, medium-length brown hair that had an almost blonde aura to it in the sun. He had fair skin, but was very bronzed. He appeared to have a skinny face by his cheekbones and jawline, and he was mildly thin, although about the same height as Tristan, but nowhere near the amount of mass that Tristan carried. Vini wore a dark purple t-shirt, light blue board shorts, and sandals.

"Nice to meet you," Vini greeted, shaking the hands of both Diana and Tristan.

Vini spoke in perfect English, although it was still apparent that he was of the island by his accent that shared hints of his home. He took the couple to the beach where they stopped so that he could explain some fundamentals, such as the anatomy of the surfboard and the attached piece known as the leg rope. He then took the couple into the shallow water so he could teach them how to position themselves atop of the board, in the middle, centered. They practiced hopping on and off to reach this optimal position before moving on to how to paddle, feet together and chest raised. They then practiced how to paddle between two markers that the boy had set up. After thirty minutes or so of practice, Vini began to teach them how to 'duckdive' under a wave as well as how to 'eskimo roll,' and the couple were then set to practice these skills for another thirty minutes or so.

Tristan brought his hands to the edge of his board, pressing down with the help of his chained knee so that he would submerge, or dive before rising up again. Meanwhile, Diana practiced how to 'eskimo roll,' tipping herself over and submerging herself with the board over her before rolling back out. They each practiced these until they were comfortable to move on to actually surf. Tristan observed the waves at Praia Icaria to be too dull, and rightly so, because once the couple were comfortable, Vini took them down to a part of the beach where the waves were fiercer.

At this beach, which was on the cusp of a coastline that wrapped around a hilled part of the town, and then came around to the ports, the water hit against the lips of the beach at a harsher tone. Vini demonstrated their next practice with his own board, swimming out with his belly on the board to catch whitewater and then ride out back to shore. Once Vini had explained the process to them, the couple set out to practice for a couple of repetitions. They then returned and Vini went over the process of standing on a board on land before challenging the couple to go out and try.

Diana stood up with careful feet as she rode a wave. The couple practiced with Vini's assistance, working on their maneuvering skills for another hour before their time was over and they had learned the basics of what could be learned. By the end of the lesson, Diana and Tristan were able to comfortably rise onto the board and ride the gentle waves that came at them from the cove.

Vini walked with them back to the surf shop at Praia Icaria.

"Is surfing a popular sport here?" Tristan questioned. "There weren't that many people back where we were."

"The beach we were at was a quiet beach," Vini answered. "The best waves are on the east-side of the island, along that side going south"

"Our hotel faces the east," Diana chimed in. "I've noticed the waves to be more tenacious there."

Once the couple had returned with Vini to the surf shop, they returned the surfboards and then went to retrieve their backpacks from the small locker room.

"Well, that was fun," Diana admitted as the couple were alone.

"Yeah, I actually enjoyed that a lot. I hope we get to do more of that," Tristan replied, going through his things and looking at his watch. "It's almost three o'clock. Do you still want to spend some time on the beach, or should we return to the hotel?"

Diana picked up her smartphone from her bag.

"I don't have any messages from Charles, which means they're still not done," Diana replied. "Let's relax on the beach for a bit. I'm going to change out of this suit and into my bathing suit."

"Okay. I need to change out of this shirt – it's all wet and stuffy," Tristan remarked.

Diana left and went into a change room. Tristan took off the sun shirt and then sat it onto the bench. He then looked up and over to himself in the mirror. He paused as he looked at himself – his torso, all covered in sporadic scars from the lashes the Huntsman whipped into him. Diana hummed in the background as Tristan became lost in his own disfigurement.

Tristan quickly pulled around his Hawaiian shirt as Diana got out of the change room. He buttoned up and then stuffed the wet sun shirt into his backpack. Diana wore a white bikini. She smiled at Tristan as he looked over to her. Diana sat down at the bench and took out a bottle of sunscreen to apply on herself. Tristan looked at the back of Diana's neck and to her own, lone scar.

Once the couple were set, they left the surf shop and walked out onto the waterfront path behind the beach. In the last three hours, the beach had become busier with plenty of people taking up a space with a towel on the sand. Tristan put on his sunglasses and walked with Diana to designate a space of their own. He could observe plenty of women, young women especially around his age and older, most of whom wore string bikinis. There were women of all sort, of the Iberian-kind, the castizo-type, and even some of mixed ancestry; mestiço. There were also some women with fair-skin, who could have been Americans, and likewise women with dark-skin, African-Americans.

"Tristan?" Diana questioned.

Tristan turned around and looked at Diana.

"Huh?"

"How about here?" Diana asked again.

"Oh, yeah. Sure."

Tristan took off his backpack and the two took out their beach towels to spread them across. They then sat down and stretched their legs out.

"I didn't expect it to be this busy," Diana confessed.

Tristan looked back at her.

"I was hoping it'd be a bit quieter too," Tristan remarked. "Hopefully there's not much a tourist-scene over at the south of the island where the camp is. Then again, I hope the camp isn't much of a zoo, period."

Tristan sighed and then turned his head to the side. His eyes attempted to evade the women, which placed his eyesight towards the men. Even the men wore lewd swimwear, swimsuits with less than six inch inseams. Some of the men were larger than Tristan, more muscular, or simply taller and older. Tristan looked away from them and back forward, bringing his knees up.

Diana looked at Tristan and saw that he was uncomfortable.

"Hey," Diana said to him.

"What?" Tristan replied in a brash tone.

"You," Diana responded, pausing for a moment and then sighing. "You look uncomfortable."

"I'm not," Tristan answered her in an annoyed tone. "I was only hoping it'd be quieter here," he said, stretching his feet out again and leaning on his side.

Tristan raised his sunglasses and looked at Diana.

"Let's just enjoy each other, huh?" Tristan said in a calmer tone.

Diana gave a soft smile and rummaged through her handbag. She looked at her phone and then took out a bottle of sunscreen.

"Well, if you're determinate to stay here, then put on some lotion because I don't want you to get burnt."

Tristan took the bottle into his hand and opened it. He began to apply some to his forearms and legs. He also took some to his nose and neck. Diana watched. Tristan stopped when he had nowhere else that was exposed to go, hesitated for a moment, and then unbuttoned his shirt to remove it. Diana looked at the scars with saddened eyes. Tristan avoided looking at her directly, looking instead briefly from the corner of his eye before then looking forward as he finished to apply the sunblock. Tristan's eyes wandered off to some women, young women, he noticed looking at him and his scars.

Once Tristan had applied to his shoulders, he turned his back to Diana. She took the bottle and covered his back before he then returned to how he was positioned before. Diana took the bottle away and began to notice some bystanders look at her boyfriend with curious eyes looking at the scars.

"You look beautiful, you know that, right?" Diana said to Tristan.

Tristan lay back on the towel and brought his sunglasses over his eyes.

"Is that why you cried the first time you saw them?" he responded brashly again.

Diana shot a glance at him and gave him a backhanded slap on the side.

"I cried out of empathy, you jerk," Diana remarked. "To think of what my other half must've have gone through…"

Tristan brought on a slightly embarrassed face over himself.

"I'm sorry, that just came out," Tristan remarked. "I didn't mean it. I knew better…"

Diana sighed. She continued to rummage through her bag, but then dropped it off on the side.

"Well, after that, I think I'm going to go for a swim in the sea," Diana expressed, standing up. "Watch our things, will you?"

"Okay."

Tristan sat up as Diana left, watching her from behind as she went towards the sea and then dropped down to swim out. He let out a sigh and then dropped back to lie down and soak in the sun.

"I'm such an idiot," Tristan muttered to himself.

Tristan's self-loathing was cut-short as his ears twitched to the sound of some females yelling out alongside the laughter of some men. Not too far from where they had the towel set up, there were some men hosing down some young women in white t-shirts by a part of the beach where people could hose down. Tristan looked away and then continued to lay down as he tried to mostly ignore them with a mild growl.

Diana swam out for quite a distance, to the point where the ambience of chatter and shouting at the beach was a mere echo. She eventually stopped and turned back around. When she returned ashore, she had travelled a fair distance from where Tristan and she had set up, so she walked over to the waterfront path and returned on foot. Diana observed a crowd of males near a restaurant by the path. She then looked with disgusted eyes at the vibrant rainbow flag that hung from the canopy of the venue. Diana promptly returned to Tristan and sat down next to him with crossed arms.

Tristan raised his sunglasses as he looked at his girlfriend. Diana was looking about, eyeing the other males, not lustfully of course, but with skepticism. She then looked down to Tristan, noticing that he was looking at her before casting her gaze forward.

"If you want to leave, I'm ready to leave," Diana said with a pout. "I'd rather we sun tan at the beach behind the hotel than around here… with all these people… looking at us, at you."

Tristan sat up and nodded.

"Okay," Tristan agreed. "Let's leave."

Act 2, Scene 5

On Sunday, Charlemagne and Diana took Tristan and Allodia to the St. Thomas More Catholic Church in town where they celebrated Mass with the local population. Once the Mass had ended, they exited from the cathedral and came outside to another square similar to Ricardo Plaza, but with a luscious park in the center. In the ambience, there was both the organ playing from the church as well as a local band from the park playing traditional folk music, *Fado*. Charlemagne looked at his watch.

"An hour to twelve o'clock," Charlemagne said. "We'll be early, but I suppose it would be better to be early than late. He'll probably be late."

"There's no rush," Allodia cautioned. "The café is not too far from here and we have plenty of time. Let's enjoy the sights and slowly make our way over…"

Diana and Tristan held hands as they walked behind Charlemagne and Allodia. Diana wore a summer dress to Mass, while Tristan was formal-casual with a polo shirt and shorts. Charlemagne was in his summer suit, and Allodia in her own summer dress. From the front of the church, they crossed the street and entered a park with a fountain in the center. Allodia sat down near the band to listen to the strum of the Portuguese guitar. Meanwhile, Tristan looked at a bust of St. Thomas More behind an enclosure of bushes. Diana looked at Tristan who had an unimpressed glance on his face.

Tristan then turned to the melancholic music that came from the folk band. Diana and he went and sat down as Allodia hoped to burn some time. Charlemagne sat with his sister at another bench in the park. Tristan became lost in the music.

Within half an hour, the band had finished another song and Charlemagne rushed the three of them onwards to walk towards the café, which was fifteen minutes from their location, or twenty minutes with Allodia stopping in front of every boutique to window shop. Eventually, they arrived at a café where there were plenty of people sitting outside, enjoying themselves on a patio. The family entered and Charlemagne looked around.

"I don't see him," Charlemagne remarked. "Typical."

Tristan turned to the left as he saw a man rise from a table. The elderly man looked distinct from the pictures that Tristan had seen of Everest around the manor. For a start, this man was completely bald with only a thin line of white hair at his eyebrows over his piercing blue eyes. Crow's feet spread out from the far corners of the eye, and his cheeks were flabby, but he had a jaw that was strong like Salmar's. His face was clean-shaven. He had a slight hunch, a firm build, but even then, a pot belly that stuck out as he no longer had the strength to stick it in. The man was dressed in cargo shorts, a light blue polo that was tucked into his shorts, and tall socks that wrapped over his calves. He also wore sandals. Tristan looked at him as he looked to Charlemagne.

"You really should have learned by now to stop being so presumptuous," Everest remarked to his son.

Charlemagne glanced at his father and his cheeks reddened with embarrassment. Everest spoke in a firm voice as he used to, but his sentences came out in a hoarse-like manner as if it took a greater effort for him to speak than it used to.

"Dad," Allodia quickly said, going over and embracing him. "It's so good to see you."

"It's nice to see you too, Allodia," Everest said, hugging his daughter.

Allodia quickly moved away from her father so that Charlemagne could face him.

"Father," Charlemagne simply said, extending his hand.

"Did you come a thousand-kilometers just to give me a handshake?" Everest questioned, taking his hand.

Everest took Charlemagne's hand in a firm grip and patted him on the side with a hearted laugh.

"I'm only joking with you," Everest remarked, giving a hearted laugh as he shook his son's hand. "What's with the gloves? Worried about the virus?"

Everest's attention then shifted to Diana and Tristan. He let go of Charlemagne's hand.

"These must be the kids your mother told me about," Everest said with a slight chuckle. "They don't look like kids to me though…"

"They don't act like kids either," Charlemagne added. "I'd like you to meet Diana and Tristan. Likewise, please meet my father, Everest Cabernet."

Everest took Tristan's hand and patted him on the side. He did the same with Diana, looking to each of them.

"It's nice to see that my son has done *some* good in his life," Everest remarked, parting hands from Diana and then turning back to Allodia. "Boy, I didn't expect this. You told me you were travelling alone," he said, turning to Allodia with a smile. "You brought the whole family, minus Salmar of course."

"Surprise," Allodia replied in a calm manner. "I hope you're not upset."

"No, no," Everest assured her. "Here, let's find a larger table. Come on."

The five of them sat down at a table on the opposite-side of the restaurant by a window. Each of them were served some coffee and ordered some lunch.

"Boy, isn't this a nice surprise," Everest remarked with a hand at the handle of his mug of coffee. "Well, what brings you down to Isla Paraiso?"

"I brought them with me," Allodia answered. "I thought it'd be appropriate if Charlie came down with the kids to relax, unwind a little, and even help you and mom out. She asked for some assistance after all, so I brought the whole family to help out."

"Yes, you really have," Everest replied with another hearted laugh. "God, how long has it been since we've last seen each other, Charles?"

Charlemagne cleared his throat and answered, "Almost thirty-two years..."

"Eh?" Everest questioned. "Wow, and look at you – I'd barely recognize you had I not seen your face in the papers. What have you been up to recently? Last I heard, you were in Asia for the U.N."

"Yes, that's really been all," Charlemagne responded, "that and managing the family company; it's been a difficult quarter with the recession, so we've been struggling to stay afloat."

"Well, all empires have their time," Everest responded. "Believe me, I was happiest when I took my leave... You really ought to consider doing the same – don't let the stress eat what youth you have left."

"Hm," Charlemagne responded, displeasingly. "Unfortunately, there's no one to take care of the company with the same care at the moment... but let's not talk about our family's legacy, and let's instead discuss other matters. How have you been, dad? You've aged a lot since we had last talked."

"We all age," Everest replied, "but I've never felt better."

"You look almost like our great-grandfather with all your hair gone; your grandfather."

"I suppose I do," Everest remarked. "I've never thought of it – I barely knew him."

Tristan could hear a slight growl from Charlemagne's throat.

"Anyways, dad," Allodia cut in. "I know that I had told you that we would have lunch before I joined you at the camp, and that's still true, but Charlie and the kids are going to join us as well. However, since there's only room in the truck for the two of us and that cargo we have to pick up, they'll be returning to the hotel to pick up some things, and then I'll be returning to pick them up and bring them to the camp. Is that okay?"

"Yes, of course," Everest replied. "No, I suppose that's okay if they'll be helping out. We can get them setup with a tent each for sure. I'm glad that Charles and his adopted kids have come. I'm happy to meet you both, and I'm glad that you'll be joining us as volunteers. I really am. I never imagined it even when I heard it from Vienna – that Charles would ever have adopted two children. Well, when you dedicate your life and obsess over all sorts of nonsense, I suppose there was never any time to have kids of your own. Someone would have to inherit the 'precious' Cabernet fortune, but don't let that deceive you kids. It isn't a glamorous inheritance."

"Dad," Allodia interrupted and scolded.

"I'm sorry," Everest apologized. "I didn't mean to belittle you, Charles, especially in front of your kids."

"You didn't belittle me," Charlemagne replied.

"Anyways, tell me," Everest asked, shifting his focus back to the kid who only sat awkwardly. "What's it like living with Charles, eh? Has he been a good role-model to you both?" he asked with a hearted laugh.

"He's done the best he could provide, which has been a lot for us both," Tristan answered, "and because of Charles, I've been able to see and learn stuff that I wouldn't have been able to from, say, Salmar."

"What about you?" Everest immediately asked Diana.

"I think Tristan's summarized it perfectly," Diana replied. "Even if we've had our share of unpleasant experiences," she added, looking to Tristan, "there's been a lot of positive experiences, interesting moments, and neither of us would be who we are now, for the better, if it weren't for Charles."

"Good," Everest replied, nodding his head. "No, I'm glad – that's good to hear. Well done, Charles."

Everest raised his mug to him.

Charlemagne looked to Diana and Tristan as they looked back at him. The three of them then looked over to Everest who looked at the mug of coffee before him.

"Anyways," Everest remarked, looking to the kids again. "Tell me about yourselves. I want to know about my grandkids."

For the most part, the conversation at the table was dominated with Everest asking questions from Diana and Tristan with Allodia chiming in every so often, especially as Diana and Tristan were both timid and seldom spoke more than a few sentences. However, Charlemagne was unusually silent throughout the conversation up to when lunch was served when everybody quieted down. Instead, he sort of lingered at the corner of the table, listening and keeping to himself.

Once the five of them had finished lunch, they exited the café and stopped at the sidewalk.

"Well, I suppose I'll see you again later today," Everest stated. "There's lots to do at the camp."

"Yes, but first, we need to stop at the airport to pick up those supplies," Allodia reminded him. "We shouldn't take more than two hours since everything should be ready, but the drive from here and to the other side of the island takes about forty-minutes. I'll send you a message, Charlie, when we leave and if I have a signal, then I'll let you know when I'm on my way back."

"Sounds good," Charlemagne replied. "It was nice to see you, father. I look forward to getting to see mum."

"Yes, she'll be happy to see you too," Everest noted.

"Have a safe drive," Charlemagne lastly expressed.

Allodia and Everest left down the street, leaving Charlemagne with the kids. Charlemagne let out a sigh. He then looked to Diana and Tristan.

"Wasn't that nice and awkward?" Tristan remarked to Charlemagne with a sly smile.

"You have no idea," Charlemagne agreed with another sigh. "I'm afraid it's going to be a long summer for me."

Act 3, Scene 1

Later in the afternoon, Allodia returned to Villa Paraiso, but not with the truck, but a jeep, and she parked it in front of the hotel where Charlemagne was waiting with Diana and Tristan. Charlemagne carried two bags, one for his own personal belongings and another with Allodia's. Diana and Tristan each carried their own medium-sized gym duffel bags with their own personal effects. Charlemagne sat in the front of the jeep, while the couple took to the back. Once they were set, Allodia drove off, but made a quick stop to refuel before they continued on and left town.

The eastern road on the outskirts of town was by the shore and looked out to the ocean on one-side and the farmland on the other. The further they travelled the sooner the farmland was replaced with the outskirts of jungle as they drove along the elevated road that looked to the shoreline. Tristan observed that as Vino had said, the waves on the east coast were in fact a lot fiercer than on the northside. Even further along, the paved road was replaced with a dirt track, and finally, nothing.

Allodia drove over the sand of the beach as they approached the southside, and within a few minutes, Charlemagne could make out the camp further ahead. There was a lot of movement around the campgrounds, and as they got closer, Charlemagne observed there to be a lot of tents pitched around. Allodia parked the jeep near the trucks, which were parked at the outskirts of the beach.

"You know, it really amazes me how these two have travelled around half the third-world and not become convinced that they could use private security," Charlemagne remarked, exiting from the jeep.

"They're usually more discrete than this," Allodia answered. "I think this is the largest project they've ever undertaken in their lives to be honest, which was all the more reason for them to call me. A lot of this was initially a part of a smaller charity's efforts, but they ran out of money, so now they've taken over, kept the volunteers, and here we are."

"Yes, and here we are," Charlemagne repeated.

Allodia and Charlemagne walked towards the camp with Diana and Tristan behind them. The volunteers were noticeable by their light blue t-shirts and the large words that read, '*Voluntario*,' at the back in white font. Within the camp, there were various tents with signs at the top of the entrances that designated important areas, such as the kitchen, medical tents, and supply tents. Allodia took them to one of the supply tents where she picked up and distributed a large canvas bag to Charlemagne.

"We're short on tents apparently, so we'll have to share Diana," Allodia remarked.

"No matter," Charlemagne responded. "You'll be in good hands with her, and likewise, I think I can say the same about myself and Tristan."

"We need more tents, so maybe in the future we'll each have some privacy and each a tent to our own, but until then this'll have to do. They're really not a priority at the moment as much as food and water is. Each tent has enough space for at least two cots, so I'm told. They're not big tents, though. These are the personal ones," Allodia explained. "Here, Diana."

Diana took a cot into her hands. Tristan took two into his hand. The four of them then left and went to the far-side of the camp where they proceeded to set up their tents with ease as all four of them were fairly experienced at pitching a tent. Once the tents were set up, the cots went in with their personal belongings, and they were set. Diana sat down on her cot.

"Better than the bed I had in Harlech," Diana remarked.

"I know my brother was being a bit lippy about security, but this is a public space, so I hope you didn't bring too many valuables with you," Allodia remarked. "I only brought stuff I was okay with losing. When you've been in the business I've been though, pretty much everything you're prepared and ready to lose though."

"I left my phone and wallet behind in the safe in the suite," Diana responded, taking her camera and bringing the strap around her neck. "Charles already warned us before we left. He also moved some of your things into the safe too."

"Of course he did," Allodia replied, wiping her hands from the sand on them and sighing. "He's that type of brother, Charlie is. Always looking out for me…"

Diana smiled.

"Come on, let's go and see how the boys are doing. Also, Diana?"

Diana stood up and looked at her with attentive curiosity.

"Yes?"

"If I can get more tents in, would you prefer a tent with Tristan rather than splitting with me? Or would you prefer a tent on your own?"

Diana hesitated to give an immediate answer.

"I'm fine with whatever accommodation needs to be made, whether I'm alone, with you, with Tristan, or sleeping outside," Diana stated with a smile. "I'm flexible."

"Okay," Allodia responded.

The girls left their tent and came back outside. The boys' tent next to theirs was set up, but Tristan had returned from the supply tent with another cot for Charlemagne. He entered, while Allodia took Diana to see the beach.

"There we are," Charlemagne remarked, folding out the cot with Tristan. "Home sweet home."

"It's really humid in here," Tristan remarked. "This fabric is trapping all the heat in."

"Yes," Charlemagne agreed. "Perhaps we can make an adjustment later on, but in the meantime, I want to go and meet my mother – I've been dying to see her ever since we landed. Come on," he said, before stopping, "and Tristan?"

"Yeah?" Tristan questioned with a dull expression.

"Forgive me for intruding, but I hope you understand that when I make arrangements for bedrooms, and such, I do keep in mind the fact that you and Diana are an item, but also the fact that we're a Christian household, and Diana in particular is religious... My point is, I do not deliberately divide you two. I am honoring her religious beliefs – if the circumstances were different, I wouldn't care if you two shared a bed, or whatever..."

"It's alright," Tristan acknowledged. "Thanks, but it's fine. To be honest, ever since I came clean with you about the truth, I've made the effort to do the same, but not because of her beliefs. We never really honored that, because, well, we already broke the deal and believed, naively, that we'd be together forever. I made the effort because... I don't know because," he said with a sigh. "I don't know why I'm telling you this... Forget I said anything."

"No," Charlemagne responded, looking at him carefully. "I understand perfectly, Tristan, but although you may have been naïve to think then, don't think it to be naïve now. You and Diana complete one another, and that is good, and she loves you a great ton."

Charlemagne paused for a moment and then sighed.

"Every man needs his space," Charlemagne remarked. "This conversation is between us, okay?"

"Thank you."

"I too would also prefer that we keep you and Diana separate for the simple reason that Diana is skilled and trained in self-defense, and will keep Allodia safe if anything were to happen. Likewise, you too are trained in self-defense, so I know I'm safe with you. Don't let Allodia know that – she'll take offense to it."

"Okay."

"Come on," Charlemagne encouraged, slapping Tristan's right shoulder with a smile. "Come and meet my mother, Tristan. Next to my grandfather, she's the other half of my world who I owe my ego to."

Charlemagne exited the tent with Tristan behind him who continued to hold a sort of depressed expression. The expression faded as he was met with the hard sunshine and glances of the girls as they saw them. Charlemagne held a flat hand over his eyes as he looked to them.

"All settled in?" Allodia questioned.

"Quite," Charlemagne remarked. "We were discussing the fact that it is quite hot in those tents, so I'm thinking of perhaps making a few modifications to help them breathe better. If they go alright, I'd like to share the modification with your own tent."

"Well, we'll see," Allodia replied.

"Anyhow, where's our father gone?" Charlemagne asked.

"He should be around," Allodia responded. "I left him to unload the trucks with the volunteers, so who knows where he could be. We'll have to ask around."

"Nevermind that," Charlemagne replied. "I'd rather ask where our mother is so that we can greet ourselves."

"Good idea," Allodia agreed.

The four of them made their way into the camp from where they set up their tents and stopped to ask a volunteer.

"Excuse me," Allodia asked, "but do you know where Vienna Cabernet is?"

"Check the medical tent," the volunteer responded.

"Thank you."

Allodia and Charlemagne then made their way to a medical tent, which was a large tent with various cots spread out with island natives atop of them. A volunteer doctor could be seen alongside some nurses, around the tent. Another volunteer stopped to approach the family. She wore a face mask. Allodia approached her.

"Can I help you?" the volunteer questioned.

"We're looking for Vienna," Allodia requested. "My mother."

"Vienna is with first aid next door," the volunteer stated. "Please don't come here unless you've been sent for medical attention."

"Sorry," Allodia quickly responded, leaving the tent with Charlemagne. "Come on."

The four of them then went around to a separate tent that was part of the makeshift urgent care center. Inside the smaller tent, there were only four cots, and two volunteers looking after the wounded. Charlemagne raised his chin as he recognized his mother out of one of the two volunteers.

Vienna looked up and then waved. She quickly tied the bandage and then had the islander lay back down in his cot before she went around, taking off the latex gloves from her hands and then coming over to greet the four of them. Vienna Cabernet was a short woman, approximately five feet and four inches tall with short white-blonde hair. She had a round face with light fair skin, and wrinkles all about. She removed the glasses from her light blonde eyes and then wrapped her arms around her eldest and most beloved son. Vienna had a slim figure, wore a white blouse, and beige shorts with boots.

"Oh, Charles," Vienna remarked, embracing her son with a tight hug. "*Mein kleiner Charles. Wie gehts?*"

"*Mutti*," Charlemagne responded, "it's so good to see you again."

Vienna separated from her boy and looked up to him.

"Yes, it's been a long time," Vienna agreed in her Austrian accent.

Charlemagne then stepped aside. Tristan observed a wide smile over Charlemagne's face – a smile that he did not see too often on Charlemagne's face. Allodia went in and embraced her mother.

"Hello," Allodia greeted, hugging her.

"*Ah, Allodia, immer ein Vernugen,*" Vienna said. "*Mein kleines Madchen.*"

Allodia then parted from her mother and Vienna looked to Diana and Tristan.

"Oh, and who must these two youngsters be?" Vienna asked with a smile.

Vienna then went into embrace each of them, starting with Tristan. Tristan took the hug awkwardly. She then parted from him and brought a hand to his cheek.

"Yes, he's a big boy, Charles," Vienna noted, lightly tapping his cheek. "Very handsome. Very nice to meet you."

Vienna then went and hugged Diana, who received the hug less awkwardly than Tristan.

"Oh, she really does appear like she is part of the family," Vienna boasted, looking to Diana. "She has the eyes – not just the color, but the focus."

Diana blushed.

83

"Thank you."

Vienna stepped back and looked at them both.

"What a beautiful couple, Charles," Vienna remarked. "What beautiful children you have brought into your world. Oh, when your father told me that you were here, I had been just dying with anticipation to get to see you all. What a lovely turn of events this has been. No?"

"Ah, so my father told you we were here beforehand..." Charlemagne said.

"Yes," Vienna stated. "Yes."

Charlemagne did not respond.

"Oh, let me take a moment of rest so that I can properly give you a tour of the camp," Vienna remarked, removing a fanny pack at her side, which held various first aid items.

Vienna left the pack behind and then exited from the tent with the others.

"Welcome to the camp," Vienna said, walking with them as they began their tour. "It started out much smaller than it is now, but that's been mostly thanks to the various donations we've received and the volunteers we've been able to co-opt from around the world."

"Perhaps you should tell them what this is all about," Allodia suggested. "I haven't really told them what the mission of the camp has been."

"Oh, of course," Vienna responded. "Well, where do I begin? For a start, we're here because a lot of the indigenous people who have lived on this side of the island for centuries have been forcibly evicted from their homes because of legal problems over the ownership of the land. Your father could explain it better, but for the most part, the American courts had decided that Obelisk Corporation was entitled to the property they had purchased from a private individual, who had owned this part of the land for decades, but never developed it and purchased the land from the U.S. government shortly after they had acquired the island from the British during the war. The problem, however, was that the local people claimed to have been given this land by the British before they had left in a treaty, but since this treaty was done with the British and not Americans, that was the whole point of contention. They couldn't find the treaty either. And so, the local authorities evicted all of them people from their villages and they are now stuck here as refugees."

"What will be done then?" Charlemagne asked. "You can't hold them here forever."

"No, and while some have been offered to leave, and they've taken that offer, most don't speak even Portuguese and have nowhere else to go than here. The plan is that we assist in the development of the nearest village, which the courts had ruled to be a permanent reservation for the Kathunoacan people, but even then we've been facing resistance from those local people who don't like these people, especially since they have this sort of rivalry, been blaming them for bringing some recent bad luck with their missing children, and between that and some other problems, it's been madness here," Vienna said with a sigh. "I'm glad you're here though. We could use your help – all of your help. We're very short-handed at the moment."

"Hm," Charlemagne responded, "well, I don't think there's anything from a legal standpoint that we could do to earn these people their ancestral land back. When it comes to matters of the law, it's a losing battle for me even if one were to uncover that treaty. Tell me more about these missing children though."

"Oh, I don't know anything about that other than the locals from the village blaming these people," Vienna replied. "Ask your father, Charles, because he knows more. He does business with the villagers more than me. Hopefully, you can go and see the village with him tomorrow and also ask some of the people there. Your father and some volunteers have been constructing houses over there and I'd like it if you helped him. He can't keep pushing himself like he used – he's going to throw his back."

"Yes, perhaps I'll take the kids in tomorrow then," Charlemagne responded. "Where is he now?"

"Oh, I don't know, but he should be around. He might be in the kitchen if he's finished organizing the supplies," Vienna stated. "Have you set up a tent?"

"Yes, we're set up at the northside," Allodia replied.

"Oh, I was going to suggest that you set up to the south. That's where your father and I are with the other volunteers. It's okay... it's not a problem. Are you hungry? What about the kids? It's almost time for supper. We can finish our tour and then go and eat."

"Sure," Charlemagne agreed.

"There's a lot to do," Vienna repeated. "Once you're familiar with the camp, you can help out with some chores before you rest for the night. You'll have an early start tomorrow if you're to help out with your father. They head into the jungle early in the morning."

"We'll be sure to join him," Charlemagne assured her.

Act 3, Scene 2

The tour that Vienna took Allodia, Charlemagne, Diana and Tristan on was short-lived as there was not much to see around the camp other than tents upon tents stationed about. The entire camp was setup like a small community for the displaced people of the other village, who numbered to be approximately three-hundred in total, or about forty families, a majority of which consisted of children. In total, there appeared to be at most thirty volunteers, including the arrival of Charlemagne, Allodia, Diana and Tristan as well as the elderly Cabernet couple. Other than the tents where the islanders now lived in, the dining tent, the kitchen tents, and some tents where supplies were stored, there was little recreation in the camp other than a net and the beach at the side.

Early next morning, Charlemagne, Allodia, Diana and Tristan left with Everest and a team of six male volunteers to venture in the thick of the jungle and go to the village where the island natives would be resettled at. Charlemagne sat in a jeep that Everest drove with the kids in the back.

"I'm surprised a lot more villagers didn't accept to go and live in Villa Paraiso," Charlemagne remarked as he sat next to his father.

"The local city council does not provide welfare," Everest answered, "so while some of the indigenous people have been free to start a new life, most of them don't have the means to support that new life, so the only option for them is to start life anew in the United States, which is what the minority did when they left."

"I'm surprised the solution on your part hasn't been to phase them into urban life rather than to pour all these resources into constructing houses," Charlemagne remarked.

"We don't have money to support that kind of effort, Charles," Everest said in a stern voice. "I'm not sure what your mother's said to you about our financial situation, but we only own what is given to us, including our pension, and that is it and that is all we've believed we've ever needed. Everything else comes from donation, and that is barely enough for us. Of course, you're the billionaire, but I very much doubt that you'd own up to rehouse all these people, would you."

Charlemagne went silent.

"Perhaps you should put that brain of yours into use and attempt to win over the courts so that these folk can return to their rightful land," Everest remarked.

"It would hardly work like that, would it," Charlemagne responded in a distasteful tone. "Even if I were to find this alleged treaty, which I have thought of, a treaty signed between the locals and the British would not hold up in an American court. I've seen it rejected before, and even with today's justice system, it would not hold up. Americans value their property rights more than any right, believe it or not."

"What a vile system it is then," Everest replied. "Property rights…" he said, shaking his head. "Bah."

Charlemagne sort of scowled at him and then turned his face to look out the other side. Diana and Tristan rode silently in the back of the jeep, listening in on their conversation while they also looked around the jungle from the bumpy dirt road they travelled on. The jungle was extremely dense and consisted of tall trees, thick and wide, and very green with moss covering the bark and all sorts of shrubs and ferns leaving nothing of the ground to see beneath the flora. The humidity in the jungle was worse off than in the town and there was a lingering mist that acted almost like a fog above them. The ambience consisted of various critters in the background, tropical birds chirping away, and the high-pitched screech of cicadas, all of which was part of the diversity of this tropical rainforest. Charlemagne continued to scowl as he looked out the side of the jeep.

Tristan wore a white wife-beater underneath an open flannel shirt, while Diana wore beige shorts and her own flannel shirt. Both of them wore hiking boots. Charlemagne wore a different summer suit and Everest wore a light blue collared-shirt with sleeves-rolled up, tucked into a pair of beige shorts. Behind them, Allodia was in a truck that carried lumber and the other volunteers. Tristan merely sat in his seat, looking out the side of the jeep as they continued to drive through.

Within a couple more minutes, they crossed a makeshift bridge over a small river and then reached the village in the midst of the jungle, which took up a large open space covered in shade by the tall trees. Everest parked the jeep on the side of the dirt road, allowing the truck to pass and continue on. Tristan stood up in the jeep and looked over to the village, which only consisted of a couple of traditional structures, or huts. The construction site of the homes being built by the charity stood out as they had a modern appeal to them.

The four of them exited the jeep and made their approach over. Tristan quickly realized the presence of islanders around, having not noticed them by their dark skin. The islanders around them had even darker skin than the dancers they had seen at the hotel. Behind them, on the banks of the river, there were groups of men and women tilling at the land at the side of the river where they had a small farm that stretched on either side. The men and women here looked nothing in comparison to the dancers, who were well-built and fit. These people looked of average-size, of average-shape, and were not well-defined although they may have been as fit as they needed to be. Their skin was like mud though and their hair as dark as black hair could be, long, thick and unkempt. Both the men and women were shirtless, but they wore Western shorts as opposed to traditional clothing. From the river bank, the villagers looked over to them, and from the outskirts of the old village, more began to show, these people wearing Western clothes too.

"Come on, we've got lots of work to do," Everest remarked, walking over to the construction site. "We have to build a lot of homes by the end of the summer."

Charlemagne walked with Everest over to where Allodia had parked the truck. Many of the villagers continued to look on at them in curiosity. Tristan observed some elderly women raising their cupped hands up and bowing up and down. He also observed the children who were curious, but silent, and some older men who looked over at these foreigners with intimidating and plain faces. At the front of this crowd appeared a man in a white suit with a silver tie and a sort of white cowboy hat. He had long black hair that was tied in a ponytail. Charlemagne walked with Everest as they went to greet him.

"That is Dr. Waomoni," Everest explained. "He is the half-brother of Chief Arari and acting-chief at the moment. Please be respectful."

Charlemagne didn't respond.

"Good morning," Everest greeted, extending a hand to the acting-chief.

"*Bom Dia*," the doctor responded in a neutral expression.

"This is my son, Charlemagne Cabernet," Everest said, introducing Charlemagne. "He's here to help with our mission here in any way that he can."

"Mr. Cabernet, it is a pleasure to meet you," Dr. Waomoni remarked, shaking Charlemagne's hand. "I've heard much about you. I hope that we can get together some time, all three of us to better discuss ways in which you may help my people, but if you'll excuse me, I must return to town for some business to attend to."

"Very well," Everest responded.

"It was nice to meet you," Charlemagne replied.

"I have arraigned twelve of our own to help you with the construction of these houses," Dr. Waomoni remarked. "If you require any sort of further assistance, please seek out one of the elders in the village."

"Will do," Everest affirmed.

Dr. Waomoni promptly left the two of them and went towards an SUV that was parked and protected by some men in suits. Charlemagne and Everest watched as the car drove off.

"You said he was a doctor?" Charlemagne questioned.

"A medical doctor," Everest responded. "Yes. He stops by on occasion and has become the leader of the village ever since the chief caught COVID-19. He's been in critical condition at the hospital in town ever since."

"Oh dear," Charlemagne replied. "Has any other villagers caught the virus?"

"Not that I'm aware of," Everest responded. "Our volunteer doctors have become all the medical help they can get, and between us and Dr. Waomoni, nothing that I've heard of, but that's enough of that, we're here to build houses."

Everest left Charlemagne, who turned around to look back over to the villages. Half of them had dispersed. Everest began to organize the labor when Charlemagne was suddenly approached by some of the elderly females, mothers and grandmothers, from the village. One of them, a short, but large lady spoke in the indigenous tongue and was speaking rapidly to him. She held her head sort of down and her hands were together grasping a handkerchief. It appeared as though she was muttering a prayer to him.

"S-sorry, but I don't speak your language," Charlemagne apologized before looking around him. "Where's that volunteer who can speak Kathuno? Oy! You there! Come over here!"

Charlemagne waved a volunteer over. He ran over and stood next to Charlemagne.

"Do you have any idea what they're saying?" Charlemagne asked.

The volunteer paused for a moment and then said, "They think you're a doctor, probably by your clothes. She has a son who is ill and she wants you to cure him."

"I'm no bloody doctor," Charlemagne remarked. "Tell her that I'm not a doctor."

The volunteer spoke to them in their native tongue, but the women were persistent and did not listen.

"She's saying that her youngest boy has a bad fever and that he's been seeing visions of the devil, or a demon," the volunteer translated. "Nothing has worked to ease his pain."

"Well, tell them that they can see one of the doctors in the camp or the village chief," Charlemagne replied.

The volunteer told them this, but they became more upset.

"They've already seen both," the volunteer remarked. "None have been able to help."

Charlemagne was defeated by these words. He sighed and paused for a moment.

"Okay," Charlemagne replied. "Fine, I'll take a look at their son, but I'm not a doctor – make that clear to them. I'll do my best to try and make a diagnosis."

The volunteer translated this and the women were happy by these words. The volunteer then attempted to leave.

"Ah, not so fast," Charlemagne said to him. "I may need you if I have any questions."

Charlemagne and the volunteer walked with the women into the village. She took them to a hut where he entered and observed the interior. There was no basic floor in the hut, but it was instead basically dirt. The windows had no glass, but the beds did appear to have mattresses. In this sense, the homes were a sort of hybrid between new and old. Charlemagne was taken to a separate room in the house where he saw a young boy, perhaps eight-years old, on a mattress.

"Ask them if anybody else has fallen ill," Charlemagne remarked before he approached the boy.

"She says nobody else," the volunteer replied.

Charlemagne brought a hand to the forehead of the child and he was extremely hot. He then went onto assess his breathing, having the boy sit up so he could assess his breathing, bringing his ear to his back to listen on the lungs. He then compared the coloration of the skin with the others to see it to be about the same. Lastly, Charlemagne checked the boy's eyes. During this assessment, the boy sort of muttered incoherently as the volunteer was unable to make any of the words aside from the Kathuno word for a demon or devil.

"Well, fever indicates an infection, or toxin," Charlemagne remarked. "Breathing appears to be good though. Ask if there's been any coughing or shortness of breath."

The volunteer asked.

"Nothing like that," the volunteer translated. "Only delusions and a fever."

"The fever would be causing the delusions…" Charlemagne remarked. "I don't think this is respiratory if there are no respiratory symptoms."

"Has there been any change of behavior before this? How long has he been like this?"

The volunteer asked and he translated, "A couple of days – it was spontaneous."

"Hm…" Charlemagne responded.

Charlemagne looked back over to the crowd by the doorway as they were shoved aside by an angry man, yelling in the local language. He waved a hand to Charlemagne and then pointed to the boy. The mother began to argue with the man.

"Er," the volunteer remarked. "He's questioning why you're here since the last doctor was unable to do anything… He's saying that the boy isn't sick, but cursed and that he got what he deserved for going into the ruins he was forbid from going to…"

Eventually, the father was taken out of the room by some of the other males. Charlemagne pondered for a moment and then looked at the boy.

"Well, I'll try and get a volunteer to come over and take some blood samples, take vitals, and perhaps move him to the camp so that he can be monitored. Ideally, he should be taken to a hospital, but we have to work with what we realistically have available…"

The volunteer translated to the women Charlemagne's instructions.

"Can I go now?" the volunteer asked. "Everest will be mad if I'm not out there instructing the others… I'm the only one that can speak Kathuno here."

"Yes, you can go," Charlemagne remarked. "Wait, one more favor. Can you quickly ask these women what their opinion is on the missing children?"

The volunteer paused for a moment and then asked the women. Each of them gave an account, which the volunteer then briefly summarized.

"None of them have personally lost children, but their mystified and don't know what's happened to those that have lost kids," the volunteer translated. "There have been accounts though of a mystic, or a witch doctor who preys on young boys and girls, but I have heard, and this isn't me translating what they've said, that this witch doctor is just an urban legend."

"Hm," Charlemagne responded. "Okay. Thank you."

Charlemagne and the volunteer left the hut. The volunteer returned to his duties, while Charlemagne looked around the village before making his way back over to the construction site. He found Allodia who was near Diana, looking at blueprints for the homes while Diana took photos.

"Isn't this nice," Allodia said to Charlemagne. "By the time we're finished, this entire village will be modernized with their own energy supply even."

"Yes, quite nice," Charlemagne responded in disinterest. "I need a favor. I can't do much to help with these houses, but I just met with a little boy who appears to be quite ill. I was wondering if I could commandeer the jeep for a moment while I go deeper into the woods to look for some ruins. I believe it was possible that this boy may have eaten or touched a berry or plant of some kind, but I need a sample before I can develop an antidote."

"What?" Allodia questioned. "You want me to enable you to go out on a little quest?"

"I'm not going to ask our father, am I?"

Allodia did not respond. She then sighed.

"Fine, but be quick about it because I don't want him to start to complain about where the jeep is when it comes time to return home."

"Thank you," Charlemagne replied.

"Can I come?" Diana asked. "I'm not doing anything here either and I've taken enough pictures. I want to go and do some hiking with you."

"Certainly," Charlemagne agreed. "Good idea. Where's Tristan?"

"Tristan's with dad," Allodia answered as Charlemagne looked for Tristan among the volunteers ahead. "Right now, he's the most useful out of us, putting his strength into helping with the house building."

"Oh," Charlemagne remarked. "No matter, you'll be safe with him. Come on, Diana, let's go."

Act 3, Scene 3

Everest had quickly divided the labor into three groups to work on three of the houses today. Afterwards, Everest took Tristan on a quick tour of the project.

"Have you ever taken part in constructing a home?" Everest asked Tristan as they walked through the construction site.

"Never," Tristan responded, looking around.

"When I was about your age, I had a summer job helping to build homes," Everest remarked. "Every teenager should have to live through the experience of laying down a foundation or bringing up the walls of a home. It gives you an appreciation for places that most take for granted. By the end of the summer, I'll make sure you're familiar with the whole process and can feel the same sentiment. I for one, take great joy in getting to create something as simple as a home. It is by no means though a simple process."

Everest stopped in front of one of the homes. Before them was an unfinished concrete brick foundation in a rectangular shape. There were various plots like these spread around the entire construction site, or clearing of lands where the homes would be placed. There were also some machines, such as a bulldozer and an excavator parked around the site alongside various palettes of lumber, bricks, and other equipment.

"Did you help build the manor back in Allabrese?" Tristan asked.

"The manor?" Everest questioned. "Oh, you mean the family home. No, my father built that when I was only about six-years old. I didn't take part in that."

Tristan didn't respond.

"Do you see this, though?" Everest remarked. "Each of the homes start with a stemwall foundation made of these bricks.

We stack them and keep them together with mortar, and once that's set, we'd set the wood atop to create a frame and then lay sheets over to make the floor. The alternative process to that is lay down a concrete slab, but 'cause of the climate, it'd be better for the folk here if we built each home with a crawlspace. We'll lay down some more foundations once we get these first few houses here finished, but enough on that... Come over here where I can use your help laying down some walls."

Tristan walked with Everest over to one of the plots where a foundation had been laid down with sheets of wood atop, setting the ground floor. Next to the house that Everest had stepped up to, there was a more completed home with walls all around the perimeter, including exterior sheets. At the moment, the team assigned to that house was setting a frame above, which would become the ceiling of the house, and involved individual pieces of long wood being brought up and then sat down. Tristan looked as they carefully navigated around the tops of the walls to place each piece down.

Everest picked up a belt from atop of some lumber and handed it to Tristan. On the belt were pouches with various tools. Everest also picked up a nail gun before looking to Tristan.

"Go on and pick up some of those two longer pieces of wood over there," Everest said to Tristan.

Tristan put on the belt and then walked over to pick up the two long pieces of wood that Everest had pointed at.

"Bring 'em over here," Everest requested, walking up onto the ground floor of the house.

Tristan brought them up and slid them over. Everest pulled them further and then sat them apart.

"Good, and bring over those twelve shorter pieces up," Everest requested, "and then those stints I left over there."

Everest proceeded to measure the pieces of wood with a measuring tape while Tristan gathered the rest of the lumber. Once all was gathered and set above, Everest had Tristan climb up and join him on the platform.

"I measured these last night, so it should all be well and done," Everest remarked, checking on the measurements. "Right, now, we're going to build this left wall, so help me place those medium-sized pieces of wood in the middle. We want them spaced-out at each mark here."

Tristan looked at the longer pieces of lumber as he saw markings for where the medium-sized pieces would go. Once he saw these, he set off to place them down properly before Everest returned with another nail gun.

"I don't suppose you've ever used one of these before," Everest remarked to Tristan.

"No."

"Well, luckily for you, there's not much to it," Everest replied. "Come on, I'll show you."

Everest knelt down next to the longer piece of wood and simply shot a nail into the piece of lumber like it was a gun, a nail gun. He made the insertion twice to properly secure the piece of wood together.

"You see?" Everest remarked, giving the tool to Tristan. "Do that on both sides just as I did it, while I go on and do the sides."

"Okay," Tristan responded, taking the nail gun into hand.

Everest went to the side of the wall they were building and put two identical medium-sized pieces together and then proceeded to bind them from their lateral side to the face of another medium-sized piece. He properly secured these pieces together before joining Tristan to bind the larger pieces together. Once that was done, Everest had Tristan help with setting the smaller pieces of wood between the medium-sized pieces of lumber, strengthening the structure. The smaller stints were placed in a pattern, one slightly above the former, but the third lower again. Tristan did this task while Everest focused on some openings in the wall, which were to be windows. Everest routinely looked up to check on how Tristan was doing as they worked on their separate tasks.

Once the wall was put-together, Everest and Tristan immediately placed sheets of wood over top and secured them with more nails. After, Everest quickly drilled some holes into the bottom of the wall before he called some workmen from the site next-door over to help them push the wall up.

"Alright, on three," Everest said to the men. "One, two, three…"

Tristan assisted in raising the wall up and then bringing it over to the edge of the platform where there were small rods poking up and out from under the floorboards. The wall went carefully into the platform. Everest let go and hopped down to make sure that everything inserted correctly. Once he saw that it was good, the team were permitted by him to lower the wall down. Tristan carefully let go of the wall at his own caution, but the wall was secured into the rods.

Everest climbed back up and the two proceeded to secure the wall further by punching nails to connect the wall with the foundation. Once that was done, Tristan stood up and stretched his back. He also wiped some sweat from his forehead before looking over to see Diana approaching him. Tristan walked over and hopped down to see her.

"What's up?" Tristan questioned.

"Charles and I are going to go for a hike," Diana remarked. "I see that they've got you busy here, and I think Charles would prefer if you stayed with the crew in case something were to happen."

"Okay," Tristan responded. "Be careful."

Diana gave a warm smile at Tristan's words of caution, blushing almost. She kissed him on the cheek, but quickly took it back as she felt the sweat on his face.

"Do you want me to take your flannel with me? You're going to get a heatstroke if you keep that on and keep on working here," Diana remarked.

"Oh, yeah, okay," Tristan responded, taking off his flannel and handing it to her. "I'll see you later then."

"For sure," Diana replied before leaving.

Tristan watched her off and then climbed back up to rejoin Everest who had been watching them.

"You have an awful lot of scars on your arms," Everest said to him.

Tristan looked at his arms and then back over to Everest.

"Yeah, they're from sports," Tristan replied.

"Sports?" Everest questioned.

"Yeah," Tristan remarked to him. "So, what's next?"

Everest refocused and looked behind him.

"Next? We've got to finish the rest of these walls," Everest said.

Tristan continued to help Everest as they made the front wall of the house and then raised it up. Afterwards, they made the right wall and then finally the rear-wall, which left them almost enclosed. Everest left Tristan to put together the first interior wall that would mark a bedroom, while he took a saw and began to cut out the spaces where the windows would go. Everest routinely switched from sawing out spaces for the window and helping Tristan with the walls until it was almost noon and time for them to take an hour break. By then, they had completed the entirety of the ground floor and started to work on installing the roof. However, after six hours of work, it was now break time.

Tristan sat down to eat the lunch that some volunteers from the base camp had brought.

At the end of the break, the volunteers resumed for another six hours of work. Tristan resumed to work with Everest as they began to cover the ground floor with a similar frame so that they could lay down a ceiling. The two worked close together from above as they installed each rib of the frame.

"There's nothing more refreshing than to be outside and to work from outside," Everest remarked to Tristan. "Don't you agree?"

"I guess," Tristan responded in a lame tone.

"Did your own father ever take you outdoors, Tristan?"

"My father never raised me," Tristan clarified. "My uncle did, and he did used to take me outdoors. What about yours?"

Everest paused for a moment and kept his eyes away from Tristan. He then resumed to work, inserting nails into the side of the piece of lumber Tristan had just brought down.

"Yes, as a matter of fact, my father used to take me outdoors quite a lot in the summer when I was young, to camp," Everest replied. "Some of my fondest memories with him were in the forest."

"Huh," Tristan responded in a plain tone.

"As a matter of fact, the moments we spent outdoors were some of the only memories I ever had of my father. He was not a man who spent a lot of time with me. He was either working, or overseas for one of his petty adventures, or sometimes overseas for work. Does Charles travel a lot?"

"Sometimes," Tristan responded. "He usually takes us if he can, but more than half the time we can't join him because of school."

"Good," Everest replied, nodding. "I'm glad that he at least has the decency to share in his (mis)adventures."

Tristan didn't respond. He instead continued to work as he laid down another beam.

"I'm quite impressed by Charles," Everest noted. "Never in my years did I ever expect him to adopt not one, but two children."

"We were sort of an unexpected twist to his life," Tristan replied, focusing on his work. "I used to be in Salmar's care, but then... well, I suppose you know what happened with him, right? Charles adopted me... well, I don't know why to be exact. I always thought he did so just so I wouldn't have to go to a foster home and since we had a lot in common back then – because he liked me and I liked him. Then again, I still like him..."

"You and this Diana girl..."

"She's my girlfriend," Tristan clarified. "In case you didn't know."

"The two of you remind me of my wife and me," Everest commented. "To have someone like that in your life is special, let me say that as much. Not a day goes by that I don't consider myself lucky – we've been married for almost sixty years, you know! She's the center of my life and she's made me the happiest man in the world... We've known each other since high school!"

"Yeah, I sort of figured, Tristan responded. "I know you were only sixteen when Charles was born."

"Right," Everest replied. "You seem like an intelligent boy, Tristan."

"You deduced that from the fact that I knew a minor detail of your life?" Tristan questioned.

"No, because I've been observing you quietly as we worked," Everest replied. "You've been very meticulous in your work, and I can only suspect because you don't want me to criticize you. You've also picked up this craft very quickly… and I've heard positive remarks about you from my wife, but that is a minor detail. I don't take the words of men (or women) with great consideration. I judge men by their actions. When I was chairman of Cabernet Industries, this was what I had learned from those corrupt investors."

Everest shook his head.

"What a state that Cabernet Industries was in when I was in charge. All of them… a pack of wolves. I don't know how Charles has had the temperament to cope with them, or how he continues to work for that crooked corporation."

"Cabernet Industries is corrupt? I've heard nothing but good things about it from Charles. I mean, I've personally seen some suspicious activities, but they were minor and Charles has always told me, and I've known, that Cabernet Industries was an honest company."

"Well," Everest replied, pausing from a moment. "I don't know for certain what it's like now, but when I was in charge, it was miserable. I had entered the position with high hopes of change, to bring change, and in the end, I found myself to be used by these greedy men for their own benefit – a benefit that hurt others. I didn't see any hope to change that, but there was no way out until I made the decision to cut my ties and divide control between my three children."

"Why didn't you liquidate your assets?"

"I couldn't," Everest responded. "Salmar and Allodia were young and didn't deserve to have their lives changed because of me. Charles too. I retained Cabernet Industries and did what I did for them, so that I could do what I wanted most with the woman I loved, for us."

Tristan didn't respond.

"Anyways, we've become carried away," Everest remarked. "Pass me that board. We'll never finish if we keep lollygagging."

Tristan continued to work as he asked, "But tell me about your work. Why travel the world and help others?"

"Why not?" Everest questioned. "You must understand, in my time with Cabernet Industries, I had seen a lot that I'm grateful for, but that which was also unjust and the sort of greed no man should have to see. I saw the exploitation of the livelihoods of others for the gain of a few rich men, especially from the third-world. Ever since then, I've committed myself to this – to purge myself of the spirit of my family, our people, because the world is unfair... Why would others live in poverty while rich men bask in luxury? I've spent the last years of my life dedicated to raising others, using my skills to achieve that for them, which is only useful motive I have for my life. Just because the world is a cruel and corrupted place, does not mean that I have to tolerate that."

"Right..." Tristan responded, "but do you feel like you've made the world a better place because of your work? I mean, isn't it still a dreadful place?"

Everest paused for a moment again. He then sighed.

"Less so than before," Everest remarked, avoiding eye contact with Tristan as he responded. "Come on, we're slacking..."

"Sorry," Tristan apologized, slightly dissatisfied by the respond. "Sorry."

Tristan focused on his work while Everest took a moment to wipe some sweat from his forehead. He then took a moment to look around. Everest and Tristan stopped talking for almost ten minutes until Allodia came around.

"You've done a lot of fine work here," Allodia commended from the exterior of the house, looking up to them. "Are you having fun, Tristan?"

"Allodia," Everest responded, interrupting a response from Tristan, "where did Charles go? I've just noticed that he's not around. Wasn't he supposed to be helping us?"

Allodia stuttered for a moment and then replied, "He took the jeep and went off to investigate some flora nearby. He thinks a local kid may have eaten or touched something, and that's made the boy ill."

Everest scoffed and said, "He's been lured into looking after that boy with the fever, hasn't he? He's already been examined by our doctor and their own chief... They said it was most likely the flu made worse by the heat. Where does he get these wild conclusions from? Who does he think he is, using our resources so that he can go off on one of his selfish adventures?"

Allodia and Tristan were silent. Tristan simply continued to work.

Act 3, Scene 4

Earlier, after having talked to Tristan, Diana returned to the jeep where Charlemagne was, moving around to the front passenger seat door as Charlemagne entered and sat down at the driver's seat. Diana opened the door to her side and noticed a backpack at the foot of the seat.

"Sorry about that," Charlemagne said, taking the backpack. "Just some of my things I thought I'd bring with me."

"You came prepared?" Diana questioned. "Why am I even surprised?"

"Honestly, you've known me for as long as it's been. Why are you surprised?"

Diana neatly folded Tristan's flannel shirt.

"Let me put Tristan's shirt in," Diana requested, opening the backpack and placing it inside. "I don't want to lose it. Tristan can be pretty stringent about losing his things and this is his favorite shirt."

Diana took the backpack and kept it at her feet while Tristan started the jeep. He then pulled out and drove through the rest of the village and then continued down a dirt track that went further and deeper into the jungle. Charlemagne looked to Diana as he drove.

"I can't remember the last time the two of us ventured on our own," Charlemagne remarked. "It's not like you to want to join me on an adventure. Did you really want to join me, or...?"

"I don't know," Diana replied. "Are you really interested in finding some plant, or did you just want to escape from your dad?"

Charlemagne didn't respond.

"And for the record," Diana carried on and said, "I enjoy when we spend time together."

Charlemagne gave a light smile.

"But it's not healthy that we indulge on escapism," Diana remarked. "Between Tristan and your dad, they're two people we shouldn't be running away from."

"Bah, they'll be fine together," Charlemagne replied. "*And for the record*, I am concerned about that young boy, and since I don't believe in superstitious nonsense, I refuse to believe a 'curse' afflicted that young boy. For all we know, he could have eaten an interesting-looking berry or leaf. The emphasis on the berry, since that's more of a likelihood."

Charlemagne sped up and continued to drive on. The trees in the thickness of this forest were like those behind them. The density was worse however, and the road was very unsteady and eventually ran out. At the end of the path, Charlemagne stopped the jeep and turned it around. He then shut off the engine and had Diana hand him his backpack so he could retrieve a handheld GPS. Charlemagne fiddled with the device.

"I'm setting our location," Charlemagne said. "We'll hike the rest of the distance."

"Do we even know where we're going?"

"We're going to just hike around," Charlemagne replied. "Not all ruins can easily be found. There's rarely ever a map with an X that marks the spot."

Diana didn't respond. Instead, the two of them got out of the vehicle. Charlemagne put his backpack around him. Diana then joined him around the other side and they ventured forward through the dense jungle.

The trees in this part of the island were wide and tall with branches sprouting upward from the trunks and then spreading out with a dense foliage of avocado green leaves. From these branches, vines fell downward towards the ground. Around these trees, there were bushes that were about as large as small trees, but they had thin trunks. Alongside these two types of trees, there were also extremely large ferns and philodendrons with large and thick leaves. At the base of this vegetation, there were occasional patches of extremely tall and thick grass as well as a covering of moss and groundcover with fair-sized leaves. Likewise other than moss at the side of trees, there were also coverings of ivy.

Charlemagne and Diana continued through the tropical forest, eventually finding themselves to be climbing up a slope before they then turned down to reach a ridge with a river. The river water was a thick and dark green, reflecting the surrounding trees. The pair followed the river as far as they could until the ridge elevated itself even further with a rocky cliffside that had multiple small cascades of water flowing from the stream that came from a greater height. The larger stream that the pair had been walking along converged at this point from three smaller streams that had joined at this point and flowed from each respective cascade. Charlemagne eventually led Diana to a low-bridge made of wood that allowed them to cross the water.

At the end of the bridge, Charlemagne and Diana eventually reached the other small stream where they found another bridge and then another. The pair continued forward as Charlemagne checked his GPS. Within a couple of minutes of walking along the forest, they eventually reached a large cliffside wall that was approximately fifty feet or so tall. Instead of continuing left, Charlemagne instead took them right as he looked at his GPS.

"I want to stay within an area close to the village," Charlemagne remarked. "If we venture too far, we might miss the ruins. We'll stay close for now."

Charlemagne and Diana followed the cliffside wall and eventually began to climb up the side of the cliff as they reached another slope. At the top of the slope, the earth blended with the top of the cliff so they found themselves at a high altitude where the forest continued on. Charlemagne stopped again at the top of the cliffs where they looked behind them to a view of the large shrubs of leaves that were the treetops. Unfortunately though, any magnificent view of the greater forest was obscured by the heads of trees that faced them as the trees were taller than the cliff they were on. Charlemagne and Diana carried on and walked to the right, following the top of the cliff until they began to hear the roar of a waterfall in the surrounding area.

After another few minutes, the trees at their side were replaced with a view of a minor drop towards the river they had been following with the trees on the other side. From here, Diana was able to see some of the palm trees and palm shrubs she hadn't noticed before that were scattered around on the shore of the river. The space they walked on was less dense than the rest of the forest and was a sort of a minor clearing in the space of all the vegetation as there wasn't much to brush against as they walked. It was a sort of a natural dirt path that they followed with trees and bushes to their side as below. Among these bushes, Diana noticed some shrubs with a beautiful magenta flower with thin petals and an orange-yellow center. The edges of the petals were a light pink-purple. Diana also noticed some groundcover flowers that were a goldenrod color with red centers. The trees at the side were of the same kind, ivy, vines and moss at the trunks, but Diana now began to take notice in the distribution of some palm trees and palm shrubs with the tall ferns and philodendrons.

Charlemagne, as Diana had observed, was paying close attention to their surroundings as he walked. He took advantage of the fact that his hands were gloved to touch the foreign foliage, which was something Diana abstained from. Instead, she attempted to avoid skin contact with the bizarre tropical plants. Diana eventually stopped on the path as she saw an anomaly before them. Charlemagne, who had not really been paying attention to his front path, took a moment to notice that Diana had stopped moving to see what was before them.

In front of the pair, a sort of pillared statue loomed down on them at approximately ten feet tall. The base of the statue was constructed in a chiseled, light grey stone before extending upwards to a sort of totem figure with a face that sort of looked like a puma. However, this cat had a sort of mane with turquoise feathers carved out of stone and held its arms up at its side with paws pointed outwards at either side. Charlemagne observed the statue for a moment, walking around it to look at its details while Diana took out her camera to zoom in on its face and nab a shot. The statue had some minor runes or emblems around certain edges to even the eyes, and some parts of the statue had been painted in an assortment of terracotta red or gold.

"Hm," Charlemagne simply noted. "Well, we must be close if this is here. Perhaps this devilish figure was used to ward off unwelcomed guests. Come on."

Charlemagne took out his GPS to check on their location and then the two carried on, reaching another slope that wrapped around and left the side of the ridge. They climbed even further up and began to find themselves moving left again. From the height they had reached, Diana was finally able to see the greater forest around them with the treetops below. Instead of continuing either left or right, Charlemagne and Diana went deeper into the forest behind them, inwards, to reach the other side of the plateau where they ran up to another steep cliff wall. The roar of a waterfall seemed closer. Charlemagne took them further left until they reached a small canyon that led them to the other side of the mound.

Here, there was another small plateau that looked to the greater forest behind. The breadth of the island seemed a lot larger than from the skies. To the left, the edges of the cliffs led to a canyon where a river ran below, but connecting two sides of the canyon was a rope bridge. Further to the left was another, separate plateau separated by a canyon that joined with the former. From this third plateau, a wide cascade gushed down around the side and spilt into the canyon river below.

Charlemagne and Diana stopped at the side of the cliff by the rope bridge to marvel at the enormous waterfall with its stream of white water and the mist that floated up from below.

"Wow," Diana awed. "Now that's something you don't get to see every day," she remarked, taking a picture.

"Indeed," Charlemagne replied before looking over to the bridge and the heights around them. "I hope you're not afraid of heights, because we appear to be navigating around tall lands."

Diana didn't respond. She put her camera down and continued to observe around her. She then looked across the bridge and into the forest beyond. Diana pointed forward.

"Maybe we don't have far to go – look over there. I see some sort of structure."

Charlemagne squinted.

"Perhaps another statue. I wouldn't be surprised if the ruins were around here."

Charlemagne approached the wooden rope bridge and examined it. He crouched down and checked the panels of the bridge and the supports. He removed his backpack and took out some rope, securing it on his own spike before bringing it with him as he crossed the bridge.

"I don't trust this bridge, so I'll go first. If all is safe, then you can cross."

"Sounds good to me," Diana replied.

Charlemagne took his rope and proceeded to cross the suspension bridge. The bridge swayed as he crossed, but held. Once he was on the other side, Diana took the rope and crossed with careful steps. The two reunited at the other side, left the rope behind, and then carried on. Charlemagne and Diana reached the structure she had seen, which turned out to be a gate made of a similar stone as the statue further behind.

The pair passed under the gate and carried on to notice more man-made structures around them in absence of dense trees. There were still trees, shrubs, and other plants around, but in less of a density and more spread out as they were in a sort of clearing that was not clear, but littered with these structures.

"I can see why the local children would come here," Charlemagne remarked, looking around. "Between the falls, and these ruins, this would be like a playground to them."

Charlemagne went to some shrubs around the ruins to examine their fruit, collecting some samples, but he found very little. The pair carried on and eventually came back into the density of the jungle, but they had not left the ruins as some man-made works could still be seen around them, wrapped in moss and vines. Charlemagne cautiously led Diana forward where they eventually reached another clearing that housed a temple of sorts in the center.

The temple was surrounded by the ruins of ancient walls. There were some gaps in the walls, such as where the pair had come out of, as the state of the ruins was poor. The temple in the center of the grounds, the ground of which was merely a tall grass, was pyramidal in shape with a set of stairs in the center that led up to entrance. In comparison to the other pyramids the two had seen, this one was vastly smaller than the Great Pyramid in Giza, and perhaps the same size of one of the smaller Egyptian satellite pyramids. The temple was greatly smaller than the temple in Burma that Charlemagne had visited last spring. Closer to the temple, the ground was integrated with a stone floor. Between the palm shrubs and trees that could be seen around, there were also some statues similar to the one seen in the outskirts of the ruins, before the grand waterfall. The temple entrance was below a sort of terrace at the top of the pyramid where another entrance came out from within. There were then a set of second stairs that went to the very top of the temple. The temple itself could not be taller than a four-story modern structure.

"Hm," Charlemagne remarked, "shall we go inside and take a look?"

"Why not," Diana replied. "The thought of entering the probable sight where human sacrifices took place certainly isn't going to have any sort of bad omens or demons around."

Charlemagne proceeded to lead on as he replied, "Well, the father of the ill child did state that these lands were cursed."

Diana stopped and looked at him. Charlemagne looked back.

"You're kidding, right?" Diana questioned.

"No, I really am not," Charlemagne responded, "but don't be silly. The boy wasn't cursed. He most likely ate a bad berry – you know that to be more likely, don't you?"

Diana didn't seem convinced.

"All I know, is that in the last three years that I've known you, I've seen ghosts, a Yeti, aliens, zombies, an anarchist cult, and a dragon."

"The zombies and dragon were a figment of the imagination," Charlemagne reminded her. "All of those had rational explanations behind them. A curse – it's improbable. The rational explanation for that, is as I said… perhaps even, a mold or gas of some sort."

"Do we have gas masks?" Diana questioned.

Charlemagne frowned at her. He then took off his backpack and took out two respirators. Each of them took one.

"Happy?" Charlemagne questioned.

"A little," Diana replied, voice muffled.

Act 3, Scene 5

Charlemagne and Diana entered the temple through the main entrance, which brought them to a square room with a set of two stairs before them that went up and another wider staircase between these two sets that went down. At first, they took the set of stairs that came up to the top of the temple. From here, where the ceiling was low, they could exit from the open archway above the main entrance and then take a set of stairs at the sides that went to the very top of the temple, but they did not go up to the top. Instead, they looked out from the terrace and then returned down to come into the depths of the temple. Charlemagne and Diana both carried with them a spotlight in one hand that shined the way for each of them, and Charlemagne also carried an air quality detector in the other hand.

Upon reaching the bottom of the temple, Charlemagne checked the air quality around him before removing his respirator.

"We're safe," Charlemagne concluded. "No presence of any harmful fungi or gasses."

Diana did not respond as she looked around the interior of the temple. The shape of the room was like a reverse pyramid with the floor that they reached being the smooth top and the walls around them diverging outwards. The stairs they had come down were lined against one of these sides and were raised out in large steps, except before them where instead there was a large mural. To the left and right, there were tunnels in the center that expanded outwards. Diana removed her respirator as she finished examining the central temple space.

"So, what's the significance of a place like this to these people?" Diana questioned. "Doesn't look much like a mausoleum."

"If the local people are anything like the other ancient Mesoamericans, then it could be like the more traditional pyramids, a place of internment, or a ceremonial site where rituals are conducted and they honor their deities."

Charlemagne shined his light towards the mural as he finished examining around him.

"The sort of rituals are as you surmised earlier – human sacrifice and torture – the bizarre and inhumane practices that appease these false gods. I could never make sense of their primitive actions, and perhaps it would be folly to attempt to make sense of such a senseless act."

Diana took pictures of the murals as Charlemagne continued to look at them.

"I'm not an expert on this ancient civilization, but if it would be alright, could you send me a copy of the pictures of these hieroglyphs?" Charlemagne asked Diana. "I'd like to study them later."

"Yeah, that'd be no problem," Diana replied.

"Thank you."

The pair continued from the central chamber and went left to enter a separate room where there were more murals. Diana took a picture of the mural in this room while Charlemagne looked around.

"Empty," Charlemagne concluded. "Whatever used to be housed in this temple or tomb is long gone."

From the room on the left, the pair then went to the room on the right. Diana could not make sense of the paintings on the wall as they displayed an array of strange characters in a typical Mesoamerican art-style. Once they had finished looking at the art, they returned to the room in the center before they exited and looked around the grounds once more.

Charlemagne returned to Diana with a plain expression on his face, similar to the one that Tristan would typically carry. He was focused on the task at hand and environment around him, and he seemed frustrated. Charlemagne avoided eye contact with Diana as he spoke.

"Well, this is quite disappointing," Charlemagne remarked. "I have some samples, but from what I've seen, there doesn't appear to be anything that from my own knowledge, could have caused the condition of that poor child."

"What are you going to do then?" Diana asked.

"Well, I need to identify these plants and perhaps visit a local library to do some reading," Charlemagne responded. "Portuguese isn't an easy language for me to read, but hopefully there'll be some texts in English or even Spanish. If that fails, then I'll have try my luck on the Internet, but to do that I'll have to return to the hotel."

Diana didn't respond.

"Anyhow, we've spent half the day out here," Charlemagne remarked, looking at his watch. "We better return... I'm sure you're hungry as am I. Come on, we've got quite a hike to the jeep – it's never a pleasing moment when you must return from a long journey, is it?"

Charlemagne and Diana returned to the jeep within an hour and a half, and then they drove back to the village where they made a brief stop. Diana stayed in the jeep as Charlemagne went to speak with Allodia, and then he returned with her, and the three of them came back to the camp where Diana and Charlemagne went to eat a late lunch. Charlemagne seldom spoke as the two ate alone in the mess hall, and Diana observed that he was pensive.

After the two had eaten, Diana returned to her tent, while Charlemagne went to find his mother in the first aid tent. She was sat at a desk as Charlemagne went and sat on the chair next to her desk, facing the opposite way.

"Oh, Charles," Vienna remarked, "you're back early. How was your day at the village?"

"Very interesting," Charlemagne replied before explaining his experience between the sickly boy, his father's belief that the boy was cursed, Charlemagne's own hypothesis, and the trip he took to the ruins. "I'll be needing some supplies to run some basic tests to determine whether the samples I took were toxic or not – very basic tests, I won't need anything extravagant. Is that okay?"

"Certainly," Vienna answered, listening carefully to her son's story with a hand at her head.

"I think I might also return to town to do some research... I want to know more about the local people, as I've hit a stub in my own knowledge. I'm going to try and return by tomorrow..."

"If you want to learn more about the local indigenous people, Charles, you should speak with the matriarch," Vienna suggested. "She's an old woman, older than the men, and she is very respected by the others for her wisdom. She's here in one of the tents... You should go and speak with her before you decide to leave."

"Good idea," Charlemagne replied. "Does she speak English, or... will I need to find another translator?"

"I believe she speaks a little bit of English," Vienna answered. "Not much, but a bit."

"Hm," Charlemagne responded. "Well, I better go and speak with her then. I might not find a better source than the people here. I'm afraid there won't be much information for me to seek out."

"Come," Vienna said, standing up. "I'll take you to her."

Charlemagne and Vienna left the first aid tent and then went out to one of the refugee tents which had various cots laid out. The two looked for the matriarch and found her after a short search. The matriarch was indeed an old woman, but she was also a small woman with long greyish-white hair and wrinkled skin like dark leather. She appeared to be in her eighties, if not, possibly even in her nineties. Her eyes were slightly closed and her hands were wrapped around a sort of wooden cane carved out of a branch with a handle atop. She was not alone, but sat on a cot in the corner of the tent accompanied by four others, some women who were frail and old like her, but also some younger women. Charlemagne lingered back as his mother went forward.

"Hello, Ch'aha," Vienna greeted. "Do you remember me? It's me, Vienna Cabernet. I'm here with my son, Charlemagne. He's a historian and an archeologist, and he wants to learn more about your people. Would you like to speak with him?"

A woman with Ch'aha had to translate what Vienna had just said to the old woman. Charlemagne observed that the woman's eyes didn't move, but she could hear around herself.

"Is she blind?" Charlemagne quietly asked his mother.

"I'm afraid so," Vienna responded. "I haven't spoken to her in quite some time, and she looks like she's become worse off than how she was. It'll be better if these assistants to her translate your questions."

The woman smiled as her assistant finished translating and then she spoke in her native tongue. She held a happy look on her face and simply looked slightly upwards.

"She would be happy to answer questions you might have," a woman to her right translated.

"Excellent," Charlemagne replied, finding a chair nearby and bringing it around for him to sit down. "My dear, I'd like to learn more about the sort of society that used to live here before

European colonization took place. Would it be okay if you could give me a general idea of that if possible?"

The woman translated Charlemagne's question while Vienna brought a hand to Charlemagne's shoulder.

"I'll be back in the first-aid tent if you need me," Vienna whispered.

Charlemagne nodded. The matriarch then began to speak in her native tongue while the woman translated.

"She says, what she knows about her people has been passed to her from her own great-grandmother and likewise to them for generations… Before the white man came to the island, this was a land that was simply known to the people as 'Kathu,' which means 'home' in our language. Back then, almost six-hundred years ago, there used to be nine tribes on the island divided between the entire land. Me and my people," the woman translated, "are all that remains of one of these tribes, the 'Ha'huo' as well as the K'achuo. These are the only two groups that exist as others had assimilated and become part of the society, while others were killed off."

"By whom?" Charlemagne interrupted.

Charlemagne waited for the woman to translate, the matriarch to answer, and then the answer to come to him in English.

"When the first Whites arrived, there was a war between them and the war-like K'achuo and other tribes, and that resulted in the extermination of three of these tribes, the destruction of the ancient capital of the K'achuo where they were banished from, and the end of the civilization as it was. The I'chuo and Lu'chuo people, who used to live where the modern port town is, and who allied with the White people remained as they were, converted to their religion, and these people were then assimilated and no longer exist as they were. Only the K'achuo remained with few of the other tribesmen who assimilated into this tribe, and our very own because we chose not to fight. In this time, we lived at a part of the island that no longer exists. Our capital city was a mirror of the K'achuoan capital, but laid on flatter lands that have returned to the sea. The word 'Ha'h' in our language means 'water' as we were a people of the water, and likewise, 'K'ah,' in our language means fire as the Ka'chuoan were a fiery people…"

"Tell me more about the capital of your people… Did it have a large pyramid-like temple? I've visited what I believed to be the Ka'chuoan capital and they had a pyramid, and inside this pyramid, they had lots of drawings on the wall. Did your capital have a pyramid like this?"

The woman translated Charlemagne's statement and then the matriarch responded. Charlemagne listened to the translation of this response.

"The pyramid in the Ka'chuoan capital is a replica of the one that was constructed in our old capital, but the uses were not similar. The pyramid in our capital was built for ceremonial purposes, but also as an observatory so that our people could study the skies. The Ka'chuoan people used their pyramids for similar purposes, but also as centers of their rule and their mythology. They were also more cold-blooded, as a warrior tribe, and they often performed human sacrifices in these temples… rituals like these were a reason why the White people went to war with these tribes and forced their conversion. The Ha'huoan people never performed rituals like these…"

"And what became of your capital? You said that it returned to the ocean?"

The woman translated Charlemagne's question and the matriarch then gave a breadth of an explanation.

"As time went on after the White men had arrived on the island, the sea levels rose and rose, and then there was a terrible explosion of the local volcano and an earthquake, and the flood that came brought the city down. Our people then moved inland and we made our lives here for almost three-hundred years, that is, until we were recently evicted. In that time, we had made contact with the new people that shared this island with us, and we traded with them, and lived in peace. When the British took over the island, they treated us with the same hospitality, and we accepted into our lives what they had to offer in terms of faith and knowledge, but with this, we gradually lost our own sense of our past... but the culture of these people had less to do with that than our migration and the destruction of our capital by nature."

"Hm..." Charlemagne responded, "and approximately where did this ancient capital of yours exist? Relative to us?"

Charlemagne waited for answer.

"She says, the capital was towards the southeast, not too far from where we are, but on a separate island that no longer exists just off the coast."

"Has there been any attempt for an archeological expedition to visit the site? Is it still there?"

Charlemagne waited for an answer.

"She does not know," the woman confessed. "From what she is aware of, there has not been any attempt to visit the location."

"Would it be dangerous to do so?"

The woman asked. The matriarch shook her head.

"I see," Charlemagne replied, stroking his chin. "Tell me, though. I expect that your people must have a good understanding of the local plants that must grow on this island... Is there any type of plant or berry that has been known to cause hallucinations or feverish delusions?"

The woman asked the matriarch and she seemed confused.

"No," the matriarch answered herself, waving a finger. "No."

"Seeing that you are of a different tribe, I must also ask..." Charlemagne said before explaining the situation with the young boy in the K'achuoan village. "What do you believe could be the problem with this boy?"

The woman finished to translate for Charlemagne, and then the woman paused to think for a moment.

"The locals said that the boy may be cursed, but not all of them seemed convinced," Charlemagne added as they thought.

The woman told the matriarch of this addition. She continued to think for a moment before speaking slowly.

"She says, she does not know for sure since she's not too familiar with the customs over there, but she has in her time heard of a local myth from their village of a... 'Witch Doctor' who practices witchcraft and has been known to kidnap children... and this may be where the idea of the boy being cursed could have originated. What troubles the boy though... she does not know."

"Right," Charlemagne replied, "well it was worth a try. Please, let her know how thankful I am for her time and knowledge."

Charlemagne stood up. The woman translated this, resulting in the matriarch talking quickly as Charlemagne was about to leave.

"Oh, she says... to be careful, if you are going to keep on studying their past, especially the past of the K'achuoans... Although they, like our own people, are remnants of the past, there is a danger that surrounds them, which is why she does not want her own people to have to come and live with them. She fears for us, and wants you to know that and to help us."

"Oh… there's not much I can do in that regard, but I will be careful. Thank you for your words of caution," Charlemagne responded.

Charlemagne promptly left the tent to return to his own.

・・・・

Later that night, Charlemagne sat at a desk he had made in his tent, which was lit by a gaslight. He sat in his foldable chair, looking through the images on Diana's camera ported onto his laptop. Charlemagne hopped through them until he came to the first image saved on Diana's camera, which was a picture of Tristan's face taken as a portrait. The picture was taken slightly of the side of his face. He stopped for a moment and studied the picture, which was extremely detailed as Diana's camera was of good quality. The picture grabbed a certain pain in Tristan's tired eyes. He had an almost cold stare to him. Charlemagne quickly reverted back to the pictures from the tomb as he heard footsteps outside.

The tent flap opened and Diana entered.

"So, have any luck?" Diana questioned. "Solve the mystery?"

"Unfortunately, no…" Charlemagne responded. "I've looked at the pictures you've taken, and sadly, because of the damage on the stone murals, it's hard to make out what is attempting to be exhibited, but that's a minor point. I also did some quick tests for heavy metals on some of the samples, but that got me nowhere. Tomorrow, I'm going into town to have some samples flown to Harlech for some more extensive testing, and I'm also going to go to the library to do some research… something I haven't done in a long time. If that's of no use, then I'll go to the hotel and simply browse open-sources on the

Internet, but that is rarely of any help. Before I go, I'm going to try and get a sample of blood if the parents would be okay with that."

"And then?"

"And then, hopefully I'll have something to help that poor child," Charlemagne responded. "I've also become interested in some of the pre-history to this island, particularly in the existence of another temple like the one we saw today."

"Oh yeah?"

"Yes, according to the matriarch of the people refuged here, they used to have a marvelous capital on an island of the coast of here that sunk, and on this island, there was a temple like the one we saw. In fact, it is supposed to be a 'mirror' of the other, so I'm interested in going to go and look for this temple."

"How?"

"When I go into town, I think I might rent a yacht, some scuba suits, and then take you and Tristan out this weekend on a trip offshore so we can go and find this ancient site," Charlemagne expressed. "If I can't be satisfied in helping this poor child, then the least I can do is learn more of the local people in hopes that I can piece-together something, right?"

"I guess so," Diana replied, crossing her arms.

"Where's Tristan?"

"He's with your dad," Diana answered. "They're at the campfire, I think."

"He must be exhausted," Charlemagne said. "He had him working for almost twelve-hours straight."

"Yeah, I think I might go and pull him out so that he can get some rest, but when I last saw him at dinner, he seemed to be doing okay. In fact, he seemed a little happy…"

"That's good," Charlemagne commended. "A little work goes a long way… it is liberating, really, for the soul."

"Oh yeah, and when was the last time you... oh wait."

"I've been at the helm of a company for the last twenty-or-so years, longer really, but I don't consider myself to have been a businessman in those years. I was more of a figurehead..." Charlemagne said. "Tristan's almost eighteen-years old, and I don't think he's had a serious job. If we hadn't come here, I would have almost have made him get a part-time job."

"What part-time job did you have when you were his age?" Diana questioned.

"When I was about Tristan's age, I was in the army," Charlemagne answered. "I spent two-years of my early life in that misery in hopes that I could understand my grandfather better, but instead, it gave me a contempt for the military-life. At the same time, I learned a lot in those two-years, and a lot of the skills I learned I put to use when I was roaming around with the Protection Squad..."

"Right..." Diana replied. "I forgot... you've told us about this before."

"Yes," Charlemagne said, standing up and stretching. "Anyways, it's getting to be late. Why don't you go and pull Tristan from the clutches of my father so that he can rest. He has an early rise tomorrow, and so do I. Allodia told me that they moved my patient to a bed nearby, so I'll be up early to get some blood and then I'll be off with a convoy to town so I can get my samples on the plane headed back to Harlech after dropping off some supplies. I most likely won't see you tomorrow, so in that case, please... well, I don't really have to say it, do I? I know the two of you will be careful... you're both quite capable to take care of yourselves, especially together."

"Thanks," Diana responded. "It means a lot to hear that from you."

"Well, the pair of you have earned it after all you've been through," Charlemagne replied, "and you better be able to if you're each to live on your own in Harlech this autumn..." he remarked, "but that aside... goodnight, Diana. I'll see you in a day or two."

"Goodnight, Charles," Diana responded before she left.

Act 4, Scene 1

The following weekend, Charlemagne took Diana and Tristan away from the camp after being absent since he left Tuesday morning, and took them to Villa Paraiso where a yacht awaited to meet them in the town's port. Charlemagne wore his white suit with a white panama hat. Tristan wore light beige shorts and a light blue polo shirt, and Diana wore a white summer dress with a matching summer hat. Charlemagne looked at the yacht from the pier-side and pointed it out to the couple. The *Miranda* was a ninety-six feet long sailing yacht with an outboard motor at the rear. In the center of the boat was a small cabin with slanted windows all around that extended outside with cushioned seats surrounding the steering wheel. Within the cabin, the seats around the side surrounded two wooden tables left and right with an aisle in the middle that led to two seats behind at front, which looked forward out the front window. Behind this small, entrenched area there were more lounge seats that looked out the back of the boat from where one boarded down a stair-ladder. The floorboard of the yacht was a light beige. The boat floated gently over the water from where it was moored and docked. Once they had finished admiring the boat from afar, Charlemagne took them down so they could get a closer look.

"So, you really went and rented a yacht so we could do a little scuba diving?" Diana questioned.

"No," Charlemagne denied. "I didn't rent this boat. I bought it…"

"You bought this boat?" Diana questioned, looking to Tristan with concern.

"Yes," Charlemagne replied without a care in the world. "Why not? I was never one for boats, seeing that it's never been too interesting to sail the Nattau River than to admire it, but I suppose if I own a jet, why not a boat too? I'm taking a liking to this island, to be honest, and could consider buying a villa to retire here if, well…"

Charlemagne didn't finish his thought. He instead continued on until he and the couple arrived at the side of the boat, which proved to be a lot larger than it appeared from afar.

"Come on," Charlemagne said, taking them to the back. "Hop aboard, we've got a pyramid to find."

"Don't we need scuba gear, wet suits?" Diana questioned.

"Yes, and it's all aboard. Come on, before the day passes us," Charlemagne replied with haste.

Charlemagne led the couple to the back of the boat where they boarded onto the back of the boat, which extended out to reveal the stair-ladder up to the top deck. Tristan observed that the ladder could be moved out of the way so that a medium-sized motor boat lodged behind the stairs in a den could be taken out. The couple climbed aboard the boat and looked out from atop while Charlemagne went and made preparations for them to set sail.

Tristan entered the small area around the steering wheel and sat down, stretching his arms out around the seat.

"Well, I suppose I can't say I didn't expect this, but I'm all for it," Tristan remarked.

Diana frowned at him and then looked over to Charlemagne.

"So, where's the gear?" Diana asked.

"It's downstairs," Charlemagne remarked. "In the bedroom."

"Bedroom?" Diana questioned.

Diana entered the small pit where Tristan and Charlemagne were and then she entered the cabin, walking past the tables, down the aisle to reach an opening between the navigation equipment with another set of stairs that went down into the depths of the boat. Tristan stood up and walked with her to go down into the main living space of the yacht, which lit up on its own as they entered a quaint and luxurious living room with a blue carpet floor. The living room contained a dining table to the left with chairs on the outside and a white sofa against the wall, and another sofa on the right with a coffee table. Above these two sides were small windows that looked out the side of the boat. Before them, immediately forward to the left was a doorway that went onwards into the sublevel, and next to this door was a cabinet made of a reddish-wood that most of the furniture and walls consisted of. The cabinet consisted of two glass cabinets on the sides with main doors in the center that opened up to reveal a television. Tristan ventured inwards into the boat and entered a small kitchen with a refrigerator, stove, and sink to the right, and a small dining table on the left. Diana joined him and they went on to reach the final room, which was a single bedroom with a king-sized bed. Next to the bed was a large mirror on the left and a door on the right. Next to the mirror at the side was a loveseat, and next to this loveseat was a small cabinet bookshelf. The door next to the bed led to a moderately-sized bathroom. Behind the bed was a large modern painting in light blue. In front of the bed, to the left from the exit was a small closet, and to the right was a cabinet and some drawers.

"Hm," Diana remarked, looking at the bed.

"Here they are," Tristan said, opening the closet to see two wetsuits with scuba gear on the floor below inside. "I've never been scuba diving before... this'll be interesting."

Diana looked at the gear inside, two suits and two tanks and gear, and then she looked at the large bed and around the room with a sort of worried expression on her face. Tristan noticed this emotion and dropped a quick concerned look back.

"What's wrong?" Tristan asked. "I would have thought you'd be a little happier to be in a yacht about to do some deep sea exploration, or do you not want to dive?"

"I'm looking forward to it, but two suits mean Charles isn't going to join us below and that these are for us," Diana said. "I don't know why Charles bought this yacht either when he could have rented, and this... it seems a little off."

"What seems off?" Tristan questioned, looking at her.

Diana avoided Tristan's eye contact as she continued to look about. She was thinking.

"Maybe I'm just over-thinking it all," Diana replied. "Nevermind me."

Tristan continued to look at Diana with suspicion. She left the room before he could inquire further and when she did, all Tristan did was shake his head and refocus. Diana returned above and sat down near the steering wheel as Charlemagne took *Miranda* out of port and into the Caribbean Sea for their journey to the other side of the island.

"I didn't know you knew how to sail," Diana remarked, sitting politely.

Tristan sat down next to her, observing that she had returned to have a smile on her face. He observed her carefully, noticing her eyes look to Charlemagne's gloved hands briefly for a moment. Tristan looked at them for a short minute too before focusing on the conversation again.

"It's one of those peculiar skills you study when you're bored," Charlemagne replied. "If I wasn't slightly color-blind, I would have also learned how to fly, but they won't let me do that."

"I didn't know you were color blind," Diana said.

"A tad bit," Charlemagne responded. "I have a bit of a trouble with certain shades of red and green, but it isn't severe and has never been a problem."

• • • •

There wasn't a cloud in the light blue sky and the sun hit down hard, but with the breeze from the sea, it was easier to be outside as the yacht sailed freely approximately a few hundred kilometers from the shore as they made their approach towards the approximate location of the former capital of the Ha'chuans as it became noon.

Diana and Tristan exited from the inside of the yacht dressed in wetsuits, each carrying the scuba gear allotted to them as they went to the rear of the boat. Charlemagne was on the platform below, readying the panel for them as they joined him.

"So, what's the rundown of anything important we should know before we head on down?" Tristan asked.

"Well, scuba diving isn't a difficult sport," Charlemagne stated, preparing the air tanks, "and I have no doubts that the pair of you will be able to manage yourselves down there. What you do need to know is to never hold your breath. I kept in mind that the two of you have never been underwater before, so I took the liberty of purchasing full-face masks with a PTT (push to talk) system and ear-piece. The mask is a tight fit so you should have no problem with water entering, but if you do, you can hit this purge button."

Charlemagne pointed to a button at the front of the regulator.

"Don't worry about these devices attached to the regulator," Charlemagne said, pointing to the second stage and pressure gauge. "If you do need to take out the regulator, simply blow a stream of air out while you do. Do not hold your breath, especially as you submerge. You could blow a lung."

"That's reassuring," Diana remarked.

"With this mask, you should be able to hear me and talk with me if anything were to go wrong. The waterproof body cameras on the fronts of your vests will allow me to see what you see."

"Why aren't you coming with us?" Tristan asked.

"I'm not in shape to be exploring under the sea," Charlemagne replied. "If I could, I would, but I'm not feeling it right now. When you do enter the water, even with these masks, you will need to equalize the pressure in your ears, and I'll guide you through that. Simply put, these nose plugs will allow you to block your nose, and when you do that, breath gently into your nose while blocked to relieve the pressure in your ears. I'll have the pair of you do it together to make sure it's done right. You should see some air bubbles come out from your ears if done properly. If not, you risk blowing your ear drum."

"Again, very reassuring," Diana remarked. "Anything else?"

"The swimming techniques should come naturally to you," Charlemagne said. "This is a weight belt and this is your buoyancy compensator. Fiddle with this button to achieve a neutral buoyancy once you're at an appropriate depth. Any questions?"

"No," Tristan replied.

"Right then," Charlemagne remarked, "let's finish suiting you up then and we'll do a radio check."

Charlemagne helped the pair into their vests with the tanks of air. Diana and Tristan pulled over hoods attached to the wet suits that covered their hair. Afterwards, the masks went on and Charlemagne checked that each was tight and there was no chance of leaks.

"I feel like I'm going into doing my space training in that pool again," Tristan said, voice echoing in his mask.

"It'll be similar, but less dangerous," Charlemagne responded. "God knows I've placed the pair of you in enough danger as it is…"

Charlemagne finished checking Diana's system while Tristan put on his flippers.

"Radio check," Charlemagne said, speaking into the mic attached to a headset he wore. "One, two, three."

A minor bit of feedback came through.

"Good," Charlemagne replied. "We'll do another radio check once you're below."

Diana put on her flippers and then stood up.

"The ruins should be somewhere within the vicinity of this area," Charlemagne briefed the couple. "We'll attempt to sweep this immediate area for it within an hour, but if no luck or something goes wrong, I'll pull you out and bring the boat around to pick you up."

"Got it," Tristan responded, turning to face the water and then Diana. "Ready?"

"For sure," Diana replied, jumping into the water.

Tristan followed suit and the impact of the two into the water as they jumped splashed Charlemagne's trousers.

"Be careful, you two," Charlemagne saluted as they submerged into the depths of the Caribbean Sea.

Act 4, Scene 2

Tristan delve down into the sea with Diana until they reached the bottom of the shallow sea, less than a couple of meters from the surface. The water around them was crisp and almost clear, displaying in a light blue. They could see around themselves to up to almost fifty meters. From where they had entered, the sand below their feet was smooth and clear at a light beige, and this stretched out all around them as far as their visibility could see.

"Radio check," Charlemagne spoke over the radio. "One, two, three... Do you copy?"

"I copy," Tristan replied.

"Copy," Diana answered.

"Good," Charlemagne responded. "The feed from your cameras is clear. All seems to be well so far. Let's equalize your ear pressure before you press on. I need you to both look at each other as we do this."

"Got it," Tristan responded, looking towards Diana.

"On the left sides of your masks there should be a button that pushes the nostril plugs into your noses," Charlemagne explained. "Press it."

Tristan pointed at the button as he saw it on Diana's mask. He then brought his hands to the same button on his own, pressing it.

"The button on the right side is your push to talk button for your microphones. Once you've plugged your noses, breath gently from your mouths into your nostrils whilst looking at the other," Charlemagne explained further. "You should see some bubbles of air escape from each other's noses as well as a mild pop as the pressure in your ear equalizes."

Diana and Tristan looked at each other as they did this. Tristan saw the bubbles of air escape from Diana's ears. Diana let go of the button.

"I saw them," Diana said to Tristan. "I also felt mine."

"Yeah, I saw yours," Tristan confirmed.

"Good," Charlemagne replied. "You may need to repeat that again if you travel further down, but the waters around here appear to be shallow, so I'm not too worried about you having to travel further below the current pressure you're experiencing."

Tristan looked around their immediate area. He then brought two fingers back to his mask to talk.

"What direction should we go towards?" Tristan asked. "It all seems to be pretty deserted around here."

"Have a swim ahead of the boat, to the west," Charlemagne recommended. "I'll keep a track of your location by the strength of our signal, and if you're about to hit the limit, I'll warn you and sail over to pick you up."

"Got it," Tristan confirmed, looking back to Diana. "Let's go."

Diana led the way as they swam off into the deep sea. The diversity in the underwater landscape began to develop the further the two swam. The ground soon became rugged with encrusted sea life, which became more sporadic. The pair spotted their first fish amidst the reef where inches of kelp and coral began to form. On the sides of some of the larger formations there were large growths of soft coral sea fans and other forms of sea-life such as sea plants in an array of different bright, tropical colors. Diana continued to follow the fish as the two of them admired the coral reef.

Around the reef there appeared more fish with a majority of them being very small fishes. Diana looked to her left and spotted a large growth of brain coral with its folds like the gyrus of the human brain. She pointed the coral out to Tristan who was looking to the right.

"Be careful," Tristan cautioned. "I've heard coral can be really sharp, so don't touch anything," he said, holding his hands politely together as they hovered in place.

"It's all so beautiful," Diana replied. "I need to find something that I can take home with me as memorabilia."

Tristan looked about and then back over to Diana.

"We have all summer to find something right," Tristan replied. "Maybe we can find a conch shell though. That'd be pretty neat."

Diana continued to swim as they went on, exploring around the reef as they became distracted.

"Look," Diana said, pointing. "A sea turtle!"

Tristan looked and saw the junior sea turtle swimming around a ridge ahead of them. They briefly observed the sea turtle with respect towards it before it swam off and they continued onwards. Towards the edge of the reef, Diana and Tristan spotted a larger fish than the small ones they were seeing. This fish had silvery and shiny scales and was long and rigid. It sort of hovered ahead of them, not really moving about, but maintaining its position. Tristan observed that it had some large teeth poking out from its mouth.

"That's a barracuda," Charlemagne warned. "They're predatory, but shouldn't give you any problems as long as you don't bother it."

"Good to know," Tristan responded.

From the coral reef, the couple moved onwards over the rugged landscape. The barracuda proceeded to follow them for a moment, but the further they went, it suddenly broke off and disappeared.

Tristan looked forward and began to spot some man-made structures in the water, which told him that they had found what they were looking for. A set of chiseled stones poked out from the sand ahead. Diana saw some markings on the stone similar to totems seen in the jungle. She stopped before them, straightening out vertically so that the body camera at her torso could see the stone. Tristan continued forward.

"Well, that didn't take long…" Charlemagne remarked, "but from the looks of it, a lot of the city appears to be submerged in sand."

"I'll say," Diana replied. "It's like an underwater graveyard around here."

"A pyramid will stick out no matter what," Charlemagne replied. "Have a look around."

Tristan led the way as he looked around the ruins of the submerged city. In comparison to the ruins seen in the jungle, this city was a lot more intact although the chiseled stone that composed the buildings ahead were encrusted with barnacles and other crustacean sea life as well as algae. There were even some small fish wandering around the site. Tristan saw some submerged trees that had collected algae against the trunks and lost all of their leaves.

"This is pretty eerie," Tristan remarked, stopping to take a look around him.

"Tell me about it…" Diana replied.

The couple continued to wander around and between the structures of the old city.

"Some of these buildings have a pyramidal shape to them," Tristan said. "I imagine the temple you're looking for is bigger and stands out from the rest."

"That'd be it," Charlemagne replied. "You'll want something that looks like a temple."

"The temple in the jungle was further from the initial village," Diana said. "We should move on and head out if we want to find this place."

"Good call," Tristan responded.

The couple moved along and proceeded to reach the outskirt walls of the former city, which they floated over. Tristan pointed out the top of a distinct and larger pyramid that stuck out from the sand. Approximately a quarter of the temple had fallen under the earth at a slant. The temple stood out from the rest of the city as it was surrounded by a courtyard of nothingness just like the one in the jungle. Around this nothing, there were some totems like the ones in the other city. The pair swam closer to the pyramid, moving towards the top, which they could see reach to. The top of the forty-foot or so tall pyramid was approximately another forty feet from the surface of the sea. The couple stopped at the top to look around.

Tristan looked ahead and saw a sudden break-off in the ocean floor at the side of the temple into a ridge that reached another hundred feet below. The bottom was difficult to see, but barely visible and not completely obstructed by the field of vision. The canyon was large though and marked a large portion of the sea ahead. Once Tristan had finished surveying the land around them, he followed Diana as she was about to enter the temple.

The design of the inside of the pyramid followed just like the other, but the couple entered from the very top, swimming down to enter the main atrium where they turned on the lights of the cameras to guide them as they entered the depths of the pyramid and went further down. The design of this inner chamber was like the other as well, but the mural on the wall made of tiny stones was not as decayed. In addition, the temple was decorated almost as if it was maintained in its original state with statues armed with a two-pronged spear.

"Are you seeing what you wanted to see?" Diana asked, floating vertically as she looked towards the mural.

"I'm... but the... not good," Charlemagne responded with static.

Diana looked to Tristan with a look of concern hidden behind her mask.

"Charles, we're receiving you poorly," Tristan spoke. "I repeat, we are receiving you poorly."

"No matter... exploring. The... recording. Be... have a good look," Charlemagne said. "I'm... the boat."

"Not helpful," Tristan muttered. "Let's be quick, huh?" he said to Diana. "We'll grab what we can on our cameras and then bounce. I don't want to be out of comms for too long."

"Don't worry, there's not much to grab. The pyramid in the jungle wasn't that big, so if this is a mirror image, then it shouldn't be as big either."

Diana focused the camera on her torso with her hands as she slowly began to pan the mural and document the artefact carefully. Tristan had a look around to see if there was anything peculiar he should record with his own camera while Diana worked on the largest piece. He looked at the stepped sides of the chamber and then at the stairs. He also looked up to the ceiling and then around to the other side of the staircase. Diana continued to pan around the mural until she stopped to notice a set of two entrances into tight corridors at either side of the mural from within a trench before the mural and behind a ledge.

For the time being, Diana ignored these two entrances and went with Tristan as he took her to the lateral chambers, which were similar to the ones in the jungle temple. After she had finished the left chamber, Tristan took her to the right one.

"We should head back to the yacht now," Tristan stated.

"We're not done," Diana said.

Diana quickly explained the two side entrances that went into narrow tunnels at the side of the main mural. She noted to him that she couldn't see these tunnels in the jungle temple because of the elevation and darkness.

"Well, let's check them out quickly then," Tristan replied, swimming off to head back to the main chamber.

Tristan stopped as he was about to reach the main atrium. He looked onwards with worry. Diana caught up with him and the two of them looked ahead to the pair of sharks that were circling close to the ceiling, near their exit point.

"Oh, great," Tristan remarked with sarcasm. "Right on schedule. Turn off your light so they can't see us."

Diana quickly shut off her camera light with Tristan.

"What are we going to do?" Diana questioned. "Neither of us are equipped to handle something like this."

"Charles, are you listening?" Tristan questioned.

No response came.

"Great," Tristan remarked.

Diana continued to stare towards the brown-grey sharks with their dark, soulless eyes. They were both lit up by only the light that seeped in from the exit. Each of the sharks were approximately the length of a small car, or around twelve feet long. They were not large sharks, but sleek and shaped like torpedoes with flat-heads. Each of them had large dorsal fins, striped sides, and whitish heads. Diana looked more fearful than Tristan as they observed the beasts.

"So, what do you know about sharks?" Diana asked.

"Not much, if not, hardly anything," Tristan replied. "You?"

"All I know is that you're supposed to punch them in the nose if they get too close, but the more I look at them, the more I'm starting to doubt that."

"Yeah, I'm pretty sure that's just a myth."

Tristan continued to observe the creatures for another moment until he began to move forward slightly with initiative. He went towards a statue next to the entrance into the corridor they were exiting from and grabbed the spear from the statue.

"Well, we're not going to just wait here for our oxygen to run out," Tristan stated. "I have a plan. I'll lead us forward, and hopefully they'll ignore us, but if anything happens, I'll jab at them, and worst case, dislodge my O-two tank for them to take a bite out of."

"Wait, Tristan, I have a better idea," Diana said, stopping him. "Our cameras. We can flash them – blind them. Think about it. It's dark here, and a brief flash of light would surely annoy them."

Tristan looked at her camera and nodded.

"Plan B then," Tristan replied. "Let's just do our best not to provoke them as we try to pass, okay?"

"Right."

"Come on," Tristan said, swimming forward.

Diana followed from behind as they began to make their approach towards the circling sharks. The pair of them swam slowly towards the exit. Tristan caught a glance of the face of the shark, which looked at him. The other shark, which was swimming lower than the other, looked towards Diana and swam close to her, but then swam around. Diana breathed slow, sharp breaths, turning her neck to face the other side as she tracked the shark with her eyes.

The shark closest to Diana began to circle her closely.

"Tristan…" Diana remarked with minor distress.

Tristan looked down to her and saw the shark in its proximity to Diana. He tightened his grip on the spear, but then quickly jerked his head as he saw the shark closest to him get a little too close. He lurched back slightly and it made its pass around. Tristan attempted to keep track of both of them as they came to a halt so close to the exit.

Diana detached her body camera from her vest and quickly raised it up and ignited the flash as the shark opened its mouth and made a quick dash towards Diana's head. At the same time, Tristan quickly grabbed Diana with one hand to pull her up and out of the shark's path while with the other, he pierced down with all his underwater strength, and stabbed the shark from above. Diana then quickly looked up as she saw the other shark attempt to take a bite out of Tristan, causing her to flash her camera towards him.

"Watch out!" Diana shouted.

The flash of light caught Tristan's eyes and blinded him partially as he raised the stake out from the shark's head below and pulled himself back. Tristan saw double as he took the spear and jabbed it into the side of the shark that just passed him. The other shark had rushed off. Tristan took the spear out from the side of the shark and gave another jab, but when he attempted to pull out, the spear was stuck. The rush of the opposing shark to jet off caused the stake to slap Tristan upwards against the jaw like an uppercut as it was went off with the spear stuck in its side.

Without hesitation, and with Tristan's vision recovered, the two of them swam off and escaped from the temple hand in hand. Once they had left the depths of the temple and returned to the open water, Tristan could see the underside of a vessel ahead, which he aimed for as he and Diana swam for the surface.

Act 4, Scene 3

Diana and Tristan emerged from the water next to the vessel. Diana saw past them and towards a small island ahead of them where a sort of modern mansion sat atop of, while Tristan looked up the side of the boat and to the men that pointed rifles towards them. She eventually joined Tristan to look to these men. They were not locals, but were diverse in appearance, some fair-skinned and others dark, and each of them had a stocky build. They wore black cargo pants and dark black t-shirts with ballistic vests atop. They appeared to be some sort of private security. The couple continued to look to them.

"Stay where you are!" a merc shouted.

A zodiac was lowered from the vessel and a small team of mercenaries came to pull the couple out of the water and remove their masks. Afterwards, they were taken aboard the ship where they were put into ties and kept on their knees.

"Do you understand that you are on private property?" a merc stated to them, kneeling down to face them.

Tristan scowled at the man.

"We didn't know, honestly," Diana answered before Tristan could get them into more trouble. "We're just tourists doing some scuba diving and we thought your boat was ours."

Tristan looked to the side and was able to see the yacht in the distance.

"Hey, there he is – over there," Tristan remarked.

Diana looked and said, "Yes, that's our boat! We're sorry – we'll leave right away if you let us."

The merc looked at them for a moment and then stood up.

"As long as you understand that all of a hundred feet from that island over there is restricted, you are free to go…" the merc said. "We'll escort you back to your ship, but after that, I insist you leave at once."

"Thank you," Diana replied.

Diana and Tristan were kept in their ties and taken onto the zodiac where they were let free and then escorted to the yacht. Charlemagne met with them at the rear of the ship.

"Sir, are these your children?" the merc questioned.

"Yes, what seems to be the problem?" Charlemagne asked.

"Your children were trespassing on private property. Do not let it happen again, or there will be consequences," the merc simply stated.

"Private property? You cannot own the open waters," Charlemagne argued, assisting the kids aboard the rear platform.

"Do not let it happen again," the man repeated before they went off.

Charlemagne looked at them suspiciously and then to Diana and Tristan.

"Are you both alright?" Charlemagne asked.

"Well, we're alive," Tristan replied.

"We got the footage you wanted," Diana said, taking off her body camera again. "Hopefully it's clear enough for you to study."

"Excellent," Charlemagne commended, taking the camera. "I'll take both your cameras so I can review the footage tonight. Come aboard and we'll debrief."

"Charles, we got attacked by a shark on our way out," Tristan noted as they followed him.

"Really?" Charlemagne responded, turning around to them from atop of the top deck. "Shark attacks towards scuba divers are relatively rare. What happened precisely?"

Diana and Tristan climbed up top and then explained.

"Hm…" Charlemagne thought for a moment. "Perhaps it was the equipment in your helms. Sharks are attracted to electrical impulses, and your helmets are wired with transponders. They were most likely curious, but… I'm glad you're both alright. I'm sorry you had to live through that."

"It's okay, we managed," Tristan replied in a neutral tone, removing his equipment.

"Right…" Charlemagne responded, holding the cameras before moving back over to the steering wheel. "Well, if that's the case, then…"

"Hey, Charles, what's with the smoke over there?" Diana questioned. "I don't remember any smoke coming from the island when we went under."

"Hm?" Charlemagne queried, looking over to the island where there was a thick plumage of smoke coming from ahead.

Tristan looked and observed where they were relative to the island. They were closer to the base of the volcano to the southwest. The small island with the manor was connected to the main island via a long plain bridge. Around the base of the volcano was a thickness of the jungle, but slightly towards the middle the smoke originated from.

"Oh dear…" Charlemagne stated. "I didn't even notice – it must be new."

"You don't think it could be coming from the village, do you?" Diana asked.

"No… surely not," Charlemagne responded.

Diana and Tristan didn't look any more certain.

"Perhaps we should return to the camp immediately," Charlemagne remarked. "We can take the speedboat once I anchor ourselves from the coast."

"Okay…" Diana replied.

Diana and Tristan changed out from their wet suits, showered, and changed back into the clothes they had come to Villa Paraiso in while Charlemagne steered the yacht around and towards the camp at top speed. Once they were close, Charlemagne dropped the anchor to secure the ship and then prepared the motorboat for them to disembark at the camp. Diana and Tristan followed Charlemagne as they took their steps into the camp, which was amess.

"My God, what's happened here?" Charlemagne questioned, looking about. "Hello?! Hello?!"

Charlemagne and the couple entered into the camp, looking about. A lot of the tent canvasses had been ripped and some of the crates of goods had been taken from the storage tent, left about open with leftovers left on the ground. There were also small and random fires set about, some of them put out already. The three of them saw various refugees, bundled together, women and children. Eventually, Charlemagne met with Allodia who was with some of the other volunteers as they assisted some of the refugees.

"Allodia," Charlemagne remarked, rushing over to her. "What's happened here?"

"Oh, Charles, it's a disaster!" Allodia replied, going to him, tearful. "We were just raided – I don't know by whom, but they were some sort of bandits. They came in a couple of a semi-trucks and just pillaged what they wanted, started to harass some of the locals, and... and..."

"Where are our parents?" Charlemagne questioned.

"They took them both..." Allodia stated. "Dad... he couldn't keep his mouth shut and tried to stand his ground. They took both of them and went into the jungle..."

"Not long ago I saw loads of smoke coming from the jungle – that's why I came as fast as I could," Charlemagne explained.

"They may have gone to raid the village afterwards – I need to get after them. Call for help, Allodia. Call Henry Heavner via the satt phone and have him dispatch my personal guard ASAP. Understood?"

"Y-yes, Charlie," Allodia responded. "What are you going to do?"

"Go after them of course," Charlemagne replied. "What else?"

Charlemagne turned around and looked to Diana and Tristan.

"Tristan, come with me. Diana, stay here and protect the others. Do not let anyone come near – Allodia is going to contact Heavner and get Lukas and them here at once."

"Got it," Tristan replied. "Will you be okay on your own?" he asked Diana.

"Of course," Diana responded. "I've got this – don't worry. Just go."

Tristan nodded to her and then went with Charlemagne to the other side of the camp where the vehicles were parked. Charlemagne took one of the jeeps and Tristan sat next to him as they ventured off and into the jungle.

Charlemagne drove as fast as he could atop the rugged road that went towards the K'achuoan village. The stench of smoke was rife and became more potent the closer they arrived. From a distance, the fire could be seen. Charlemagne drove faster, with anticipation and anxiety.

Tristan looked forward with concentration and determination. Upon arriving at the village, they could see the village houses set ablaze and the residents in chaos. The pair of them exited from the jeep and immediately went forward before ducking at the sound of gunfire. At the sound of gunfire, Tristan and Charlemagne went and took cover behind the foundations of some of the under construction houses.

"Looks like they're still here," Tristan stated, eyeing a white pickup truck with a machine gun in the back.

Charlemagne took out a pistol from his suit and readied it. Tristan looked to him and the pistol.

"I'm always prepared for trouble," Charlemagne remarked. "You think I'd let my guard down after what happened in France?"

"Stay here and I'll take control of the machine gunner," Tristan stated. "After that, you can move in."

Charlemagne didn't respond.

"Charles?" Tristan questioned, looking to him.

"Sorry, yes. Of course."

Tristan kept low and went over to the left-side of the construction site, using the cover of the developing houses. All of the houses had been set ablaze, but the foundations proved useful for Tristan to use as cover as he snuck around. He stopped at the other side of the foundations and then proceeded to move forward and towards the truck. Stealth was not much of a problem given the volume of people screaming. Once Tristan was close, he pounced up and attacked the bandit.

Charlemagne observed from afar as Tristan took the man down with brutality and ease, smashing his head into the rear window of the truck. Tristan then took control of the machine gun and quickly assessed it as an MG-42. Charlemagne moved up and took cover before opening fire as he spotted some bandits wielding AK-47s. Tristan looked up from the machine gun as Charlemagne opened fire at the bandits and he retook control and aimed the gun towards them. With hands on the handle, he hesitated to open fire. Charlemagne took out the two bandits and reloaded.

"Tristan, get down from there," Charlemagne shouted, moving up. "Come on!"

"Right," Tristan muttered under his breath.

Tristan neutralized the gun and then hopped over, running towards Charlemagne who recovered the weapons dropped by the fallen foes. Tristan observed that the bandits were of the local population.

"Keep your head up," Charlemagne remarked. "Let's move."

"Got it," Tristan responded, readying his assault rifle as they moved into the village.

Charlemagne followed the tracks and noticed some fresh tire tracks that went in deeper to the village. He looked about and saw a lot of distress from the villagers as their homes burned down. Charlemagne followed the tracks and then looked about from where he stood.

"I don't see any more of them," Charlemagne said, wiping his forehead. "We'll need to pursue further – this is a one-way road that goes only deeper into the jungle. The idiots will have cornered themselves."

"Let's go then," Tristan encouraged.

The two of them left the main body of the town to return to the jeep. They then drove through and went on into the deeper depths of the jungle in pursuit of the culprits.

Act 4, Scene 4

At the end of the road, Charlemagne saw two white pickup trucks parked, but nobody around. He blocked the cars in with the jeep, parking with the right-side towards them before they then exited. Charlemagne rushed towards the trucks with eyes to the ground while Tristan looked about to make sure they were alone.

Once Charlemagne had found footprints, he pointed at them and proceeded to follow the figurative trail that took them into the deepest depths of the jungle. At the beginning, the path they walked followed similarly to the path that Charlemagne had walked with Diana last week, but differed as they arrived at the river where they continued along the opposite-end, going down the stream until they reached a bridge where the trail of footprints continued from the other side. Charlemagne and Tristan continued through until they met some hills that soon became rough with sharp stony sides, not sleek, and with lush and tall lively bright green grass.

At the start of this ascent, Charlemagne saw some statues, which took him on the path upwards and had him stop focusing on the footprints, which became too hard to track. At the top of the climb, they had arrived at the ancient city from another, shorter direction. From the outskirts of the city, Charlemagne and Tristan kept low as they spotted some more bandits around, armed and patrolling about. The length of the grass covered them.

"They're surely here," Charlemagne muttered. "We'll have to take them out."

"Right," Tristan affirmed.

Tristan went silent for a moment.

"There's no way we could outmatch them in a gunfight though…" Tristan noted. "We're outnumbered."

"I don't expect these lot to compare to us – we're trained in this craft. You more than all of us…"

Tristan grunted.

"Let me go on my own again," Tristan remarked. "I'll pick them off one by one and clear a path. It's the safest method at these numbers… It'll be just like at the Medici construction site."

Charlemagne looked at Tristan. He hesitated to respond.

"Very well," Charlemagne responded. "I can no longer constrain you Tristan… every time I've tried, I've only placed you in worse situations, and for that I'm sorry. Go on – I'll cover you from here if things go awry."

Tristan looked at Charlemagne for a moment and then nodded. He then turned around and proceeded to make his approach, crouched and in the cover of the tall grass, hiding behind the thick trees that were scattered about. Tristan scoped ahead from where he was now closer to the ruins.

Immediately ahead, Tristan could see two bandits on patrol at the ruins of the wall with at least three more patrolling about the decayed structures within. He took his AK-47 by its sling and brought it behind him as he continued to move in closer. Of the first two bandits, one of them was still by the entrance into the former town while the other went back and forth on the other side.

Once Tristan was close, he waited for this bandit to move away so he could close in on the static bandit and jump him from behind. Tristan grabbed ahold of him and he began to squirm, but with Tristan's strength and size, he was able to silently subdue him, tightening his biceps around the man's neck until he was unconscious. Tristan then hurried to take out the other before he turned around.

With the two bandits by the old town's decrepit gates down, Tristan moved into cover by some of the fallen wall and assessed the interior of the ruins. Charlemagne moved up and took point closer. Tristan looked to him and Charlemagne motioned his hand for Tristan to lead on. Tristan nodded and vaulted over the crumbling wall to take cover behind an old fallen structure. There was another bandit to the left-side on the rooftop of an old structure, another by the other exit out of the ruins, and a bandit on patrol near the way towards the pyramid, behind some ruined structures to the right-side.

Tristan assessed the area and then proceeded to move to the right, stopping at the corner and peeking out to see the third bandit that remained made his way over, calmly and unaware. Tristan waited for him to come closer before he sprang upon him, placing his hands over his face and letting his hardwired and programmed instincts take over as he took the bandit to the ground and knocked him out.

The brutal takedown made a minor noise as it was quicker, but the others were unaware of what was going on, or what came for them. Tristan moved behind the cover of the ruins and stopped at the gate that went towards the pyramid. He noticed a sixth bandit of the five behind this gate, moving about, silently. Tristan looked at him for a moment until his back was turned and then proceeded in to take him out.

Afterwards, Tristan continued on his set path as he came around the other side of the village, but stopped at a corner to peek towards the fourth bandit by the opposite ruined gate. This bandit was static by the exit, barely moving at all and keeping his back to the decayed walls so that Tristan couldn't spring upon him from behind. He was also too in the open to attack him from any other angle. Tristan waited for a moment and picked up a small stone in the dirt as he thought.

Finally, Tristan threw the stone immediately across from where he was, hitting the stone wall and making a minor noise. The bandit was immediately startled by the noise and pointed his rifle towards it. He then proceeded to make his way over. Tristan backed away and retreated. He moved back to the other side of the ruins where he had come from and proceeded to make his way around so that he could enter the structure the fifth bandit was sat atop of.

The interior of the old building was simple and contained a poorly crafted staircase chiseled out of solid rock that went up. Tristan made his ascent carefully so that the bandit would not see him. Once he was above, he slowly made his way over and grabbed ahold of the bandit and took him out.

From where Tristan was, he could see the final bandit moving across the opposite-side of the city. Tristan jumped down from the building and ran over to take cover on the other side. The bandit stopped at the sudden rush of noise. He began to look about, realizing that he was completely alone. Tristan moved around the other side of the structure he was behind and began to make his way to the corner to get a better look of the terrified grunt.

Once the man had turned his back to Tristan, Tristan moved in for the takedown, hurried along and then stood up at the final one as he was taken down. Tristan brought his AK-47 around and rushed over to where Charlemagne had been positioned.

"All clear, let's go," Tristan reported.

"Excellent," Charlemagne commended.

The two of them moved into the ruins and made their way towards the pyramid. The torches at the entrance to the temple grounds were lit, but the area was quiet. They took cover by statues at the entrance and then moved in with Charlemagne at the lead and Tristan scanning the space behind them as they went to the stairs.

Tristan took point at the base of the staircase as Charlemagne went up. He then followed and the two of them entered the temple and proceeded down into the depths of the main chamber. There was nobody to be seen. The main chamber was empty. Charlemagne circled around and lowered his rifle.

"Nothing," Charlemagne remarked. "There's nobody here…. Were we too late?"

Tristan looked about and then over to the mural.

"No," Tristan replied. "We forgot to mention, but when we were underwater, Diana said that there was a space behind this wall that you two didn't explore."

Tristan approached the ledge before the mural and then climbed up it. The ledge was just about the same height as Tristan. From atop of the ledge, Tristan looked towards a caved in tunnel on the right, but an open tunnel on the left at the side, accessible from a similar trench before the mural and behind the ledge.

"Here," Tristan stated, pointing. "They must be beyond here."

Tristan assisted Charlemagne up the ledge and the two then came down into the trench.

"Remarkable," Charlemagne replied. "There's more…."

The two went on and entered the narrow, dark tunnel that wrapped around and went behind the mural, uniting from both entrances and continuing to the left and straight forward at the middle in a similar, slightly wider tunnel, but rough cave-like tunnel.

"Hang on," Charlemagne said, stopping at the intersection of the tunnels. "It's too dark."

Tristan could barely see Charlemagne from where they currently were, but the tunnel ahead was indeed pitch black.

Charlemagne took out the body cameras that Diana had given to him. He then gave Tristan one and kept the other. They turned on the light with the camera and each held one as they proceeded down the tunnel. Within a short while, Charlemagne and Tristan could hear whispers and voices coming from further ahead. The two proceeded with haste.

The tunnel was long and went on for several minutes until they finally came to a bend and began to see some warm light pouring in from the end. The voices that were echoing in the tunnel became clearer as a sort of chanting in the native tongue of the local people. There were some additional voices in a group that chanted the same words in unison. Tristan could hear the roar of a cascade as well. At the end of the tunnel, the pair came out and reached a well-lit natural cave with torches set about.

Tristan observed the posterior of a cascade at the opposite-side of the room where the cave opened out. The two of them moved forward to the end of a ridge that looked down to the cave where there were several of the local indigenous population, bare-chested and in their natural straw skirt garb with red tattoos over their bodies. They were all on their knees and looked forward to an altar where there was a chieftain, or priest, in a peculiar attire that stood out from the others. He wore a sort of dry grass garb that covered his entire body like a ghillie suit, but at his face was a large black stone mask of a sort of idol. This witch doctor stood behind the altar where there was an indigenous man stretched out and atop of the altar with only a loin cloth. Two locals dressed like the others held him down by the arms and legs. Behind the altar was a small mural positioned before the cascade like a backdrop. Tristan could see Vienna and

Everest at the side, on their knees and being held hostage by two bandits.

Charlemagne and Tristan positioned themselves in the prone position with their rifles pointed from above. They were too high for anyone to see them as at the sides there were slopes that went down to the chiseled floor of the natural cave. The ritual continued as they could only watch. Charlemagne paid close attention to his parents.

"What do we do?" Charlemagne questioned in a whisper. "There's too many of them, and I have no intentions of letting these savages carry on with this demonic procession."

Tristan didn't respond and instead continued to observe. The witch doctor was in the midst of stirring an unknown, but reddish-pink substance in a granite mortar with a pestle. Once he had finished, the witch doctor raised the mortar with both hands and began to show praise. He then lowered it and dipped his black, possibly gloved hands in and proceeded to brush the substance onto the chest of the unfortunate local. Tristan cringed as the man began to shout out in pain, while Charlemagne tightened his grip around his rifle. Tristan moved his peripheral vision to Charlemagne as he noticed the tension.

Suddenly, out of revolt, Charlemagne turned the aim of his rifle and shot at the bandits that held his parents hostage, killing both of them in an instant. The startle of the gunfire caused the worshipers who were holding the sacrifice down to let loose their grip and for the man to escape. The witch doctor shouted to them in his native tongue while he moved sideways, quickly. Tristan saw the crowd below react as they stood up and turned to face up. He opened fire on them, but didn't aim straight at them, instead providing a suppressing fire that would keep them at bay. Charlemagne attempted to shoot at the witch doctor, but he grabbed Vienna from the ground and brought her up to cover him.

Vienna struggled. The witch doctor placed a hand on her throat. Tristan saw at least four bandits appear from the cascade, two at each side, and proceed to open fire at them. Everest attempted to keep his head down at the gunfire, but his rage overwhelmed him as he stood up and bashed his body into the side of the witch doctor, causing him to let go of Vienna. The two bandits closest to them immediately moved forward to restrain Everest while the witch doctor escaped. Vienna fell to the floor and began to tighten her body over the continued gunfire.

Charlemagne shifted his aim to the other side of the room while Tristan reloaded. He shot at the immediate threats, killing them, but then moved to the others to notice they had disappeared with Everest.

"Dammit!" Charlemagne shouted, standing up.

Tristan stood up with Charlemagne and the two of them moved down. Tristan kept his weapon pointed at the crowd, most of whom had started to panic and escape, which he permitted so long as they kept their distance from them. He gave a couple of warning shots to some daring natives who attempted to face them, but instead rushed off. Charlemagne went to his mother on the floor and attempted to help her up. Tristan covered him.

Vienna was in a sort of epileptic fit as her body shook. Charlemagne observed a red mark on her neck from where the witch doctor's tainted hands had grabbed hold of the neck with the unknown substance. Charlemagne looked over to the floor behind the altar where the mortar had fallen and smeared all of the remaining substance on the floor. There was little left.

Charlemagne then looked back down to his mother as she had entered a sort of trance, squirming and moaning in pain.

"*Mutter*," Charlemagne remarked. "*Können Sie mich hören?*"

Vienna didn't answer. Charlemagne removed a glove from his hand and placed it over her forehead.

"She's hot," Charlemagne noted. "and she's not responding to my words. We need to get her out of here at once."

Charlemagne picked up his mother and began to carry her in his arms.

"Come on," Charlemagne hurried Tristan.

Tristan nodded.

Act 4, Scene 5

Charlemagne carried his mother back to the jeep from the temple with Tristan at his side. By the time they had returned to the vehicle, the sun had gone down, but there was still plenty of light as the moon was bright, but only at third quarter. Once at the jeep, he drove as fast as he could to return to the village while Vienna continued to suffer from a fit of delusion, muttering inaudibly with only one word identifiable from them all, 'Charles.'

Diana with Allodia heard the jeep arrive at the perimeter of the camp and then saw Charlemagne exit and raise his mother from the back of the vehicle. Tristan exited and watched as Charlemagne rushed Vienna to the medical tent.

"Charles...?" Allodia questioned as Charlemagne passed her.

Tristan caught up with Diana and Allodia.

"What happened?" Allodia asked Tristan.

"Charles' mother's been poisoned," Tristan explained.

"Oh my God," Allodia responded, going into the tent after her brother.

Diana gave a look of concern to Tristan, which he exchanged for an equal look back.

Charlemagne brought Vienna into the first aid tent where there was nobody else and laid her down on a bed. He then proceeded to look through the supplies as his mother continued to suffer. Allodia entered the tent and looked over to her brother.

"What can I do to help?" Allodia asked.

"Get some ice," Charlemagne requested. "Whatever ice that's available. She has a violent fever and if we don't lower it, we could lose her."

"Okay," Allodia affirmed, leaving.

"Charles…" Vienna muttered again.

"*Behrugen…*" Charlemagne responded, attempting to soothe her.

Charlemagne took out a small bottle of a type of painkiller and a syringe. With shaking, ungloved hands, he extracted the drug from the small bottle and then went to his mother to inject it to her thigh. Afterwards, Charlemagne took some wet towels and attempted to wipe down his mother's neck and her forehead. There was none of the unknown substance left on her neck, but instead the area that the witch doctor had grabbed was left inflamed, red, like a rash. Despite Charlemagne's efforts, the area remained like that.

"Ch- Charles…" Vienna said, weak and looking up to her boy.

Vienna raised a hand up to Charlemagne's cheek.

"I'm sorry…" Vienna said to him in a raspy voice.

"No," Charlemagne replied, shaking his head at her.

"I should have been a better mother to you."

"No," Charlemagne denied again. "You were the best."

Vienna slightly scoffed at her son's suggestion.

"A good mother… doesn't leave her son with- with his grandfather, while she and her love travel the world…"

Allodia returned with two bags of ice. Charlemagne brought his hand into his mother's hand. He had become tearful. Allodia quickly became tearful too.

Vienna began to struggle for breath as she attempted to say more until suddenly, her hand collapsed down from Charlemagne's cheek and her head rolled to the side as her neck muscles gave in.

"No…" Charlemagne muttered, checking her pulse. "*No! Aufwachen! Bitte, Mutter! Aufwachen!*"

Charlemagne quickly assessed her airway and saw that it was clear. Allodia dropped the bags of ice and began to cry into her hands. He brought his face to her mouth, but felt no breath. He placed his hands below her breasts at the rib cage, but felt no expansion. Her skin was still warm, but she was lifeless. Charlemagne shook at his mother's corpse, but there was no response.

"No..." Charlemagne remarked, wiping the tears at his face.

Charlemagne proceeded to attempt to resuscitate her by breathing two breaths into her mouth and then proceeding to do chest compressions with hope.

"Wake up!" Charlemagne encouraged. "Wake up!"

After thirty chest compressions, Charlemagne gave another two breaths and repeated the process while Allodia sat down to continue crying. After several minutes of non-stop attempted resuscitation, Charlemagne became weak and fell over his mother's corpse. He carefully brought himself up and began to look about.

"No..." Charlemagne said. "It's not over..."

"What?" Allodia questioned as her brother frantically searched the room for materials.

"I can resurrect her- I can do it!"

Charlemagne's desperation worsened as he tore the tent apart in search of anything he could use. He grabbed a couple of items, random items, and then laid them down next to his mother with a scalpel in hand.

"Charles, stop!" Allodia pleaded, going over to him and bringing a hand to his wrist. "Please, just stop!"

"I can bring her back to life!" Charlemagne argued. "The drug – she might not be dead at all... We don't know!"

Allodia tightened her grip around Charlemagne wrist, bringing his arm up and then looked at him.

"You can't raise the dead, Charlie," Allodia stated. "Please, just let her be…"

Charlemagne became more tearful as he looked at his sister.

"Please…" Allodia pleaded, letting go of him.

Charlemagne looked down and wiped the tears from his eyes. He then looked at his watch and to his mother.

"Time of death… eight thirty-five."

Allodia went back to the chair and sat down. Charlemagne sat down on a chair behind him and stretched his arms out on the rests as he simply looked forward in defeat.

Diana and Tristan had listened in from outside. At the moment that they had heard that Vienna had died, Diana grabbed ahold of Tristan and buried her face into his collarbone. Tristan consoled her.

"What the heck happened over there?" Diana questioned in a quiet voice.

Tristan briefly explained what had occurred from the village fire, the bandits there and at the ruins, and the human sacrifice.

"All of that sounds awful," Diana responded. "I'm glad you're safe."

Diana tightened her grip around Tristan.

"Everything fine here?" Tristan asked.

"No sign of trouble… We tried to do some cleaning up before you returned, but they raided a lot of equipment… Allodia phoned Heavner and said that a team would be dispatched as soon as possible…"

"How soon is soon?" Tristan queried.

"For the Protection Squad, probably by tomorrow or Monday," Diana responded. "The difficulty though is that the island is on lockdown to foreigners, so we'll see."

"Hm…"

Allodia exited from the tent and the couple faced her. She gave a saddened look to them and then walked over to confront them.

"Is Charles alright?" Diana asked, letting go of Tristan.

"He- he would rather be alone for the time being, and I think we should respect that," Allodia replied. "He sent me out to fetch a doctor to properly assess our mother, but I'm afraid she's gone."

"I'm sorry," Tristan responded.

"You are not at fault, Tristan," Allodia scolded. "Neither of you are at fault... Where's dad?"

Tristan explained to Allodia that Everest had been taken away during the conflict that arose at the temple.

"Oh dear..." Allodia replied. "This has all turned into a disaster... How did it come to this?"

The couple remained silent.

"Why don't you two go and get some rest?" Allodia suggested. "There's nothing more you can do – I'll keep watch of Charles, okay? He'll be okay, I'm sure."

"Okay," Diana replied.

The couple watched Allodia off and then looked at each other.

"Come on, I'll walk you to your tent," Tristan said in a soft voice.

"Wait," Diana responded, "there's something I want to show you. Come on."

Tristan raised an eyebrow, but walked with Diana as she took him by the hand and the two went to the other side of the camp.

"When we were doing some cleaning up, I walked into Everest and Vienna's tent and found something in the garbage can," Diana explained. "I didn't make much of it, but when you told me about the ritual you watched and put together with all that's happened, I thought it might be relevant."

The couple entered the tent and Diana took Tristan to a desk where there were loads of items, mostly personal items that belonged to Vienna – makeup and beauty products. Diana picked up the trash bin and then took out two rectangular postcard-like items that were bent in half and in the bin.

Tristan took each of the cards into his hand and looked at them. On the back, they were a crème white and on the other side, it stated in a royal font, 'You are cordially invited to a masquerade ball at the Windsor International Resort at Villa Paraiso, Isla Paraiso.' Below this message, each of the cards had their respective names, 'Everest Pepin Cabernet' on one and 'Vienna Edelweiss Cabernet' on the other. Below these names, tomorrow's date and a time of nineteen hundred hours was written. In the corner of the card was an emblem of what either looked to be either a pointed, or triangular heart or a pair of horns brought together of a devilish triangular head shape. Tristan looked at this insignia with intent.

"I recognize that logo," Tristan stated. "It's the same one that Charles told me about – the one used by the Committee."

"I know," Diana replied, "and it looks Satanic. When he described them, I thought for sure it was supposed to be a polygonal heart of some sort, but this is a symbol of the Devil."

Tristan shrugged.

"If these were thrown out, then I think it's safe to assume that they had no intention of attending this party," Tristan explained.

"Do you think they're members though? Do you think Everest and Vienna – Everest mainly, as a former businessman and philanthropist, could be somehow arraigned with these people?"

"I- I don't know," Tristan confessed. "It's possible, but they seem like good people."

Diana sighed and said, "What bothers me is what could have provoked this attack – I feel as though there's something more here, especially since you told me about that ritual. I couldn't help but put two-and-two together."

"When I arrived at the ritual, Vienna and Everest were prisoners, not partakers. The priest killed Vienna when he touched her with that weird paste he had used on that man. Why would they be held prisoner if they were members? Maybe, and just maybe, this wasn't some sort of random attack by a bunch of bandits, but a strike against those two because they refused to cooperate with the cabal?"

Diana didn't respond.

"Should we show these to Charles?" Tristan questioned, moving aside slightly to leave.

"No," Diana denied. "No, he's in grief, Tristan. We can't push this on him without knowing for sure. He might take it too seriously without proof and it'll only push him into madness. No. I have a better idea..."

"Better idea?"

"The meeting is tomorrow, so let's go with these invitations and attend ourselves. Look, it's a masked-ball, so if we wear masks, nobody will be able to see our faces and recognize us, and if we claim to be Vienna and Everest to get in, I'm sure they're such obscure characters that a bouncer won't look twice at our youth."

Tristan hesitated to respond.

"All we need to do is to get some masks and gowns, and then we're set," Diana stated. "Look, between this recent blow and the fact that I think there's something wrong with Charles, we cannot let him know about this until we're a little more certain."

"You think there's something wrong with Charles?" Tristan questioned.

Diana looked at Tristan with disbelief. She then sighed.

"Ever since Charles started to put on those gloves, I've become suspicious that he's been keeping something from us," Diana stated. "He's hiding something – he's got that same sort of shady attitude that you get when you're hiding something from me."

"I don't get shady!" Tristan deflected.

"You do too," Diana replied, "but at least you've been more honest with me lately. No. Charles is hiding something from us, and I think it might be something about his health. It's probably why he didn't want to go scuba diving with us."

Tristan looked at Diana with belief and nodded.

"No," Tristan replied. "No, you're right. I can believe that…"

Tristan looked to the side and out of focus for a moment. He then looked back to Diana.

"Okay," Tristan said. "Fine. We won't tell Charles, but are you absolutely sure about this? What if we get caught?"

"What's there that the two of us could not possibly handle? If it's just a social function, then so be it, but if there's something more, then it's worth the risk to find out more."

• • • •

The doctor assessed Vienna and then brought a blanket over the corpse.

"I'm so sorry, but I'm afraid she's deceased," the doctor stated.

Charlemagne nodded. Allodia became tearful again.

"I'll make arrangements to have the body moved to the city so that it can be preserved in a morgue," the doctor remarked, moving to leave.

"Thank you, doctor," Charlemagne responded, standing up.

The doctor turned around and looked to Charlemagne.

"Oh, and Mr. Cabernet, there's something more that I need to let you know of, but perhaps now is not the right time..." the doctor said.

"What is it? I can handle it."

"Your patient, the little boy from the village... I'm afraid he's passed away as well this evening. Just so you know... before you ask."

Charlemagne nodded and then sighed.

"Thank you, doctor. Please let me know when transport has arrived for the bodies... I'll speak with the next of kin about performing an autopsy."

The doctor nodded and then left. Charlemagne sat down again and looked to his mother. His face was pale and emotionless. He simply looked to the body while Allodia sat down again, and the two of them remained together in silence to mourn their loss.

Act 5, Scene 1

Charlemagne returned to Villa Paraiso to return the yacht on the following day as soon as local authorities arrived at the camp to investigate the damage done by the raid. Vienna's corpse was transferred to the morgue at the local hospital as well as the corpse of the boy that had also died that same evening. Both parents had refused to provide consent for an autopsy. Charlemagne told Diana and Tristan that he would prefer to be alone for the next couple of days, which they respected. Shortly after Charlemagne had left, Diana and Tristan left Allodia under the protection of the legal authorities at the camp while they took a jeep into town to spend some time at the suite. Allodia refused to join them and preferred to remain at the camp while Everest was missing. For most of the day, Charlemagne spent time in the depths of the yacht on his laptop, researching and reviewing the video attained underwater.

Once Charlemagne had finished reviewing the footage thoroughly, he spent some time attempting to decipher the hieroglyphics drawing comparison to Aztec and Mayan writing system. Little headway was made, especially as Charlemagne found himself distracted. At approximately five o'clock in the late afternoon, Charlemagne received a notification on his laptop of a received email from Dr. Lambert. He immediately opened it and proceeded to read what his friend had to say. Charlemagne crossed his arms as his eyes scanned the screen and he read the report.

The email contained the results of the blood analysis that Charlemagne had entrusted the Cabernet Foundation to deliver to him in Harlech. A thorough analysis had been undertaken to separate all different molecules in the blood, which included a slew of different types of poisonous chemicals and their respective structures. Most of these organic compounds were vague and nameless, but some of them were related to similar and well-known toxins that have been found in plants. Dr. Lambert provided a reference of such plants for Charlemagne to cross-reference with related species. Of all these toxins, there was one that was responsible for the delusions and fever, and it was a neurotoxin. Other toxins were not as fatal, but, for example, one of which was an immunosuppressant, which explained the low white cell count. All of this was noted in the email. The email of which ended with a necessity that Charlemagne retrieve a sample of the toxins in order to formulate an antidote and to further research the substance.

Charlemagne reviewed the report over again and re-read the conclusion that his friend had come to, in which the main neurotoxin, based on the related neurotoxin documented to be found in South America, was a type of neurotoxin that becomes fatal and is only fatal when synthesized through the reaction with a natural acid found in another common plant. In other words, the toxin found in the blood of the boy was synthetic, and therefore, he had been poisoned like Vienna. Charlemagne brought a hand to his mouth.

Without hesitation, Charlemagne began to look deeper into these plants to cross-reference them with the various species he was able to identify and take pictures of during his various hikes over the last week. None of them even remotely matched the plants that Dr. Lambert had listed. Once he had exhausted his online resources, he stood up and began to pace the room. Charlemagne brought a fist on the table he had been sitting at and stroked his chin. Afterwards, he left the room.

At the start of sundown, Charlemagne exited from below the yacht with a briefcase and came to the pier to meet with a taxi that waited for him at the curbside. He entered into the back of the cab and gave his destination to the driver, which was the Moreau Botanical Gardens within town. Once Charlemagne had given the driver his destination, the cab set off into town where it was quiet and less warm than the days earlier. The sunset painted an orange-red sky over the town with a faint mixture of striated cirrus clouds.

Charlemagne sat at the back of the taxi with a frown upon his face. He looked to the side and watched the passing buildings as they drove through town. The cab came to Ricardo Plaza and made a pass of the square on one-side and the synagogue on the other. Charlemagne straightened up as he saw the front entrance of the temple and then looked over to the driver.

"You know this town well, I suppose," Charlemagne said to him. "Are you Jewish?"

"No," the driver replied. "Are you?"

Charlemagne gave a chuckle and responded, "Certainly not. I recently read that Villa Paraiso has one of the oldest and largest Sephardic Jewish populations in the world who have been here since the Portuguese came. I remembered about it as I saw that synagogue at Ricardo Plaza... It's a very noticeable landmark."

"Ah, yes," the driver replied. "Yes, there used to be lots of them here," he explained with a minor disgruntle. "That's what my parents have said. Around the time the island went to the Americans, during the war, a lot of them left."

Charlemagne didn't respond and instead sat through the rest of the trip to the botanical gardens in silence. From Ricardo Plaza, it took approximately ten minutes before they arrived at the gardens atop of an elevated portion of the town towards the west of town. Charlemagne paid the driver the fare and then turned around to look at the structure of the botanical gardens.

The Moreau Botanical Gardens was large complex composed of domed glasshouses. A series of steps from a causeway led up to the main doors into the structure, which was composed of chiseled stone at the base and lower walls that went up approximately three meters upwards before being replaced by a reinforced glass with white beams and struts. Around the perimeter of the structure there was a diversity of palm leaf shrubs and ferns similar to the ones sighted in the midst of the jungle, but in a neat arrangement followed by a clean margin of gravel and then the freshly mowed grass that covered the entire front lawn on approach to the brick wall that surrounded the property.

Charlemagne took in the sight and then proceeded up the steps to bring his gloved hand that did not hold the briefcase to the iron handles of the large wooden doors that went into the building. The floor of the entrance glasshouse was composed of large and thick squared chisel stone tiles. From the main doors, there was a brief enclave with a low ceiling and door to the left, which read '*Acesso Restrito*' on a plaque. The walls of this enclave were made of the same smooth stone bricks as the outer walls. Charlemagne stepped out of the enclave and came to step into the entrance glasshouse.

The gardens were open to the public as there was no desk of any sort to check-in. Instead, from the entrance, one was permitted to simply walk in and bask in the humid heat trapped by the greenhouse that left a sort of haze overhead and condensation on the windows of the glasshouse. The exhibit of plants in the main atrium were divided into three sections with paths around them and low stone ledges dividing the path from the exhibits. In this room, there was a diversity of shrubs typical to the island jungle, much like the plants outside on the front lawn, but some of these were taller and included trees that reached out and upwards. Around the gardens there were benches that looked out to the exhibits where one could sit down and admire the nature, and at other spots there were metal plaques on poles that read in both English and Portuguese a short description of certain flora. The structure of the gardens also included metal beams that went up to the ceiling and supported the curved glass.

Charlemagne walked around and then continued forward into the next glasshouse, which was significantly larger and rounder than the one before. In the center of this strut there was a fountain. Plants were constrained around the edge of the glasshouse and in the center again, but these included a lot more diversity, especially with the different sorts of flower-based plants. Here, Charlemagne began to properly look at each of the plants as he searched for the one that could contain the toxin. Charlemagne searched the room thoroughly, but could not find the correct plant amidst the many planted, so he continued to the next room which contained a long corridor.

In the next glasshouse at the end of the corridor, the glass at the far-side was exposed so that one could see the open garden outside, but this park was not accessible from the structure and one had to access it from outside. The glasshouse that Charlemagne had entered also diverged left and right into the glasshouses. Above from where Charlemagne had entered there was a second-floor platform that covered half of the room. In this section underneath the platform, there was an exhibit of some plants that were being grown behind glass cases. The flower of which had a dark blackish-grey leaf and orange-red center. On the other side of the glasshouse, there were more vibrant flowers, amidst some shrubbery. Charlemagne walked up a set of stairs to the second floor of the glasshouse and examined the individual plants in pots that were being grown there, all of which had unique appearances with small bud-like bulbs and stems that sprouted out like trees even though they were small and offered not leaves, but flowers. Regardless, this glasshouse did not contain the plant that Charlemagne looked for.

Charlemagne moved on to the right, which came to a sort of aviary with tropical birds flying around. There were more platforms and less of a focus on flowers and shrubs, but instead trees where the birds sat atop of. Charlemagne quickly looked around the aviary and there he was able to identify one of the plants he was looking for, which was the one that contained the natural acid in its stem.

Quickly, Charlemagne noted the name of the plant by a nearby plaque and took a picture. He then sat down his briefcase, looked about to be sure that he was still alone, and then opened the briefcase where there were a pair of scissors inside. Charlemagne took the scissors and cut off one of the plants, placing it in a towel and then covering it before hiding it in the briefcase.

Charlemagne looked about once more and then carried on to search the last glasshouse for the other plant. He walked from the aviary to the central glasshouse that looked to the outdoor park, and then went to the glasshouse on the left, which led into a slightly longer glasshouse with a similar layout as the others. Charlemagne walked along the path and looked to the plants on the side. He soon made it to the end of the room where there was a large display of various trees. Charlemagne continued around and stopped again as he saw the plant that he was looking for.

The plant that the neurotoxin derived from was a leafy plant with thick stems that went up straight and produced a thin leaf that sprouted out. At the top of the stem, various smaller, thinner stems fell out and fell downwards around. Some of these stems carried a small pinkish-white flower with a magenta core. The flower buds of this flower were thick, but they were not the object of focus. Instead, a sort of bean grew from this flower that was long and tubular similar to a green bean or a vanilla bean. Even then, what was inside the fruit was more desirable than the fruit itself. ♪

Charlemagne took a bean from its stock and carefully placed it on a handkerchief. He took two more and then covered the plant before placing it in his coat. Once Charlemagne had finished, he took his briefcase and turned to leave.

Act 5, Scene 2

Diana presented herself before Tristan in a sleeveless thin black dress that went almost to her ankles, but was slitted at the right. Her hair was tied back, but made wavy. Tristan looked at her as he was dressed in a tuxedo.

"Do you have the masks?" Diana asked him.

"They're on the kitchen table," Tristan responded, "with the invitations."

"Perfect," Diana replied. "Then let's go."

Diana and Tristan left the suite and walked together, arms linked as they went from the coast to the main complex of the Windsor International Resort. From the main lobby, they walked down a corridor at the side of the check-in desk, past the restaurant, and then around the corner to where the ballroom entrance was. The couple stopped before they went any further.

"Let's put the masks on now," Diana cautioned, seeing people ahead with masks on already.

"Wait," Tristan said, "I won't have much of a problem being able to recognize you, but how are you going to recognize me if we get separated?"

"You have one of the most unique hair colors in the world, Tristan," Diana responded. "I won't have a problem seeing you from the other side of the room."

Tristan nodded and took his mask. They each put on the Venetian masks and placed them over their eyes, concealing their identities. Tristan tossed the plastic bag in the garbage and then took out the invitations from his jacket.

The couple linked arms again and went to the queue behind a couple. The line-up went quickly as the bouncer let people in upon receiving the invitations. There were two men at the door, each in Venetians masks too. The door to the ballroom was open and classical music could be heard from the other side. However, the doorway was concealed by a velvet cardinal curtain in which people passed through. Once Diana and Tristan were at the front, Tristan presented both the invitations to them.

"Vienna and Everest Cabernet?" the bouncer questioned.

"We're his children," Tristan replied. "Charlemagne Cabernet's children."

"One moment," the bouncer requested.

The bouncer next to him left through the curtains and disappeared.

"What's the problem?" Tristan queried.

"One moment, please," the bouncer repeated.

Diana and Tristan looked at each other. The second man soon returned and whispered into the ear of the other. Afterwards, they split up and the bouncer extended his arm for them to enter.

"Apologies for the delay, Mr. and Ms. Cabernet," the bouncer remarked, bowing. "Please, enjoy your stay."

Diana and Tristan passed them and came into the ballroom, a large room with a second floor at the sides and balustrades rail guards. At the end of the room there were a set of stairs that separated outwards to reach this second floor. There was a moderate-sized group of people, all of whom wore Venetian masks to conceal their identities. The room was dim and between the walls, carpet, and furniture, all was composed of dark-red fabric and a sort of dark chestnut wood respectively. The main chandelier atop the center of the room was large and made of a golden material, and other lamps on the wall or dangling from the ceiling were made in this curved and thin style. Towards the sides of the main floor there were tables with food and drink. A band played piano and some other instruments from a corner, but the musicians were blindfolded. Diana and

Tristan looked around for another moment before they looked at each other.

"Well, now what?" Tristan asked in a quiet voice.

"Let's split up," Diana replied. "I'll go upstairs and look around. You stay down here."

"What are we looking for exactly?"

"Anything peculiar."

Tristan rolled his eyes and then watched Diana off. He immediately then eyed the tables where drinks were being served and went there while Diana made her way to the staircase. Diana walked up the steps and came to the top. She then looked down at all the people and towards the people mingling at the railings. There were lots of older people, most of whom had fair skin or lightly dark skin. The second floor was smaller, but contained archways that led into corridors at either side. Each of these four archways, two at each side and two at separate directional points were guarded by bouncers. Diana looked to them and then proceeded to walk calmly around the many guests that were conversing with others. Meanwhile, Tristan picked up a flute of champagne and then began to make his way around the center of the main floor where guests were dancing.

"How about a drink?" a man asked Diana, picking up a flute from a tray.

"No thank you," Diana responded, shaking her head and timidly walking away.

Diana made her way slowly, walking closely to the groups so that she could listen on the sort of conversations that were being had. Tristan walked about casually, looking at the other people. He noticed that there was almost nobody his age or slightly older, but that the majority of guests were at least forty-years old or older with a mean age of fifty-five – there were a lot of grey and white-haired guests. Diana continued to make her way around, avoiding eye contact with the men.

Tristan made his way around the main floor of the ballroom and reached a large stone tablet that was hung on the wall as an art-piece. The piece displayed some figures set in the art-style of the local tribes, similar to the sort seen at the ruins. Tristan looked at the art, which displayed a group of various men giving chase to another man who had an evil appearance, but other than that looked just like the other men aside from the roundish nose.

Tristan's ears suddenly began to twitch as he heard a word from a nearby group that caught his attention, 'Zimmerman.'

"I believe it's all over for them," a man said.

"Such a shame too," a woman replied, "but what's to happen with the Wells Project?"

"Mrs. Dulles will have to decide on that – a shame she could not make it…" the man answered. "From what I understand, ever since his disappearance, the project has been put on halt until further notice."

The conversation then shifted from the topic of the Zimmerman Corporation. Tristan proceeded to move again. Meanwhile, Diana continued to wander upstairs, but with less luck than Tristan. Diana stopped at the center-front of the second floor as she listened to some men.

"I'm not sure," a man with white-hair replied to the other man. "We have to be vigilant from now on."

Diana then continued and stopped again as she heard another two men speaking.

"He was a thorn and I stomped on him," the man boasted. "That'll teach them for messing with me."

The other man laughed. Diana proceeded to move as she noticed one of them eye her and tap his friend to look at her too. She moved towards one of the doors that went into the blocked hallways, but did not go too close, staying near the wall. From here, she began to hear some voices from the other side – the voices were hushed and argumentative.

"What the hell does he think he's playing at?" a man questioned in a local accent.

"He's reckless, but he has a point," another man replied in urban American accent. "Nobody in Washington is batting an eye at any of this. He can kidnap as many children as he wants and nothing will be done about it, just like nothing's been done about the trafficking at the border or overseas. Nothing will ever change, even with this woman in custody. She'll soon know her place."

Diana felt a chill at these words and moved along. Tristan finished another pass of the main floor, placed his flute on a table, and then proceeded upstairs where he met with Diana at the top of the staircase.

"How goes it?" Tristan questioned.

"I've heard some disturbing things, but nothing related to Everest or the raid on the camp," Diana replied. "You?"

"Nothing related either," Tristan responded. "I'm beginning to doubt this endeavor."

"Let's switch floors then," Diana said. "We'll meet at the dance floor again in a couple of minutes, okay?"

"Sure," Tristan replied, watching Diana go downstairs.

Tristan looked around the second floor and immediately went for the banquet table. He picked up another flute and then looked up to the painting behind the table. The picture familiar to him – it was of an island with a mansion situated on it. Tristan looked at the painting carefully before jumping.

"Mr. Cabernet," a man said behind Tristan.

Tristan turned around.

"Mr. Cabernet, if you would kindly follow me," the attendant said, bowing. "The host would like to make his acquaintance."

"Host?" Tristan questioned.

"Please, follow me."

Tristan looked at the attendant suspiciously and then noticed the presence of two bouncers behind him. He looked at them and then back to the attendant. Tristan sat his flute down on the table and then cleared his throat.

"Sure," Tristan replied.

Tristan walked with the attendant and they came to the other side of the room where they entered through one of the guarded archways and then came into a dim corridor. Within the corridor there were several additional archways on the right-side that went into private rooms with tables. Some of these rooms were empty while the ones that were seemingly occupied had curtains drawn to block sight inside. Tristan was brought to the middle and third archway where the attendant extended an arm for Tristan to walk in. He did so cautiously, passing the curtains and entering a dim room where there was a man sat at the other side of the table wearing a tuxedo with a cloak. He also wore a more vibrant and flamboyant Venetian mask that looked expensive and like a jester mask. The man was not alone, but accompanied by two more at either side of him. All of them looked to Tristan as he entered. Tristan saw that they each had a brooch of the organization's logo at their lapel.

"Ah, Mr. Cabernet," the man in the center expressed in an English accent. "A pleasure to meet you after all this time. I take it by your presence at this masquerade tonight that you have given some thought to my proposition."

Tristan looked to the man with slight fear. He hesitated to respond.

"I had heard from my aide that you were quite fervent and opposed. A man of your stature with the history and legacy of the Cabernet family, we are quite fortunate to meet with you. However, I will not be so presumptuous to assume that we are in agreement. Please, sit down so we can discuss terms."

"Yes..." Tristan finally replied, moving his hands to pull a chair out.

Tristan sat down.

"We have existed for more than three-hundred years," the man expressed, "but only recently has our power spread to every corner of the world for us to brag about our influence. In all this time, we have focused on one simple goal and that was the betterment of the world. Is that not too what you care about, Mr. Cabernet?"

"Yes..." Tristan affirmed.

"Look at the interconnected world that we have created, and look then to the lives we have changed, the lives we have improved, the lives we will improve and think how you could not want to be a part of that too?"

Tristan didn't respond.

"We are power, Mr. Cabernet. We are absolute power. And times are changing so that it can all remain that way – this offer will not be on the table for much longer. We need your allegiance now or never. Join us."

"I- I don't know," Tristan replied. "T-tell me more..."

"Mr. Cabernet, what more is there to say? I think we've been more than clear of what is on the table. Life is short – enjoy the pleasures that there are and leave your mark. You have nothing to be uncertain or afraid of."

"I- I'm sorry, but..." Tristan responded. "I can't make a decision like that right now."

"Hm," the man grunted. "You disappoint me, Mr. Cabernet, but if that is what you so wish, then so be it."

The man snapped and a pair of bouncers from the other side entered into the room. Tristan immediately stood up in a defensive manner.

"Please see Mr. Cabernet out," the man remarked.

Tristan looked back to the man and then walked with the guards out of this area and back to the party.

Act 5, Scene 3

Once Diana had separated from Tristan, she went downstairs and avoided the crowd in the center so that she could attempt to listen in on conversations being held by others. However, like above, Diana had a hard time avoiding the lustful eyes of other men until finally, another man approached her.

The unidentified man wore a traditional mask of the indigenous population made of a carved wood and painted in red and yellow. The man wore a white tuxedo and had a light brown skin tone, darker than the others here. He also had long black hair that was tied in a ponytail. He was a tall man too, but would have been shorter than Tristan.

"Well, hello there," the man greeted. "What's a young woman like yourself doing at a place like this? Hm?"

The man chuckled.

"I'm sorry," the man apologized. "I didn't mean to be so forceful. My name is Kau. I'd take it by the fact that you're here that you ought to be or know someone who is quite important."

Kau spoke in a sort of condescending manner towards Diana.

"Related," Diana answered.

"Oh, is that so?" Kau questioned. "What is your name, Ms....?"

"Sutherland," Diana stated.

"Ms. Sutherland... Hm... the name does not ring a bell," Kau remarked. "Nonetheless, will you give me the honor of a dance? It'd be rude to say no, you know."

The man extended a hand to Diana. She looked at it and then around at the other people, especially the security guards that were around. She lowered her head and took the man's hand. The man took Diana to the dance floor and they began to dance with arms apart.

"You know," the man said, "come to think of it. I cannot recall a single wealthy family of the name by Sutherland – at least, none that would attend this function."

Diana looked back at the man as she was looking around.

"No matter," Kau replied. "It doesn't bother me, but if it is functions like this in high society that you like, only say the word and I'll take you to all you could hope to ever see."

"No, that's not it…" Diana responded timidly.

"No?" Kau asked. "A sweet, young woman such as yourself?" he said, bringing a hand to her cheek to gently caress it by barely touching it with the skin of his hand.

Diana stepped back to prevent him from touching her.

"I have lots of money," Kau remarked.

"Please, I'm only seventeen," Diana cautioned.

"No worries. No worries," Kau responded. "I am a man of fine tastes. Come, let me take you to my mansion. There awaits you a world of surprises."

Diana shook her head, but the man could not pay attention to Diana's refusal as he was interrupted by an attendant behind him. The man let go of Diana and turned around.

"What is it?" Kau asked, annoyed.

The attendant whispered into his ear so that Diana could not hear.

"Really?" Kau questioned. "Take care of it then."

The attendant then whispered into the man's ear again.

"Really?" Kau questioned again, more seriously and in more of a hush.

Kau turned to face Diana.

"I'm sorry, my dear, but I must be off," Kau said, leaving with the attendant and a group of other men that were waiting behind.

Diana watched them from where she stood. The group stopped near the entrance into the ballroom where they spoke. Diana was too far to hear what they were saying, but she watched. Once the group had finished discussing, they split up. The man named Kau left with the attendant while the others walked back into the ballroom and moved to meet with another half at the corner of the room behind a divider. Diana moved closer so that she could hear.

"All is set," a man said.

"The target was spotted at the botanical gardens. We have orders to terminate him," another man explained.

"Let's go then," a third stated.

Diana moved away as all five of them moved to leave. She quickly went to go and fetch Tristan, running into him as he came down the steps.

"Tristan," Diana said to him, grabbing his hand.

"There you are," Tristan replied, taking her hand and walking with her. "We need to leave."

"My thoughts exactly," Diana agreed.

"They're on to us," Tristan warned.

"What?" Diana questioned, stopping at the clearing where the two stairs joined.

"Hold me," Tristan asked. "They won't attack us from within here, so we'll need to make our plan here while we can."

"Yeah," Diana replied, bringing her hands to Tristan's waist.

Tristan quickly summarized what he had learned from his meeting with the strange figure. He told her that Everest had been offered to join some sort of secret society, but refused, and that they mistook him for Everest, but he refused to join, which was met with a threat. Afterwards, Diana explained what had happened to her, the man she had met, and the fact that he had to leave because they had to assassinate someone spotted at the local botanical gardens.

"You don't think that could be..." Tristan responded.

"If it is, we better go right now," Diana replied.

"Right," Tristan agreed. "Come on."

The couple took each other by the hand and began to cut through the dancing couples non-intrusively to leave through the exit. Once in the outer corridor, they took off their masks and threw them into the same bin that Tristan had thrown the plastic bag in. Tristan saw several guards appear at the ballroom entrance, looking over to them. The couple quickly linked arms and proceeded to move quickly, but subtly as to not tip off the foes that they knew.

"I can feel their eyes gazing at us," Diana whispered.

"I can too," Tristan replied, "but don't turn around. We'll get to the exit and get the hell out of here."

Diana and Tristan passed the restaurant and turned the corner so that they were in the main entrance. Diana couldn't help but turn around and notice they were being followed. Tristan didn't need to turn around to see several of the guards were already in the main lobby. The couple attempted to ignore them as they walked through the lobby towards the hotel entrance.

Once outside, Diana and Tristan stopped before the roundabout causeway and looked for a taxi, but there were none.

"Not good..." Diana muttered.

"I have an idea," Tristan replied, taking her by the hand and going over to the expensive sports car that had just parked. "Go!"

The couple quickly separated as Tristan began to run. He attacked the owner of the sports car, an older man and knocked him to the ground. He then took the keys and looked over to Diana.

"Hey!" the driver complained.

The guards immediately opened fire as Tristan assaulted the man and pulled him down to the ground.

"Get in!" Tristan shouted to Diana, ducking down as gunfire rained on them.

Diana quickly got in the other side while Tristan got into driver's seat. The vehicle was already on despite the key not being in the ignition as it was a modern car where the key was wireless and ignition turned on via a button at the side of the steering wheel. Diana kept her head down as shots were fired and people screamed.

Without hesitation, Tristan shifted gears and drove around and then off into the city. He accelerated quickly as he went away from the hotel, bringing him into the streets of Villa Paraiso where there was close to no traffic to share in his dangerous driving.

"Tristan, slow down!" Diana complained as they swerved around a corner.

"Sorry..." Tristan replied. "I- I don't know where anything is around here. Can you check your phone for them?"

"I don't have my phone," Diana responded. "It's in the safe in the suite."

"Take mine."

Tristan took out his phone from his tuxedo and passed it to Diana. After Tristan had handed his phone to Diana, he looked in the rear-view mirror at the sudden appearance of two black SUVs. He then proceeded to speed up in an effort to escape from them. Diana looked behind them as Tristan sped up and saw the vehicles gaining on them. They were immediately thrusted forward as the leading SUV bashed into them. Tristan held on as attempted to keep the vehicle under control.

"Speed up!" Diana shouted.

"I'm trying to, but these really aren't the most maneuverable streets!" Tristan replied, turning a corner.

Tristan passed an intersection on a red light, almost being hit by incoming traffic from the sides. The SUVs passed with him, but one of them had to stop as to avoid hitting a stopped vehicle while the other continued. Tristan continued to speed forward, switching lanes to drive around traffic at the risk of being hit by an incoming vehicle from the other direction. Diana held on as they had a close call. The SUV behind them mercilessly forced a car off the road in their pursuit against them, causing the vehicle to spin. Tristan focused on the road while Diana continued to load directions onto his cellphone.

"Okay- okay, keep on to the coast. The gardens are to the west. The coast is north."

"We need to lose this guy before we go get Charles," Tristan replied, "and we need to do it quickly."

Tristan drove downhill, passing stop intersections as he made his way to the coast where Icaria Beach was. Luckily, there weren't too many people on the promenade, which meant there were less people crossing from the promenade to cross the street. Those that were moved out of the way at the sight of the sport car and the SUV behind it. At the end of the street, Tristan turned right and continued along, past the beach, but along a coastal road that went uphill as they came atop of the cliffs. The sea reflected the reddish evening sky as the sun made its final descent downwards. To the left there were various luxurious villas built on the side of the hill. Tristan tensed his hands on the steering wheel as he began to hear gunshots come from the other vehicle.

Diana kept her head down as they came. Some of the shots hit the windshield while others hit the side of the sports car, some even ricocheting off the body of the car. The SUV sped up and hit the back of the sports car again. Diana looked at Tristan's phone to get a sense of where they were.

"We're near the gardens, but we need to head into this neighborhood to reach them."

"Still trying to lose this guy…" Tristan replied.

Tristan looked ahead at an intersection ahead and made a sharp turn, driving left into the hills instead of continuing on towards the airport. The sharp turn caused the SUV to drive ahead before braking. The couple could hear the screech of the brakes. Tristan held control to avoid swerving as they made the sharp turn and then continued inwards. Diana looked behind and saw the SUV turn around and follow them in. Tristan made another quick turn and continued in this manner, following the curving roads and driving in a sporadic pattern in a desperate effort to lose the SUV, but avoiding the smaller dead-end roads until finally, as soon as there was some sure distance between the sports car and SUV, Tristan drove the car into one of these roads and then into a driveway that went downhill. Tristan then quickly turned the car around with a three-point turn and turned off the engine.

The neighborhood was quiet except for the chirp of a cicada nearby. The couple remained silent as they listened for the sound of the SUV, which slowly came and then went. The couple breathed quietly and remained motionless for several minutes. In that time, it became increasingly darker as the sun had finally set.

"Pass me my phone," Tristan said to Diana, taking it into hand.

Tristan looked at the map on his phone and saw their location relative to the botanical gardens, which were at the center of the neighborhood. The neighborhood was to the northwest of town.

"Alright, let's go," Tristan stated, turning on the engine of the car and then driving off.

Act 5, Scene 4

Charlemagne walked down the path to return to the exit from the glasshouse when he quickly came into contact with a custodian that had been nearby. The custodian was sweeping the stone floor with his back turned to Charlemagne. He continued to broom, turning around to make his way towards Charlemagne. He was an older man of Iberian appearance with dark grey hair, a hardened and wrinkled squared face, and a thick moustache. Charlemagne looked at him suspiciously.

"Interested in the Fruit of Lilith?" the custodian questioned in reference to the plant that Charlemagne was looking at. "An evil plant, so they say. Of course, a plant cannot be evil. Lilith's Stem used to be uncommon in the jungle until the European's arrived and then it became extinct. Imagine that…"

"What was this plant used for? Do you know?"

The man shook his head.

"Do you know what killed all of them off? Was it an invasive species of some sort? Overcollection?"

The man shook his head again.

"I'm afraid I don't have the answer to that," the man simply said. "I've worked here for close to thirty years and only pick up little facts here and there. That plant right there though is one of a kind… there are lots of plants like that here, on this island that is."

"Right…" Charlemagne replied, nodding. "Thank you."

Charlemagne flinched as he saw a red dot from a laser hover over the man's shoulder and then disappear as it crossed over Charlemagne. With an urgency, Charlemagne tackled the man to the floor, which was met with a subsequent firing of a heavy caliber rifle. Charlemagne quickly opened his eyes and felt the blood on his suit. He looked to the man next to him and realized that the blood was not his, but without a moment to lose, he stood up, leaving the man who was already dead behind, and rushed out of the way as another shot was fired at him.

"Damn…" Charlemagne remarked as he turned the corner.

Charlemagne breathed sharply and dropped the briefcase down as he hid. He attempted to get a look from above at where the sniper could be, but he couldn't see him. Charlemagne took out his semiautomatic pistol from his coat and cocked it. He then picked up his briefcase and proceeded quickly into the corridor where he was safe until he reached the other side. Charlemagne quickly got into cover as he arrived at the next glasshouse as he saw the arrival of two men in black tactical gear arrived with submachine guns pointed.

"Mr. Cabernet, we wish a word with you," the men requested in a local accent.

"Put your weapons down then," Charlemagne shouted from behind the ledge he hid from. "I assure you, I can be more than reasonable if we have a chat."

The mercenaries opened fire and began to shoot towards Charlemagne. All he could do was keep his head down and hope they didn't close in on him. Charlemagne returned some blind shots back at them, but attempted to conserve his ammo as he started to move for an alternative route out. The mercenaries continued to fire at him.

Charlemagne looked below him and saw a valve connected to a hose system that was up against the corner of the ledge. He brought his hands to the valve and turned clockwise to cause the sprinklers to turn on. Charlemagne cranked the water up to the maximum before he made his escape through the glass window, using his briefcase to smash the glass and then his body to force his way through. Charlemagne rolled his landing as he fell onto the grass of the outdoor park and then quickly stood up with the briefcase to take cover behind a thick tree.

The mercenaries moved and broke the glass as they opened fire towards Charlemagne as he hid. Once they had run out of ammo and were forced to reload, Charlemagne dashed to the next available tree where he stopped to return some fire. Once they had reloaded, Charlemagne kept his back to the tree and looked around him at what his options were to retreat. The outdoor park was extremely open from where he was with beds of flowers and very low hedges up to the brick wall where the exit was. The mercenaries continued to fire at him.

Charlemagne reloaded with one of the two spare magazines that he had. Once the hitmen started to reload, Charlemagne dashed to the next tree and then towards the exterior wall of the botanical gardens where he was out of sight from them. He then proceeded down the wall of the aviary where he smashed the glass so that he could re-enter. Charlemagne then dashed across the room and took cover at a strategic point where he could see both the entrance that he had smashed as well as the exit. He immediately opened fire upon seeing a mercenary that was following him arrive, hitting him in the arm and causing him to fall back. Charlemagne attempted to take a shot at the other, but he backed away.

The hitman returned fire as Charlemagne moved to another tree closer to the exit. From there, neither of them could see each other. Charlemagne kept watch of the makeshift entrance that he had made in case the hitmen attempted to enter, but only for so long before he retreated again and kept watch of his behind in case he came for his flank. Without certainty of where the hitman would strike from, Charlemagne retreated to the corner on the right of the glasshouse where there were some ferns and shrubs for him to hide amidst. He knelt down and kept watch. The hitman didn't show.

Anxious to leave, Charlemagne stayed for a moment longer until he slowly made his way to the exit and took cover there. He then looked down the corridor and cautiously made his way in to return to the center glasshouse. There, Charlemagne spotted the hitman and they opened fire on each other. The water continued to sprinkle from earlier as the floor became flooded by a thin layer of water. Charlemagne ran up a set of stairs as the man reloaded to get a vantage point over him, but Charlemagne was now on his last magazine.

Charlemagne hesitated to shoot back at the man, especially blindly, so he looked around for what he could do. He looked at the lights that dangled down, but saw that they were too small to precisely shoot. He then looked behind him to where the incubators were for certain plants. There was also a cord extension nearby with an electrical trimmer against the wall. He looked at the machines and then to the thick wires that connected them to a socket in the wall. Charlemagne stood up and went for the machine, pulling it out from its socket and then connecting it to the extension cord. Afterwards, Charlemagne pulled out the incubator from the wall with its warm light that shined down on the plant inside and then went behind it to start to push it down the stairs. The machine tumbled down the stairs and then smashed into the pool of water, causing the man to shout out in pain as he was electrocuted. Charlemagne quickly unplugged the machine from the wall and then went downstairs to retrieve ammunition off the corpse of the electrocuted man as well as the Uzi that he was using. Likewise to Charlemagne, the hitman had been running out of ammo so he only retrieved two magazines.

After Charlemagne had restocked on munitions, he moved into the next room with caution. Immediately, the third hitman with the sniper rifle could be seen ahead on the rooftop at the other side of the dome, atop of a ledge that surrounded the glass roof. Charlemagne ducked into cover as a shot was fired towards him. He returned some blind fire, which forced the marksman to get out of the way. Charlemagne moved to the opposite-side to avoid being flanked. He continued to rain down returning fire at the marksman, but at this range, the submachine gun was extremely inaccurate and the bullets simply sprayed. However, the marksman soon rather held his ground as Charlemagne came close to the exit.

Charlemagne's shots were ignored as he spent one of his two magazines, forcing him to reload. The marksman proceeded to move back to his former position, which prompted Charlemagne to retreat. Once Charlemagne had reloaded, he opened fire again before ducking down. The shots came from the sniper rifle. Charlemagne stayed in cover and looked at his options – the handgun with several bullets left or a submachine gun with more, but less bullets.

From the sounds of the gunfire, Charlemagne was able to deduce that the rifle was a bolt-action, which gave him time when the shots came to stand up and let loose a volley of sporadic fire from the submachine gun. The sniper moved to reposition himself and escape from the shots. Once Charlemagne was spent, he tossed the submachine gun aside and took out the pistol to aim with both hands a clean shot at the man as he aimed the rifle to him. The gunshot hit cleanly into the shoulder. The sniper dropped the rifle and fell over. Charlemagne went quickly to retrieve the rifle and take it with him in one hand, putting his empty pistol into his jacket while he held the briefcase in the other hand.

Charlemagne came to the entrance glasshouse and could hear a struggle from outside as well as sirens in the distance. He immediately went into cover as he saw two more hitmen towards the entrance, dropping his briefcase again to use both hands. They opened fire on him as he ducked beneath the ledge. Charlemagne readied the rifle and shot back a clean and precise shot through the bushes as the two attempted to pincer him.

The other hitman attempted to close in on him, but Charlemagne rushed to the other as he had just shot him and took his weapon. He then held his ground behind the ledge to the right and opened fire at the other, knocking him down. Without a breath of hesitation, Charlemagne dropped the rifle and picked up the briefcase. He then ran to the exit where the doors were open and several reinforced SUVs, different from the ones that had chased Diana and Tristan, were parked atop of the hill on the causeway. Two more hitmen were at the front of the gardens, but on the floor as Diana and Tristan had just managed to subdue them.

Diana and Tristan looked to Charlemagne as he exited. His hair was amess and he had cuts on his cheeks, blood on his suit jacket, and a torn seam on his trousers. Likewise, the couple were dressed oddly in their formal attire. Tristan stood up from the man he had subdued.

"What in hell are you two doing here?" Charlemagne questioned, grabbing his side.

"Ditto," Tristan replied. "Come on, we need to get out of here before the cops arrive."

Tristan led Charlemagne to the sports car. Before the car was the second hitman who was before the car, which now had dents at its front. Diana hopped into the backspace of the car, which was small, but space nonetheless for a person to fit. Charlemagne got into the front passenger seat while Tristan was at the wheel. Tristan backed out of the causeway and drove so far back that he went onto the grass, but without a care in the world, he simply set the car back into drive and then drove off as fast as he could to leave the botanical gardens.

Act 5, Scene 5

Tristan drove Charlemagne and Diana back to the pier where they ditched the car nearby and then went to the yacht, which had recently been renamed *Vienna* by Charlemagne as a tribute to Charlemagne's mother. They boarded the ship and then went downstairs to get out of the public light.

"By now they've probably broken into our suite..." Charlemagne remarked, entering the below deck of the yacht. "We'll have to remain here until further notice. Perhaps deliberately, the Protection Squad have been denied entry onto the island, so we're on our own."

Charlemagne placed his briefcase atop of the coffee table and then sat down. Diana and Tristan looked at him.

"The two of you have a lot of explaining to do, particularly in how you were able to find me..." Charlemagne said. "Not that I'm ungrateful for the rescue, but I am curious."

Diana and Tristan looked at each other and then Tristan let out a sigh. The two of them proceeded to explain to Charlemagne what they attempted to look into starting with the discovery of the invitations in Vienna and Everest's tent and then the ball. Tristan explained the meeting that he had with a masked man with a British accent while Diana explained what she had heard about some kidnapped children and the meeting she had with the man named Kau. She also explained how the man left after being informed about something, most likely Charlemagne's location, and that she then heard from his goons that they were going to go and terminate him at the botanical gardens. From there, Tristan explained the chase they had before they could arrive to rescue him.

"Well, I am glad that you rescued me..." Charlemagne remarked, standing up and going to the kitchen.

"And?" Tristan questioned. "Aren't you going to tell us your side of the story?"

Charlemagne fetched something from the freezer and then returned into the living room. He sat down and placed the cold bagged steak onto his eye.

"Where do I begin...?"

Charlemagne recapped his case with the sickly boy, informing the couple that he too died on the same night as his mother. Charlemagne expressed his intent to learn more about the poison that killed his mother, and he received more motivation after reading the forensic report sent by Barry, which stated that the boy was poisoned by a synthetic neurotoxin. With Barry's help, Charlemagne was able to identify some related plants and then the actual plants that are grown on the island, one of which was known as Lilith's Stem, which used to be an uncommon plant grown on the island, but had gone extinct. Specimens, such as the one at the botanical gardens, are all that remain. Charlemagne then produced the preserved fruit that he took from the plant in the gardens. He placed it on the table.

"They refer to this bean as Lilith's Fruit," Charlemagne stated. "Lilith is a reference to the mythological Talmudic character that was Adam's first wife."

"You mean Eve?" Diana questioned.

"No," Charlemagne denied. "Contrary to popular belief, Judaism and Christianity share little in common as Judaism as we know it is a religion that was organized well after the death of Christ, around 500 A.D. This faith and tradition revolves not around the Holy Scripture, or Mosaic Law, but around a separate, unholy book known as the Talmud. Before the organization of 'Rabbinic Judaism,' the faith of the Israelites was an unorganized religion passed on by oral tradition and based on the Mosaic Law. People we know as Jews today are those that refused to convert to Christianity, the Pharisees, and instead hold on to their ancient beliefs, which they modified and expanded through this Talmud to compete with the deep-seated theology that Christianity developed. The Talmud, more appropriately known as the Babylonian Talmud, and appropriate because this faith became Babylonic and true to its Canaanite roots, is the foundation of modern Judaism. Jews in that sense did not exist beforehand, at least as they are now, but that is a semantics problem which I won't get into because I'm digressing too much as it is. Lilith is one of these additions into the canon of their mythology and it is not an accepted belief in Christianity because it's utter Kabbalah nonsense. The idea is that Lilith was the woman made out of the same clay as Adam in contrast to Eve who was made of his rib. She is not a nice woman. In fact, she is quite an evil woman – a demon. The idea came from Sumerian mythology, and her name from a demon that is mentioned only once in the canonical Bible, but not in Genesis – in Isaiah. The name, or word I should say, likewise makes an appearance in Sumerian mythology, which should make sense given the relation of the two languages. Sadly, the myth has also seeped into Western thought, particularly in the Christian occult even though it's not regarded as a part of Christianity. There is a related character, a temptress known as Lamia that is very much like this woman, but in Greco-Roman mythology. However, I am digressing again. Accordingly, the prodigy between her and Adam are demons. Thus, this plant, is named after her – this 'evil' plant which has been the source of so much suffering and pain by its fruit, Lilith's Fruit."

"So, what does all of that mean?" Diana questioned.

"When Europeans came to the island, the evil that was Lilith's fruit was made extinct, or so we thought. There exists certain plants like the one in the gardens, and I'll hazard there to be more in private possession of certain people. Whoever this Kau man is, he is obviously the man responsible for all of these misfortunes on the island, if not some and if not him, someone he works for. You said that he offered you to go to his mansion... Did he ever state precisely where this mansion was?"

"No," Diana answered, "but I have an idea. What about that mansion close to the volcano and near the underwater temple? There's no home like that around here that someone could call a mansion."

"Hm, that is true," Charlemagne responded. "It is perhaps in our interest to look into this mansion and infiltrate it."

"How are we going to do that though?" Diana asked.

"Easily," Tristan boasted. "We wait for a cloudy night when the moon is not as bright and swim to the coast underwater. After that, we sneak our way in."

"It won't be as easy as it sounds," Charlemagne replied. "All I have is my P99 to arm us."

"Who needs guns?" Tristan deflected. "All I need are my two hands – I'm trained in Sambo."

"What if there's another way in?" Diana questioned. "Think about it... If the two temples are exactly alike, then perhaps it isn't a coincidence that this mansion was built so near the underwater temple. What if... the temple is somehow connected to the mansion past ritual chamber that Tristan and I didn't get a chance to explore?"

"It's possible," Charlemagne remarked. "It wouldn't be a waste of our time to investigate that further. However, for that to be likely, the tunnels would need to go to some sort of cave system beneath the building."

"I think that could be possible based on my memory of the area," Tristan replied. "We were really close to the mansion island when we submerged."

"Very well then," Charlemagne responded. "We shall make preparations to go and infiltrate the mansion then."

"It's settled then?" Tristan questioned. "You'll join us?"

"Join you? I'm leading this operation... My father may be held in that home, and if my suspicions and fears are true, there is a terrible evil that awaits us in that home. Ever since I met the Committee in Harlech and saw them with their face masks, the devilish emblem, I was disturbed. The whole subject makes me sick to my stomach – these pedophilic elites... How dare they approach my father and mother with their sick intentions! For all we know, we may encounter more than my father, but the missing children, or something much worse... Nothing is off the table."

"Then let's do it," Tristan encouraged. "Let's infiltrate the island and uncover what needs to be uncovered."

Charlemagne gave a minor, slightly sarcastic chuckle. He stood up and went to the kitchen.

"Be careful there," Charlemagne cautioned, returning to the kitchen and placing a hand on the cabinet to steady himself. "In what you desire, you may be opening more than just Pandora's Box. These people are not to be trifled with... I can only imagine what the repercussions for myself will be having gone so far, but from what it sounds, we are not dealing with the people of that Committee directly. You may have upset them today with this little stunt of pretending to be my father, but don't think you've fooled them entirely. These are sick people, but they are also intelligent people. I wouldn't put it past them that they knew this entire time that you were not Everest or Vienna, and even then that you were really Tristan Merrick and Diana Cambridge. That being said, the people that gave chase to you were taking orders from this secret society, while the people that are after me are not directly tied with this secret society. No, when it comes to the matter of my father, these vandals that raided the camp, etcetera, we are dealing with a subsidiary of this greater evil... A spring that does not bear fresh water, but the blood of innocents to the lake of evil. People like this have been exposed before... the most recent and voluminous example has been Jeffrey Epstein, but even then it goes to show that these people will go to great extents, even consuming their own, in order to protect themselves."

"I'm not afraid," Tristan stated.

Charlemagne looked to him and nodded. He went and picked up his briefcase, setting it on the table on its back and then opening it. He retrieved the acidic stems and Lilith's Fruits, and then took them to the kitchen. Charlemagne then returned after placing them in the refrigerator.

"It's been a long day for all of us..." Charlemagne expressed. "We can discuss more tomorrow, but I need to have a rest."

"Where are we going to sleep?" Diana questioned. "There's only one bed."

"The sofa pulls out and forms a single bed..." Charlemagne said. "I can take that, I suppose, and give you two the king-sized bed."

"You don't need to give us your bed, Charles," Tristan replied.

"Tristan and I can share the sofa," Diana agreed.

"No, it's quite fine," Charlemagne responded. "Just give me a moment to use the washroom and then the room is all yours. I have the handgun, and if someone attempts to break-in, then I'd rather be the one that greats our sly friends."

Diana and Tristan looked at each other. Charlemagne left without their opinion. The couple simply looked at each other. Tristan sat up from the sofa with Diana. Diana proceeded to make the sofa bed as she removed the cushions and then extended the bed out.

"We can't dethrone him," Tristan expressed. "I can take this couch. You can have that bed. Charles can have his bed."

"You won't share with me?" Diana questioned.

"Look at that thing…" Tristan replied. "It's almost as small as the cots. Besides… I don't think one of us should sleep just yet…"

"What do you mean?"

"Somebody needs to keep watch in case… In case they come for us. I can take the first watch…"

Diana looked to Tristan. Charlemagne soon returned without his suit jacket or shirt, but instead a white undershirt and his trousers.

"Charles, Diana and I have been talking, and… we think one of us should stay awake for at least half of the night to keep watch in case of any intruders," Tristan expressed. "It's the safest option at least for tonight. I can do the first watch so that Diana can sleep in the sofa bed. Just go and sleep on the mattress and get some rest, okay?"

Charlemagne looked at both of them.

"You'll stay awake all night?"

"I'll try," Tristan replied. "Just get some rest and leave it to me. Please."

Charlemagne looked to him and nodded.

"Very well then" Charlemagne stated. "Thank you. I'm not that much of a sleeper these days, so I'll be awake fairly early to relieve you."

"Sure thing," Tristan replied.

"Let me get some blankets for the bed," Charlemagne remarked leaving. "You better use the washroom now, Diana, while you can. Can I lend you a shirt to sleep in?"

"I would appreciate it," Diana replied. "I'll just be right back."

Diana left the room and went to the bedroom to use the bathroom. Charlemagne went and fetched a couple of blankets from the bedroom cupboard and then returned to place them on the bed. He also brought a pillow and set everything up while Tristan went and sat down on the coach. Tristan looked at Charlemagne with intent and his hands together by the fingers.

"Charles..." Tristan said in a quiet voice. "There's something I need to talk to you about if you have the time."

Charlemagne looked to Tristan and asked, "What of, my dear boy?"

"You, Charles," Tristan answered, "and your health. I know about your hands. I mean, I've seen them without the gloves on and have seen them bruised. I also know you've been attempting to refrain from any vigorous physical activity, which is why you didn't go diving with us."

"I will be underwater with you when we go to the mansion," Charlemagne rebutted before pausing for a moment. "However, I suppose it is useless to lie to you. In truth, there is something that I have not been honest about with you and Diana. I have no reason to lie to you though, because you are not one to worry. There has been so much that has happened to you in the past year that you've changed significantly for better and for worse, and become more hardened even if you continue to struggle with your own pains. However, if I tell you, promise me that you will not tell Diana. She is one to worry – anxiety is written into her. She will grow anxious and begin to panic if you tell her about my pain."

Tristan looked to the side and then back to Charlemagne.

"Sorry, but I can't do that," Tristan confessed. "I can't lie to her – not deliberately or on a scale like this. Our relationship is as strained as it is at the moment. She won't forgive me if I keep something serious like this from her, and I won't be able to keep it from her."

Tristan paused for a moment as he attempted to phrase his next words correctly.

"For some reason, over the last couple of weeks, there's been a change between us. I don't know if it is a good change, or a bad change, or even a neutral change, but we seem to be extremely in sync recently, especially in terms of our thoughts. I can't keep anything from her anymore because of it, not that I've kept anything serious from her... I've been extremely open to her, but... I can't keep anything new, especially like this from her."

"In that case, I believe it is in our mutual interest that I do not utter another word," Charlemagne remarked. "At least, until I feel it is best to tell you both, or something happens to me."

Tristan looked to Charlemagne. Each of them had a serious face. A flush could be heard from the yacht. Tristan nodded to him and then looked away.

Diana returned and Charlemagne left to fetch a clean undershirt for Diana to wear. He promptly said goodnight to each of them and then left, closing the bedroom door behind him. Diana removed her dress and then pulled over the t-shirt that Charlemagne had lent to her. She then got into bed and looked to Tristan as he was still in his tuxedo and had only pulled at his bow.

"Aren't you going to change?" Diana questioned.

"Yeah..." Tristan responded, avoiding eye contact with Diana. "I have a long night ahead of me though, and it's not like I have any of my clothes with us."

Tristan sat up and removed his blazer, setting it on a coat rack. He then began to unbutton his dress shirt. Charlemagne returned, approaching from the dark kitchen with something in his hand. Tristan saw that it was the semiautomatic pistol, the P99 in one hand, and several magazines in the other. Charlemagne placed them on the table.

"Be very careful with these," Charlemagne said before changing expression. "Well, I don't need to say that to you, do I?"

"Thanks, Charles," Tristan remarked, taking the pistol and examining it. "I'll take care of it."

Tristan kept the pistol unloaded and simply put the cartridge into his pocket.

"Goodnight," Tristan said to him again.

"Goodnight."

Charlemagne left Diana and Tristan on their own. Diana looked at the gun in Tristan's hand. Tristan kept it in his hand as he went to sit down at the table so he could examine the gun a bit more before placing it before him. Diana looked at Tristan then.

"Do you mind getting the lights?" Diana asked.

"Hm?" Tristan queried. "Sure."

Tristan stood up and went to turn off the light, leaving them in semi-darkness as some light still seeped in from the windows and from the staircase to the top deck.

"Are you sure about this?" Diana questioned. "What time is it?"

Tristan took out his phone from his pocket and looked at his wristwatch.

"Just about nine," Tristan replied with a serious look. "I'll be fine."

"You aren't feeling the adrenaline fatigue from the last several hours?"

"I'll be fine," Tristan repeated with a slightly annoyed tone. "Please, just get some sleep."

"What are you going to do for the next eight hours?"

"I would listen to music, but I don't have my earphones. I guess I'll just sit here and muse, and when I get sick of that, I'll turn on the TV and watch with the volume low. You okay with that?"

Diana sighed and replied, "Yeah. If you want to even listen to music too, go ahead."

Diana lay down. Tristan tilted his head back and concentrated ahead of him while Diana muttered a few prayers under her breath. Tristan's ears twitched as he listened in on them. Once she was done, she fell silent and soon fell asleep. Tristan gave a sigh and crossed his arms. He looked at the pistol before him. The barrel was pointed outwards and cartridges were neatly arranged on his right. Diana slept peacefully as Tristan watched over her.

For the whole night, he barely moved until close to five o'clock when Charlemagne relieved him. Charlemagne offered him a light breakfast and then the two switched spots. Tristan was sent to have a rest in the bedroom where he fell asleep without issue. By then though, even Diana was awake even if she pretended to continue to sleep for the next couple of hours as she pondered on her own in bed.

Act 6, Scene 1

Three days later a cloudy night fell upon the island. The moon could hardly be seen. Charlemagne had purchased another wetsuit for himself and did some research on the mansion, but little information was available. Although the Protection Squad was denied permission to land on the island, citing concerns of the ongoing worldwide pandemic, equipment was sent via the Cabernet Foundation airlift, but this equipment would be reviewed by U.S. customs, so no firearms were sent. With a map of the island on the dining table, Charlemagne went over the plan with Diana and Tristan, possible escape routes, and a secondary entrance option as well as possible scenarios that could unfold. Once the details were well-established amongst the three, Charlemagne reviewed the weather report for tonight and confirmed with the couple once more of their commitment, but their answers were not met with hesitation. Diana and Tristan were committed to the cause before them.

Charlemagne unmoored the yacht, raised the anchor, and then he set sail from the pier and proceeded over the calm waters of the east of the island. Meanwhile, Diana and Tristan got ready in their wetsuits and then put on the ballistic armor that went over top. Of the equipment that the Protection Squad was able to send, the bullet-resistant armor was one of them. They also smuggled a silencer for Charlemagne, which he personally requested. Charlemagne purchased a hunting knife for each of them as well. Charlemagne took the yacht towards the mansion, but stopped before they could be visible a kilometer or so away.

Diana and Tristan surfaced from the below deck, ready to dive. Charlemagne dropped the anchor and then went downstairs to change into his own gear while the couple readied the air tanks.

"Maybe I was wrong about Charles," Diana said, readying her tank. "I mean, he's going to dive with us, so maybe he isn't ill – just old."

"Or maybe he's driven by the need to rescue his father, avenge his mother, and put an end to these pedophiles," Tristan suggested otherwise. "Either way, we need to keep watch of him in case he falls behind."

"Agreed."

Charlemagne soon returned to the top deck in his wet suit, ballistic vest and flippers. They readied the vests with the air tanks onto each other's backs and then tested the air to make sure there were no leaks. Afterwards, they attached their respective body cameras onto the fronts and then moved to the rear platform where they made their final preparations. Diana and Tristan put on their flippers and then lowered their masks. Charlemagne had them do a radio check.

"Remember," Charlemagne said to the couple. "Our mission is to simply collect enough incriminating evidence to shut down whatever nefarious operations are being done in that home, and to rescue my father. We are not vigilantes nor are we there to exact our own justice, and that goes double for me. Am I understood?"

"Yes," Tristan replied.

"Of course," Diana agreed.

"Good," Charlemagne responded. "Let's hop to it then."

Charlemagne approached the edge of the platform and then hopped in. Diana and Tristan followed from behind and the three met not too far below where they did their equal pressure checks and a second radio check. Once all was good, Charlemagne looked at a compass and pointed southwards.

"I have the temple marked in this direction," Charlemagne stated. "I'll lead."

Charlemagne lowered himself and then began to go forward in the water with the couple behind him. The darkness of the night made it more difficult to see underwater than it was possible to see the last time they were below the surface. Luckily, they had brought with themselves spotlights that could guide their way, but these powerful lights could only show so much moving forward. They swam close to the bottom of the sea, which was only a couple of yards from the surface. The area they were in was quite similar to the area that Diana and Tristan had inserted the last time and consisted of plains of sand with little sea life. They soon came to reach the same type of rugged and sharp rocks as they continued forward through the dark sea. However, simply going forward was not sufficient – Tristan looked about the area around with doubtful eyes. Charlemagne continued to lead, but he soon stopped.

"I don't recognize much of this," Tristan stated. "Are you sure you have a precise location?"

"I have an approximate location based on where you entered last time," Charlemagne responded, turning around to face him. "I've also reviewed the footage to be sure I had a sense of the path you two took to come across the ruins."

"Sorry," Tristan apologized. "It's just a little different from what I felt, and it doesn't help that it's really dark."

"No worries," Charlemagne replied. "We're bound to come across the ruins if we continue on this path."

Charlemagne carried on, but stopped as they came over a ridge. He shined his light forward and spotted some objects in the water. They were cylindrical objects attached to chains, which were attached to weights that rested on the seafloor. Charlemagne looked at them carefully.

"Hold here," Charlemagne stated. "Do you recognize that over there?"

Charlemagne shined his light towards the object in the water.

"No," Tristan responded. "Is that a mine?"

"No," Charlemagne denied. "They'd never plant mines in the water. It'd be too risky and open them up to liability. I believe that could be a sensor of some kind for detecting underwater movement. There are several of them spread around."

"Interesting," Tristan replied.

"It shouldn't be a problem – they're really for boats, but they can also sense our movements and if it seems that we're moving in an organized manner or group, they might sense us to be more than just a shark."

"We should spread out then," Diana suggested. "We can fool them if we pretend to be sharks."

"Precisely," Charlemagne replied, sighing. "I'll move forward from here. You and Tristan stick together and go from around the other side. Do not go too far – if we stick to this area, we should eventually come to the ruins. We'll regroup at the temple."

"Understood," Tristan agreed. "Come on."

Diana and Tristan split from Charlemagne and proceeded to swim eastward while Charlemagne went forward and towards the sensors. The couple went down the ridge and could see more of the sensors around. Eventually, they went below and proceeded through the field of sensors. Charlemagne soon reached the reef where there were some sensors littered throughout. He continued a steady movement as did Diana and Tristan from their side. They eventually reached the cliffside of the deep ridge that dropped off at the side of the sea. They stuck close to this part of the water and swam side-by-side. There were less sensors at this part. Charlemagne went through the reef and soon found himself at the ruins. Diana and Tristan reached the outer walls soon enough and swam over it to find the pyramid.

Charlemagne went through the ruins where there were more sensors. He then stopped moving as he felt a vibration from above. He lowered his spotlight and looked up to see the underside of a boat pass him. Charlemagne watched it until it passed his line of sight and then continued forward towards the temple.

Diana and Tristan met with Charlemagne at the peak of the pyramid where they then went down and inserted into the temple. Tristan looked around, carefully looking for sea life that could be around, but there was none. The interior was quiet. The three of them swam down into the main chamber where the mural was and then went towards the smaller tunnels at the side. Charlemagne went in first and carefully navigated through the narrow space to come around to the back where the two tunnels joined and then widened out as they carried on a sort of cavernous tunnel. Diana looked around the tunnel with estranged eyes as the walls were rough and natural.

Charlemagne led the three of them through the long tunnel that shifted slightly to the right, but stretched on for a fair distance, rising upwards until they had reached the surface. Charlemagne was the first out of the water. He removed his mask and looked around. Diana and Tristan followed from behind and they looked at the small cave they were in where the tunnel continued onwards, but from above. Charlemagne swam towards the shore and then trudged through onto the land, shining his spotlight down the tunnel to realize that the natural cave blended with a man-made tunnel.

"Interesting," Charlemagne noted. "This looks recently done, as in, not by the former people or in its former state."

Diana and Tristan followed from behind. Charlemagne took out his pistol from his hand and shut off his oxygen. The three of them removed their tanks and set them aside with the masks as well as the buoyancy gear. Once the masks were off, they hooked up their earpieces and turned on their auxiliary radios at their belts. Afterwards, Charlemagne moved towards the tunnel with his pistol pointed down the dark tunnel.

"I'll continue to lead," Charlemagne said.

"Got it," Tristan responded.

Diana and Tristan followed from behind, turning off their spotlights as Charlemagne led with his light. The tunnel was damp with water falling from above in drops. They were moving upwards still and the tunnel was much longer than the one from the other temple. At the end of the tunnel, there was a ladder that went upwards. Charlemagne went up first and then the couple from behind to reach the top. Diana and Tristan followed Charlemagne to the end of the rest of the tunnel, which was less than a couple of yards.

Charlemagne exited from the tunnel, stopped and knelt down atop of ledge that looked down to a ritual chamber similar to the one in the jungle. However, there was no cascade at the other side, but instead dark, volcanic rock and magma that oozed out into small ponds at either side. The room they were in was extremely hot, causing the faces of the three to instantly be overwhelmed by sweat. Instead of a mural behind the altar, there was a large bronze statue of an anthropomorphic bull-like creature with great horns and four arms stuck out at every diagonal point from the side of the body, two to each side. The light from the magma shined against the statue, creating a hellish glow. The idol had dark slots for eyes and dark slots at its nostrils as if it had a hollow head. The bull had a built chest with firm and chiseled pecs. Likewise, the arms and abdomen were muscular, but this statue had no pelvis or legs. Instead, where the hips should have been, there was a cylindrical oven above some steps where one could light a fire from inside, or even put something inside to cook. The room was empty aside from the three of them. Charlemagne looked at the idol with disdain.

"There is Moloch," Charlemagne said. "What an unholy sight."

"Moloch..." Tristan repeated in a whisper to himself, looking at the idol. "Why does that sound so familiar? I've heard of it before..."

"It's the name of the god of the Canaanites associated with child sacrifice," Charlemagne explained. "An idol cast out of gold or bronze in the shape of a bull. We can discuss more later though... We don't have much time to lose."

Charlemagne stood up and moved down the side of the ledge, down the ramp to the ground floor of the ritual chamber to reach an exit at the side of the room that led down a corridor. At the end of the corridor, they reached a stairwell with stairs that took them up to a wooden door. Charlemagne carefully approached the door and brought his ear to it.

Diana and Tristan watched as Charlemagne then opened the door and carefully looked out. He then opened it wider to exit and the others to follow behind him. They entered a much larger and wider corridor that was lit by lamps. The walls were reinforced while the floor was of a smooth concrete. They had entered the sublevel of the mansion. Diana and Tristan looked both ways and then took point behind them as Charlemagne went right.

Charlemagne took cover against the wall at the corner and peaked around the corner with his P99 in his hand. Tristan went forward the opposite direction and to the corner at the opposite intersection. He then checked around the corner and saw that it was clear. He waved a hand to Diana who then waved a hand to Charlemagne. Charlemagne saw the signal and then moved back to regroup with Tristan where Diana was.

"Looks clear," Charlemagne remarked, taking out a device from a pocket.

Charlemagne looked at the GPS with their location on it.

"We're in at the southside of the mansion," Charlemagne remarked. "Who knows how widespread the tunnel system could be or how extensive the security is within the property. Let's move northward and see where it takes us for a start."

"Got it," Tristan confirmed.

"I'll lead."

Charlemagne stood up and went back towards the right path where he turned the corner and then approached the door at the end of the corner. He made the same check that he performed with the last door, checking for noise on the other side, opening it slightly, and then opening it entirely. The door led to an empty room. Charlemagne turned around and went down the other side of the corridor to check the door there. The door led to another stairwell that took them up even further. Charlemagne examined the stairwell carefully and then turned to Diana and Tristan.

"I'm going to scope this staircase and see where it goes. One of you stay here and keep watch of our rear..." Charlemagne said. "A room like this should be easy to hide in if you need to," he added, referring to the furniture and crates in the room.

"I'll go," Tristan replied, looking to Diana. "Stay here."

Diana looked to Tristan and nodded.

"Right," Diana confirmed. "Be careful."

Tristan and Charlemagne left Diana and proceeded up the stairs. They came to the top and Charlemagne checked the door there. He then opened it and peaked outwards. Charlemagne closed the door and looked to Tristan.

"I'd say this is the main floor if not one of the main floors," Charlemagne stated. "I don't see anyone, but stay here until my signal."

"Copy that," Tristan replied.

Charlemagne opened the door wider. He held the P99 so that the barrel was pointed upwards. He then walked into the corridor and looked both ways before moving to a corner and peaking around the other side. The interior of the mansion was quite modern in design. The carpet and walls were simple colors, while the furniture was cubical and solid. The floor was of a simple dark wood. Around the corner, the corridor led into a foyer with doors that went outside and large windows that looked out to the dark night where it had started to rain. Within the corridor, there was the first sign of other people as there were various cloaked figures talking amongst each other. Charlemagne observed.

The cloaked figures wore a regal dark crimson robe with a royal pattern to it that covered their entire bodies, and over their faces was a simple facemask like the ones worn by the members of the Committee of Concerned Nations in Harlech. At the left breast, a golden brooch with the devilish logo was pinned – the logo of which was not of the committee. Charlemagne observed them as they conversed in the foyer of the house. He then noticed one of them make his approach towards Charlemagne's direction. Charlemagne moved back and returned to the stairwell that Tristan was in

"They're here," Charlemagne explained. "Lots of them – people from that secret society that tried to nab you and Diana. We're in the right place."

"What are they all doing here at this time?" Tristan questioned, looking at his watch.

The time was several minutes past midnight.

"I wouldn't push it past them that they prefer to congress during the devil's hour," Charlemagne replied. "That is what I've estimated from these people, but listen, one of them is coming this way and I need you to do something for me."

The member of the secret society made his appearance and proceeded around the corner.

"Take him out and bring him over. I have an idea," Charlemagne remarked.

Tristan looked at Charlemagne and then took over overwatch as the door was ajar. The man passed the door and Tristan came out, approaching him with quiet footsteps and then grabbing him from behind. Tristan knocked him out and then dragged the body towards the stairwell where Charlemagne held the door open and then closed it behind them.

Charlemagne helped Tristan carry him downstairs where Diana was.

"Find some rope so that we can tie him down," Charlemagne said, taking the mask off the man's face.

Charlemagne attempted to disrobe him while Tristan searched for some rope.

"It's a little thick, but this should do," Tristan said, finding boat rope.

The two began to tie the rope around the man and then around the mouth to mute him. The member of the secret society was an elderly man with balding white hair. They then took his body and hid it behind some clutter in the stairwell. Once that was done, Charlemagne picked up the robe and looked at it.

"A little long, but I think it's supposed to be like that," Charlemagne said, putting on the gown and then picking up the mask. "Here's the change of plan – I didn't anticipate these people to be here, but I want to learn more about them. I'll continue my part from the surface and see what more I can find and record. Remember to turn on your cameras when you are ready to film…. I want the two of you to continue through the basement and look for my father or the missing children. They should have them down here. Understood?"

"Yes," Diana confirmed.

"Good," Charlemagne replied.

Act 6, Scene 2

Charlemagne hid his pistol in the holster of his vest and then brought the hood up and over his head, concealing his earpiece and hair. He put on the mask and looked to the kids.

"Do I look incognito?" Charlemagne asked.

"Yup," Diana replied.

Charlemagne checked the emblem was still set and then looked to the kids.

"Please be careful, you two. We'll be in touch."

Charlemagne then left up the stairs and returned to the top where he opened the door and discretely stepped out. He looked to the left, in the direction that the member whose clothes he hijacked was going, and then to the right towards the foyer. Charlemagne went to the right and proceeded through the mansion to explore.

The mansion was decorated in an assortment of modern artworks, some of the paintings of which were exceptionally unique and bizarre, and some of them took on a satanic tone. Charlemagne saw a painting of a black devilish character consuming children, while another set with skeletons with the white paint of their bones dripping down along the canvas. Charlemagne later came to a wide corridor where there were artefacts and stone murals of the local tribe on display. The mansion contained an assortment of these intricacies, and Charlemagne casually looked at them until he was met with a man in a black suit and face mask similar to his.

"Are you lost, Mr. Rothschwert?" the man, a butler no doubt, asked.

Charlemagne looked to the butler who had his arms behind his back.

"I'm afraid so," Charlemagne answered in his own voice.

"No matter, sir," the butler replied, walking over to Charlemagne. "Please, follow me."

Charlemagne followed the man and he took him through the mansion, through a set of doors in a corridor and then down another corridor. They came around to a large set of doors where there were private security guards in black like the ones outdoors, but with masks on their faces. Charlemagne looked at them as they moved to open the door while the butler extended his hand for Charlemagne to enter.

"Thank you," Charlemagne said to the butler.

Charlemagne walked through the set of doors and came to a dark corridor with a smaller door ahead. Another two attendants in black suits were stood before the door with arms behind their backs. One of them stood behind a podium like a host at a restaurant while the other stood directly behind the door. Both of them wore masks.

"Good evening," the attendant said. "Will you be joining us?"

"Yes," Charlemagne confirmed.

"Very good," the attendant replied, opening the doors behind him. "Name please."

"Rothschwert," Charlemagne said.

"Very good," the attendant confirmed. "If you'll please follow my colleague."

Charlemagne followed the other attendant who opened the doors behind him. They then walked around a narrow and dim corridor shaped like a cuboidal U where he could hear the sound of a monotone female voice speaking from within. At the sides of the inner wall were sets of two doors spread out. The attendant took Charlemagne around and to the last door at the end of the right-side. He then extended an arm towards the door and bowed to Charlemagne.

"Thank you," Charlemagne expressed, bringing a hand to the door while the man left.

Charlemagne opened the door and then entered into the small, dark room on the other side. Inside there was a chair that looked towards a tinted glass, which then looked into another room beyond where there were several tinted glasses all around, looking to the center of a dark room. Charlemagne could not see past the other glasses, but stood behind the chair as the lights in the room ahead lit up and focused a spotlight in the very center where there was a low square platform.

Two stocky men in suits, wearing masks, walked in from the right where there were curtains that went to a room on the other side, and they each carried an arm of a child whose feet dragged. The young boy, who must have been ten or so years old, was a local indigenous boy with messy black hair and a flat nose. He was dressed in nothing, but a sort of gown around the pelvis. He had a sleepy look on his face as if he had just been woken up or was sedated, the latter of which was more likely. The men brought him to the center platform where he stood on his own as the men left.

Charlemagne brought a trembling hand to his mouth as he looked towards the boy. He then looked around the room as he heard a monotone voice speak on speakers.

"This item will begin at ten-thousand dollars," the voice spoke.

Charlemagne then looked forward. The voice spoke with higher numbers as time went on. Charlemagne simply stood in horror at what he witnessed.

"Sold at ninety-thousand dollars," the voice announced.

Charlemagne shook his head and then lowered his hand from his mouth. He brought it to his torso and felt the body camera. He then opened his cloak and looked forward.

"People have a right to know," Charlemagne whispered to himself, "of the obscenities that lurk in this netherworld."

Charlemagne turned on the camera and walked to the side of the chair so that he could film as two men walked forward and grabbed the boy to take him away. He then went forward and stood before the glass. The lights went dark and then lit up again as the men returned with an indigenous female this time, approximately fourteen-years old as she looked pubescent. She was dressed in only underwear and was left on the stage.

"This item will begin at twenty-five thousand dollars," the voice spoke.

Charlemagne stood before the chair and looked to the side where there was a bucket of ice with a bottle of expensive champagne, some flutes, and on the other side a device with buttons where one could insert a price and send an offer. Charlemagne refrained from touching anything and simply filmed the atrocity on the other side.

The auction carried on for up to thirty minutes until the lights in the room ahead dimmed completely. Charlemagne turned off the camera and then moved to step out of the room. He exited and went around to the front where the doors were open. The attendants looked at him as he walked past them. However, the doors to exit the room were closed. Charlemagne looked to the attendants. The room soon filled with five others, some of whom spoke closely to each other in a quiet conversation while others stood completely separate and silent, like Charlemagne. Once all of them were in the room together, one of the attendants went to the door.

"If you'll please follow me," the attendant spoke. "I will return you to your colleagues."

The attendant turned around and opened the doors. The six of them then followed him through the hall and through the mansion. They returned to the foyer, which was now empty, and they went up the staircase to the second level where they then walked forward to a large set of doors ahead. The attendant stepped aside and extended an arm for them to follow through while two private security guards at either side of the door stepped in to open the door.

Charlemagne and the other members entered into the dim room ahead, which was large and filled with other members who stood around the center of the room as a ceremony or ritual took place. The room had a checkered floor and a second level that looked down to the center where members could be seen looking down. An arcade or aisle surrounded the room from below this platform with archways, and more members could be seen from here. Like the auction room, this room with its platform and arcade was U-shaped and at the other side from where Charlemagne and the others had entered, there was a round enclave with an altar. Before the enclave, there were five seats that looked down a set of steps to the center of the room. No members stood near these chairs. The third seat in the middle was larger and empty. Charlemagne simply stood near the entrance as he observed the room. The members that he had traveled with had dispersed to join the others. Charlemagne moved aside so that he was not in the open.

In the center of the room, a man in a red cloak that was a brighter red circled a man in a cloak like Charlemagne's who was on his knees with his head before. The bright red cloaked man had a thurible, or metal censer on a chain, in his hands that was burning incense as he swung it around gently, spreading the scented smoke in a cleansing manner. The man also chanted in an unknown language, if it even was a language at all. He circled him twice as the incense burned a strong odor. Once he had finished the second pass around, he stopped before the man and used his hand to signal the man to rise up. The man stood up.

The man was then taken back by the sudden appearance of six young, beautiful adult women with firm breasts and round bottoms, and completely smooth skin. These were not indigenous women, but had range of skin tones from olive to mildly dark. They wore nothing more than the masks on their faces and the tight bikinis that covered their genitals as they strolled in and began to circle the man like fairies, brushing close to him and bringing their hands to his face. The man cloaked in the bright red robe returned to the center throne, but stood before it as he chanted. He had passed the thurible to a member who acted as an attendant, bringing it to the side and holding it. The man in the bright red robe raised his hands with his palms up. The women grabbed the hips of the women next to them, partnering up and twisting their bodies slightly as they held each other and continued to circle the man as sets of three. They stretched an arm outwards as they twirled, and then they separated out before falling to the floor. There, they lay, not motionless, but seductively as they brought their hands around their bodies as though in heat.

A member came to the man in the bright red cloak from the opposite-side as the other helper, but he carried with him a silver cylindrical tray. He gave it to the man in the bright red cloak who took it in one hand and then walked down to present it to the member in the center. The member took it into his hand and bowed his head. The man in the bright red cloak then brought his hands into the tray and took out a beige cylindrical object. Charlemagne squinted to look closely at what it was, and it was a large piece of the Eucharistic Host. The man in the bright red cloak raised the Host so that it could be seen by all. He also chanted some words before lowering it. A member then came to

227

him from his left with a dagger in one hand and a black candle that burned in the other, while another member from the right took the empty tray and backed away.

The member in the center took the dagger and then held it as the man in the bright red cloak brought the Host to the flame and singed the bottom of the Host. He then raised the Host again and chanted some words before lowering it over the dagger as the member held it with two hands at the grip. The man in the bright red cloak lowered it down onto the blade while the member that held the dagger raised it up gently. The Host was pierced in the middle and set to hold at the grip. The man in the bright red cloak backed up while the member raised the dagger upwards so that all the members could see the desecrated Host. He then inched forward again and took the candle. The member with the tray returned. The man in the bright red cloak took the candle and then began to bring the tip of the candle where the flame burned to the sides of the Host to set it aflame. The member with the dagger and burning Host then took it and gently had it slide down to land in the tray where it burned.

The man in the bright red cloak took the tray and held it before the member with the dagger. He spoke some words and then the member with the dagger brought it to his hand, piercing his flesh, and having blood flow down and onto the Host. The man in the bright red cloak then took the tray and walked back to his throne, going around and then to the altar. The member with the dagger held it in both hands like a sword with the tip pointed upwards. The women were on their knees and their bodies pointed forward as though in worship. The members at each of his sides chanted with the man in the bright red cloak, who lowered the tray onto the altar and bowed his head. The members in the room then raised their hands up before them, palms facing outwards, and spoke in the same tongue.

Charlemagne quickly did the same as to not seem out of character, but did not speak. They soon lowered their hands and went quiet. The member with the dagger passed it to the man who had carried the tray, and he then walked away as did the one with the candle. They stood at the sidelines while the member who had the dagger got down on his knees. The man in the bright red cloak came to him without the tray, which was left at the altar, and extended a hand towards him as he spoke words in the unknown language.

The member extended his bloodied hand outwards, and the two grasped hands together and was helped onto his feet. The man in the red cloak tilted his mask up, exposing his lips, which he took to the forehead of the man as he bowed his head. He kissed the man on the forehead of his mask and then the two parted backwards. The man who had been kissed and held the dagger bowed, while the man in the bright red cloak went to his throne, but did not sit down. Instead, the others on their thrones stood up with him. They raised their hands up like everybody had earlier and gave a chant that went for about two minutes as two members at the sidelines with large batons stamped the ends of their canes into the floor at certain moments. Once they had finished to chant, they sat down again. A tune began to play from somewhere. The member with his bloodied hand remained where he was, while the others began to exit.

Charlemagne looked at them as they proceeded to filter out. He then saw the man who was the subject of the ritual, with his bloodied hand, exit from the chamber with the others. Charlemagne followed him and they all came out into the foyer where they resumed to speak as they had been. Charlemagne kept his eyes on the man with the bloodied hand as a butler quickly bandaged the wound before some members approached the man and congratulated him. Charlemagne stuck around, watching and then approached himself.

"Congratulations," Charlemagne expressed, taking his hand.

"Thank you very much," the man replied in a local accent, looking at Charlemagne suspiciously. "I'm sorry, but have we met before?"

"Yes," Charlemagne responded enthusiastically. "Rothschwert."

"Ah, Lord Rothschwert. Of course," the man expressed. "A pleasure to have you in my home…"

Charlemagne looked at the man with intent.

"A pleasure to be here, Dr. Waomoni," Charlemagne responded.

The doctor bowed his head.

"I'm quite fascinated with the work you have done here on this island," Charlemagne said. "Well done."

"Thank you," the doctor replied. "I'm happy to be a part of the organization and foresee a prosperous future for Isla Paraiso. Why don't I give you a tour of my home while the Elders meet? I am due to return afterwards when they hold court, but until then, let me give you a proper tour."

"I would be delighted by that," Charlemagne expressed.

Act 6, Scene 3

After Charlemagne had left Diana and Tristan to infiltrate the upper levels of the mansion, the couple reconvened and looked out into the basement corridor. They stood in the open corridor of the wooden door.

"I guess we better get a move on," Tristan said to Diana. "I'll lead."

"I saw some doors on the other side from the staircase to the caves," Diana stated. "Let's go that direction.

Tristan nodded and then led the way as he said, going past the door that went into the staircase and into the corridor on the other side. He went forward to the nearest door and slowly opened it. The room was a storage closet for maintenance pieces. He then went to the door on the left and opened it, but it was a maintenance closet with machinery. Tristan went to the end of the corridor and attempted to open the door, but it was locked. The two then went to the other end of the corridor and attempted to open the door. Tristan peaked through the other side and saw that the corridor continued.

Diana followed Tristan as he went through and stuck to the left, taking cover by the corner of an intersection to look into the corridor on the left. Around the corner were some stacked barrels with taps as well as stocks of other bottles of liquor in crates.

"Stay here and keep watch," Tristan said. "I'm going to check the door over there."

Diana nodded. Tristan went to the end of the corridor they were in and checked the door. Through the door was another stairwell that went upwards. He closed the door and then returned to the corner of the intersection, on the other side from where Diana was. Tristan then continued through and went down the corridor with the stocked wine and liquor, reaching the door at the end. Diana caught up with him before he went through.

Tristan opened the door carefully and looked in. Behind the door was another, but wider corridor, with the left-side dedicated to shelves and crates. On the immediate right the corridor extended with a ramp at the end that went to a double door. Tristan passed this corridor and continued straight to the end of the corridor, which took them to a door that led them to another corridor, but that only extended to the right and contained a variety of gardening equipment. Tristan went to the door at the end of this corridor and stacked up.

Diana and Tristan paused for a moment as they listened to the other side. Footsteps could be heard as well as the ocean. The door was also made of metal instead of wood. Diana went to the other side of the door. She looked to Tristan and the two nodded. Diana then took a fist and knocked on the door. The couple then waited.

The door soon opened and Tristan jumped the private security guard that came from the other side, taking him down and onto the ground. Diana closed the door and then kicked him in the side of the head before Tristan punched and knocked him out. He quickly disarmed the man and detached the battery from his radio. He also took what ammunition he had and put it in his vest. The pistol was placed in a holster in the vest like Charlemagne's. Afterwards, they went to the door again and Tristan opened it. The door closed behind them.

Diana and Tristan had reached the exterior of the mansion on the farthest side, looking out to the sea from atop of tall cliffs. Tristan led Diana along the path that had presented itself, which took them to another door. Tristan brought an ear to the door and listened. He then gently turned the knob and they were taken to a garden. He went forward to a stone trough with plants in it and took cover. Diana followed. Tristan then went to the corner and looked ahead. He could see two private security guards ahead, looking out to the sea. Tristan went in quietly to sneak behind them. Diana followed and the two came close to the targets. The guards were stood by a doorway that carried on along the side of the cliffs while behind them there was a set of stairs went up to the mansion. The couple looked to each other and then they moved in on the guards, each taking one to themselves to quietly knock them out. They quickly disarmed them and tossed their radio batteries over the cliffs. Diana took a pistol and some ammunition with her. They then continued through the door once they were taken care of, stepping onto a deck with outdoor furniture organized around. The deck was sort of covered by a glass platform than only hung over some of the space. The area also continued to the right, around the foundation of the mansion.

Tristan went to this wall and took cover at the corner, looking down the other side as it seemed all clear where they were immediately visible from. A guard could be seen relaxing on the railings of the deck, looking out to some rocks ahead that extended from the coast. Tristan moved in without break and then stood up to bring his arm around the neck of the guard. He took him out and then looked over to Diana. The couple moved together past the deck and back onto a cliffside path that went to a greenhouse ahead. Tristan led the way forward.

Diana caught up with Tristan at the entrance to the greenhouse. He brought a hand to the door and attempted to open it, but it wouldn't open.

"Dammit," Tristan muttered.

"Allow me," Diana replied, moving in. "Let's see if I still remember how to do this…"

Diana took a pin from her hair and proceeded to fumble with the lock. Within less than a minute, the door was opened. She opened the door for Tristan to peek inside. He then took over the doorknob from her hands and gave a closer look only to see that it was empty. Diana followed Tristan through as they entered the greenhouse.

Within the greenhouse, the couple picked up the pace and quickly went through to the other side. However, Diana stopped as she took notice of a certain plant in a distinct pot. The pot was made of chiseled stone with engravings similar to the ones seen on stones in the ruins. The plant in the pot looked similar to Lilith's Stem. Tristan took notice and then looked to the side. In front of the pot on the other side of the room was an assortment of the exact same plant.

Diana took her camera and took pictures of the garden. She also took picture of the plant from where the natural acid comes from before placing her camera back on her torso. Diana then followed Tristan as he took position at the exit.

Tristan opened the door and stepped out onto another coastal path that curved around the side of the island. The couple stopped before they reached the top as Diana placed a hand on Tristan's shoulder. She then pointed upwards to the guard at the very top of the hill. They then continued more quietly around the corner, continuing up the path as it wrapped around. Tristan then stopped directly below the man and turned to Diana, signaling her to stay here.

Diana nodded and then watched as Tristan carried on in prone. For safe measure, Tristan took his knife out and continued around before standing up again as he reached the top. He looked ahead and saw that they had reached a large domed structure constructed out of marble that sat atop of the hill auxiliary to the mansion. He then turned to face the man that was looking out and put his knife away. Tristan quietly approached him and knocked him out. Diana heard the commotion and caught up with Tristan.

"We better check this out," Tristan stated, to which Diana nodded.

Tristan led the way to the side of the structure and then they walked around it to reach steps that led up to an entrance. They paused before the steps and then continued up them to enter through the archway of the strange structure. Tristan stopped at the entrance of strange room they had arrived at, past a simple arched corridor.

The room was round on the inside with a circular white marble platform in the middle that held an unknown insignia in black stone. At the corners of the room were fountains of water from where local indigenous girls as young as eight-years old fetched water in small kettles and then took the water and poured it over the stone in the center. Between these fountains were raised narrow archways from where natural light poured in. At the top of the dome was a chandelier lit by candles directly above the stone in the center. Between every corner and the stone in the center were columns with striated shafts. The room had a minimum of six girls in total with only two of them looking at Diana and Tristan as they had arrived.

"I don't even know what to say," Tristan expressed.

"It's certainly disheartening," Diana replied, stepping towards the girls. "Hi there," she said in a soft voice.

The girl simply looked back at her, stepping back as Diana went forward.

"We can't leave them here," Tristan said. "We- we have to get them out of here…"

Diana didn't respond. She extended a hand to the girl, but she simply shook her head. Diana stood up straight and turned around to Tristan.

"I don't think they'd come with us even if they wanted to," Diana finally responded. "We can't take them with us. It'd be impossible."

Diana looked down to her camera.

"All we can do is to record what we've seen here so that others can know and action be done by those with power to do so," Diana expressed, turning on her camera.

Tristan simply looked back to Diana with a gloomy expression. He looked down to his own camera and turned it on. He then stepped forward so that Diana would not be in the shot. They filmed a short clip of what they saw before they looked at each other. Tristan looked to Diana with the same solemn expression she was all familiar with.

"Don't worry," Diana said to him. "We're going to save them..."

Tristan nodded to her. They soon left the strange structure and continued onwards down a path that took them through another garden. However, this garden was more natural with plants growing about rather than in pots or troughs, and it took them slightly away from the cliffside. The couple were now on the opposite side (north) of the island than from where they had entered. The path eventually returned to the cliffside, but the couple came to a halt as they were about to turn the corner where the path ended. Tristan took Diana into some bushes as ahead was a guard in front of a door in the foundation of the mansion armed with an assault rifle.

"Guard ahead," Tristan said to her, readying his pistol. "Whatever is behind must be important."

Diana looked at Tristan.

"Are you willing to take a human life?" Diana suddenly questioned him.

Tristan looked slightly stunned and surprised by the question. He simply looked forward. Diana looked at Tristan with compassion and then took her own pistol. She continued to look at him.

"You're not a murderer, Tristan," Diana expressed in a soft voice. "I wouldn't expect you to kill. I wouldn't want you to kill."

Tristan's expression shifted to one of slight frustration. Diana raised her pistol up and quickly shot at the guard's thigh, causing him to fall to the ground. Tristan looked surprised again, but quickly dashed forward to disarm the guard and disable his radio. Diana assisted, knocking the man out. Tristan's expression was one of relief as they stacked up at the door. He took a deep breath and then opened the door.

Tristan entered the corridor similar in appearance to the basement from earlier. He went to the corner as the hall turned right, looked down and then went forward before coming to the corner on the left. He took cover and then looked around the other side. The corridor led into a sort of bunker or war room with desks and computers on one side and a table in the center. There were some men in suits on computers with headsets over their head, looking at closed-circuit footage on monitors while others looked at other programs, most likely information from the underwater sensors. Tristan kept his pistol in his hand and quietly approached one of the mercenaries with Diana.

Diana took out the one studying the underwater sensors, while Tristan took out the other looking at the security cameras. Tristan also took a set of keys off of the guard that he took care of. They then went to a door at the other side from the corridor they came from and stacked up. Tristan opened the door and walked through. The corridor continued forward, but had a T-intersection at the middle and was dim. Diana followed Tristan as he took cover at the corner of the intersection which went to the right.

Tristan looked around the corner, but saw that it was clear. He then stepped out and into the corridor. On either side were prison cells with two cots inside each. Tristan turned on his camera to record and then stepped forward, looking into the cells as Diana walked behind him. He looked into each of the six or so cells there were before the corridor ended and continued left and right. Within the cells were more missing children, most of whom were asleep and within bed, but there weren't many of them so most of them had a cell each. Tristan looked at both sides as he filmed.

Diana looked with silent eyes until they reached the end of the corridor and then looked both directions. Tristan continued on the left while Diana took her camera and began to record as she went right. Most of the cells in this far area were empty. Diana looked at the furthest cell and then turned off her camera as she recognized an older man sleeping in the cot.

"Everest!" Diana said. "Everest!"

Tristan looked down the corridor and turned off his camera. He then quickly met up with Diana as she grasped the bars of the cell that Everest was in. Everest woke up and looked out. He then saw the couple. Tristan quickly took the keys and attempted to try each of them on the padlock.

"W-what?" Everest questioned. "Diana? Tristan? W-what are you doing here?"

Everest sat up and then attempted to stand up, but he was unsteady on his feet. Tristan opened the cell and rushed in to help Everest stand. He brought his arm up and under Everest's shoulder and rested it on the other shoulder.

"We're here to get you out," Tristan explained. "Charles is here too. We're going to get you out of here."

"G-good God," Everest simply expressed, bringing a hand to his eyes as he was brought under the light. "Where's Vienna? Is Vienna okay?"

Diana looked to Tristan. He looked back at her.

"We can talk about that later," Tristan simply said. "Come on – Diana, tell Charles we have his father. We need to get out of here ASAP!"

Act 6, Scene 4

Charlemagne walked with Kau Waomoni through his mansion as he took him on a tour of the artworks and artefacts. He then felt a quiet vibration in his ear as he heard Diana's voice speak.

"We've secured the package and are moving towards Exit Point B," Diana said.

Charlemagne simply hit on his radio to send two taps to confirm he received the message.

"Perhaps this is my most favorite piece," Waomoni said, looking at a portrait ahead.

Charlemagne looked at the painting, which was a modernist painting on a white canvas of a man either in fright or agony. The man held his arms over his head in a sort of paralyzed manner, fingers hooked out and each in different positions. The man in the painting was brown.

"I had this one commissioned myself," Waomoni said. "Reminded me of my father… a pitiful man. Thankfully, it's not from him that I inherit my privilege to this group."

"Your mother?" Charlemagne questioned.

"Yes," Waomoni replied. "You know, this island has a special legacy to the Chosen that I wish to return to the Children. The first settlement of our ancestors was not in New York as many believe, but in Isla Paraiso through the Portuguese. We escaped persecution at the hands of the Spanish to come here where we made our livelihood."

"Our home is the entire world," Charlemagne remarked instead.

"I've heard our home to be beyond this world," Waomoni instead said. "I'm not sure I believe it though. You're a senior member of the organization though… Do you know more about our origins?"

"Even I'm skeptical, but the dogma is what it is," Charlemagne vaguely responded.

"Hm," Waomoni replied. "I suppose that is true…"

"Perhaps it is time to return to the others," Charlemagne suggested. "It's almost three o'clock."

"Yes, you're right," Waomoni agreed.

The two returned to the foyer and walked up the main steps. Various members remained around in conversation with each other. Wine and some light snacks were being served by the attendants of the mansion. The two came to the front doors to the main hall and stopped before the guards. These two guards were different from the others as they were not part of the mansion security team. They were distinguishable by their suits. The two paused before them.

"Dr. Waomoni and Lord Rothschwertz to see the Elders."

The guards opened the door and then permitted them to enter. Charlemagne walked in with the doctor and returned to the hall where the initiation ritual for Waomoni had been held. It still had the smell of incense. The guards closed the door behind them. They walked forward and came before the seven members of the secret society, who were known as the Elders.

Dr. Waomoni bowed as he came before them. Charlemagne followed.

"Dear Elders, it is I, Dr. Waomoni, your host for tonight's event and your newly initiated," Waomoni expressed. "I am with the Lord Rothschwertz of the Rothschwertz dynasty."

"Welcome, dear brothers," the man in the bright red cloak expressed in a sort of congested Londoner accent. "Dr. Waomoni, you have made us guests in your home and found your place with us as is by your birthright. We commend you over your actions in the recent months, the gentrification of the island, and the fronts you have established in this home you have referred to as an ancient home of the Chosen. However, this council is not yet satisfied even if you've made a name for yourself with the other Children. There remains an issue that you have brought forward to us of Charlemagne de la Cabernet who continues to be a thorn in our side, and as if the apple had not fallen far from the tree, there is also a deep security issue pertaining to the party last weekend in which two uninvited guests managed to escape capture and extermination under the guise of Everest and Vienna de la Cabernet. Both Everest and Vienna Cabernet of whom have refused our offer of collaboration, and surely must have sent spies into our ranks. The entirety of the Cabernet dynasty is a problem and has always been a problem, especially since the troublesome nature it has been to infiltrate their line as we have with other great families in the world. I have entrusted the issue to you, as you have reported to us that all of them are here, so what do you have to say for yourself?"

"I am afraid no recent developments have been made since my last reporting to you," Dr. Waomoni expressed. "I am unsure of whether Mr. Charlemagne Cabernet even remains on the island as my people have not been able to spot him. Everest remains in our custody and Vienna is no longer a problem. If Cabernet is no longer on Isla Paraiso, there is not much more I can do."

"What are your intentions in keeping Everest Cabernet alive? Terminate him," an Elder with a German accent spoke.

"Everest Cabernet is Charlemagne's father, and he may be important leverage should we wish to force him out of finding."

"If Charlemagne Cabernet is no longer on the island, then the problem is no longer yours anyways," the Elder in the bright red cloak expressed. "Likewise, the psychodrama of that ritual he paid witnessed to may have scared him away. We will not pursue the matter – we see no reason to, but be sure to report to us with confidence when you are sure that he is gone. The father... terminate him or set him free. I don't care either way."

"Terminate him, surely," the Elder with the German accent spoke out. "It will send a message to his son. Do not forget what Zimmerman warned us of... He surely knows!"

"Nonsense," another, third Elder responded. "Zimmerman assured us that the confidential documents were destroyed..."

The Elder in the bright red cloak raised a hand to silence the other.

"Allegations that Charlemagne knows anything about us are unfound," the Elder stated, "and I will not hear that name – Zimmerman – again in my court. You have your orders, doctor. Please don't give us reason to be disappointed."

"Of course," Dr. Waomoni responded, bowing.

Charlemagne bowed. The man in the bright red cloak looked to Charlemagne with intent. The two then left the court and returned to the foyer. Dr. Waomoni cleared his throat.

"Lord Rothschwertz," Dr. Waomoni said, turning to him. "Please come to my study and share a drink with me. There's something I wish to show you and get your opinion of before you retire for the night."

"Certainly," Charlemagne replied.

Dr. Waomoni took Charlemagne away from the foyer and down a corridor on the second floor. They walked through the mansion and then came to a set of doors. The doctor pushed against them and then entered a large study, double the size of Charlemagne's. In the center was a large model of the island. At the back was a large window that looked out to the sea. Before this window was a large desk. The study was modest in its decoration and austere. Above the fireplace, on display, was a mask similar to the one worn by the witch doctor at the human sacrifice ritual. Dr. Waomoni walked to the model of the island as Charlemagne looked at this mask.

Charlemagne discretely turned on his camera to record even though he couldn't film. He was recording audio, nonetheless. He then went to join the doctor at the model of the island.

"Please, explain to me," Charlemagne said in his modified Londoner accent. "What is it that this Cabernet family has done to upset the Elders?"

Dr. Waomoni turned to Charlemagne.

"I was told that after we had approached Everest and Vienna Cabernet to collaborate with the Children, they refused and threatened to go public with our offer."

"Really? So, for that reason they had to be kidnapped?"

"No..." Dr. Waomoni responded. "You know how it is... The organization receives dozens of threats like that a month, but they're laughed off as crazed conspiracy theorists. No, what Everest had threatened to do was much more serious, which was why I had to strike. He had information that could have ruined my entire operation for the past months. I had to take him out for that reason. Charlemagne became a problem for two reasons: he followed my men and walked in one of our rituals... a dramatic human sacrifice, and I had also heard that he was looking closer at that child that had escaped. If he knew he was poisoned, it could compromise us, especially after paying witness to that ritual. Luckily, the woman was killed in that incident that followed, or so I've heard, but he's been yet to be seen since we tried to close in on him at the local gardens."

Charlemagne looked at Dr. Waomoni with an upset look.

"What do you mean by collaborate?" Charlemagne asked. "The Cabernet family are not like us. They're not Chosen... at least as I'm aware of."

"No, they're not. Like the Elder said, the Cabernet family are one of the few families that have not been 'infiltrated' like the Kennedy, Trump, Biden, or Rockefeller family. A part of the problem has been the fact that they're an introverted bunch..."

"Psychodrama? Tell me more about that," Charlemagne insisted with a nefarious look in his eye. "Please."

"Well, for the past several months, I've revived an old myth held by these superstitious people... The idea was simple... a simple masquerade, to scare the people out of their homes and push them into the cities. I revived an old myth of a creature from the swamps that kidnaps children... and I tried to modernize it by having him go after grown men too. With that, the Elders had my half-brother hospitalized at my hospital, and I took over command of the village in his place. If I could get more than half of them to leave, I could justify selling the entire land and dispersing the income amongst them. What do they care about the tradition and history of that land anyhow? Their homes had been long abandoned, and the same is true of the other people. That's another reason why I had to chase Everest and Vienna Cabernet out... they were moving more of them in... Ruined my entire plan. No, what I had to do was to foreclose on this land so that Isla Paraiso could expand. I envision an expansion both northwest and south of the island where these people can live if they despise Villa Paraiso so much. There, we can open villas for American tourists to purchase and retreat to when they have nowhere else to vacation to because of the pandemic. The plan was brilliant that way..."

"Yes, quite intriguing," Charlemagne responded, bringing a hand into his cloak and turning off the camera. "The only problem is," he said in his normal voice, "you won't live to see it through."

"What?" Dr. Waomoni responded, turning to Charlemagne.

Charlemagne took out his pistol from his cloak and pointed it to the doctor. He then shot him in the knee, sending him to the floor.

"Ah!" the doctor shouted. "What?! Who are you?!"

"I have enough evidence about the activities on this island that I can have you made for a very long time," Charlemagne stated. "The game is over, I'm afraid, for you. You killed my mother – that alone give me plenty of reason to kill you now!"

"Charlemagne!" the doctor shouted. "How the hell did you get in here? When my people – the Chosen, find out, you'll surely be dead!"

"Except they won't find out, because I was never here. When I leave, I'll be but a ghost story, while my evidence will spread like a wildfire across the globe and the whole world will know of your misdeeds."

Waomoni laughed.

"You've spent several hours here and you still don't realize the breadth and power this organization – the Children of Moloch – have. We control the airwaves. We control information wherever it pops its head. We control truth. No major media organization will run a story about the Children so long as we exist, because we own every one of these organizations. If you go forward with what you've learned, we'll hunt you down – we'll hunt your children down. We'll hunt that sister of yours down! We'll kill your father – you forget, we have him downstairs."

"No," Charlemagne denied. "You don't. You think I came alone? All that restrains me from killing you on the spot is my moral conscience. I cannot kill a disarmed man, because that would not be honorable. Even then, I would rather see you be tried for your crimes, and then you'll see just how much your patronage with the Children, these Elders, is worth."

Dr. Waomoni scowled at Charlemagne. He shot him again in the arm and then left the room to the sound of the doctor yowling at him from where he was sat in agonizing pain.

Act 6, Scene 5

"I've received your alert," Charlemagne said over the radio. "I'm making my way to Exit Point Bravo at once."

"Copy that," Tristan responded, resting for a moment. "Come on... we have got to be almost there..."

Tristan helped Everest back onto his feet and they continued along the coast of the island. Diana went forward and rushed along to take out a guard with his back to them. Everest was extremely drowsy and had begun to drag his feet, which forced Tristan put in more force in carrying him. Diana quickly disarmed and neutralized the mercenary before she continued forward, through a natural archway formed by a rock as they continued down the north coast of the island.

Diana stopped at the edge and pointed down.

"We're almost there," Diana expressed to Tristan. "Just a little more."

"I hope Charlemagne isn't too far..." Tristan said. "I also hope this isn't a dead-end."

Tristan was panting as he carried Everest. He passed the archway and saw the boathouse below the steep cliffs.

"Probably would have been easier to just return to the cave..."

Diana looked at Tristan, semi-annoyed.

"Everest doesn't have a suit," Diana reminded him. "Now come on..."

The three of them stopped as they heard an alarm go off.

"Well, it was bound to happen eventually..." Tristan reminisced, continuing to drag Everest along. "I just hope Charlemagne's isn't in trouble and they found a body instead..."

Diana and Tristan went down a path along the cliffside that went to the boathouse. The exterior of the building was clear, which allowed them to simply reach the building door. Diana took out the pin from her hair and started to pick the lock while Tristan took a moment to rest. She had the lock picked in less than a minute and then opened the door to walk in. The dock within the house appeared to be empty, but on closer approach to the water, Diana saw some medium-sized motor boats parked below. Diana went to the furthest and then waited for Tristan to come over.

"Help me lower Everest in," Tristan said, catching up with her.

Diana took the other side and they gently lowered him down into the boat. Tristan took his knife from his wetsuit afterwards and then dropped down. He stabbed the side of the other boat and then sat down. Diana joined him.

"That should prevent them from chasing us..." Tristan said, regaining his breath. "I guess we have to wait for Charles now."

· · · ·

Charlemagne walked down a corridor on the second floor when he heard the alarm go off. He looked around and saw he was clear. He then gained a nervous expression and went for the closest window.

"Where the hell am I?" Charlemagne wondered. "I need to get to the others before any harm comes of them."

Charlemagne continued down the corridor and then around a corner when he met with two security guards.

"The area is not secure," a guard warned him. "We need to evacuate you to the lower levels..."

"No, that's quite alright," Charlemagne replied as a guard grabbed him by the arm.

Charlemagne took a step back and broke free.

"Sir..."

Charlemagne took out his pistol and shot the man before shooting the other.

"Freeze!" a man shouted from behind.

Charlemagne turned and opened fire at him, moving to take cover at a door frame. He quickly took off the mask and shot back at the man.

"I have the intruder at my location," the mercenary reported.

Charlemagne shot back at the merc and was able to graze him. He took the chance to reach the end of the corridor and continue through the other side of a set of double doors. The doors took him to the second level of the foyer. Charlemagne fired at two mercenaries ahead of him and then ran to take cover at the base of a sculpture. The mercenaries were in the open, which meant it was easy to bring them down. Charlemagne looked down and saw that the lower level of the foyer was clear. He proceeded towards the other side of the upper level of the foyer, but the doors opened and mercenaries shot back at him. Charlemagne quickly diverted to the large doors that went into the ritual hall.

On the other side, Charlemagne looked at the doors and picked up a piece of wood that locked the doors. He set his pistol onto a chair and picked it up. He then quickly placed the wood just as they bashed on the door. Charlemagne took his pistol, removed his cloak and carried onwards. The chamber was empty. The Elders had evacuated. Charlemagne went towards the corner and took a candle. He then picked it up and lit fire to the curtains. He then tossed the candle to the floor of the carpet and continued to the back of the room where there was a door out. Charlemagne entered a corridor on the northside of the mansion and saw two mercenaries approach him from the east.

The mercenaries opened fire at him. Charlemagne ducked into cover. He shot back at them, but they were too far to hit precisely. Charlemagne reloaded as they fired at him with their rifles. The window behind Charlemagne shattered. He looked down at the drop that was before him. The mercenaries continued to fire at him as he crouched where he was.

Charlemagne then noticed them approach him as he cowered. He took his pistol and fired blind shots at them before he then put his pistol into its holster and proceeded to gently lower himself from the window. Charlemagne eased himself so that he was approximately six feet from the floor below. He then dropped down, falling on his side as he landed.

"Oof," Charlemagne remarked, clutching his side. "I'm really in no shape to be doing this anymore... Not in my condition."

Charlemagne stood up and then went down the garden that he had entered, reaching a gate at a stone wall. He looked at the padlock and saw that it was locked. He then looked to the side and saw some containers he could climb atop of. Charlemagne went to them and hopped over the wall.

Once on the other side, Charlemagne looked both ways before continuing east towards down the same cliffside path from the sublevel where Everest and the missing children had been kept in. Charlemagne attempted to walk quickly, but he had a minor limp as he refrained from putting pressure on his right foot.

"There he is!" mercenaries shouted from ahead.

Charlemagne rushed into cover by a rock and took out his pistol. He shot back at the mercenaries as they spread out. They put pressure on him with their automatic rifles while he returned fire with the pistol. Charlemagne looked to the side and saw that he had an even steeper drop on his right with sharp rocks below on the beach as he sat with his back to the rock. He continued to return fire, eventually managing to graze a mercenary on the shoulder and shoot another in the chest. Charlemagne reloaded before he came out of cover as they retreated.

The mercenaries fell back, which gave Charlemagne a chance to move forward. He returned to cover at a rock ahead as reinforcements arrived. Again, Charlemagne looked to his side. The cliffs were less steep here. Charlemagne shot at the mercenaries and then brought his legs over to slide down the cliff, rolling at the end, which took less stress from the impact. The mercenaries opened fire on him from above. Charlemagne proceeded to retreat backwards, away from the exit point.

Once Charlemagne was in cover, he took his radio and brought it to his face.

"I'm pinned down," Charlemagne broadcasted. "Are you at the exit yet?"

Charlemagne attempted to return fire.

"We're here," Tristan replied. "Where are you?"

Charlemagne looked around and then around the corner. He could see the boathouse ahead.

"Less than a mile down the beach…" Charlemagne said.

"Roger," Tristan responded. "We're on our way."

• • • •

Tristan stood up in the boat and went to the motor. He then pulled at the start chord.

"Do you even know how that works?" Diana questioned.

"It's got to be like any motor," Tristan responded.

The motor refused to spring to life. Tristan continued to pull at it while Diana moved to a handle with a button on it. She pressed the button down. Once Tristan pulled the chord as she held the button down, the motor came to life and moved out of the boathouse. The pair quickly lost control of the boat as they went away from the island, directly straight up north.

Diana took the turn handle and attempted to turn left, but instead they went right.

"Other way!" Tristan said. "Other way!"

"I'm sorry!" Diana apologized, moving the other way. "The boat is moving too fast!"

The boat began to circle around.

"Is there any way to slow this down?" Tristan questioned, pulling the switch down.

The boat came to a quick stop. The couple lurched forward. Everest was fast asleep and didn't notice anything. The couple had put on a life vest on him while they waited for Charlemagne.

"What are you doing?!" Diana complained. "I said slow down, not turn it off!"

"I know that!" Tristan shouted. "I hit too far back!"

"It's a boat! Throttle it!"

Tristan brought the lever up instead, but the motor had died out. He went to pull the chord again, but it didn't budge. Diana took the lever and placed it in neutral. She then took a hold of the handle and pressed down the button. Tristan pulled at the chord and the boat sprang to life. They didn't move. Tristan went to the lever, gently raised it up, and they began to move at a more manageable speed.

"It's coming back to me now…" Tristan said. "I'm sorry."

Diana looked to him.

"You're lucky I listened when Charlemagne was lecturing us on how to work the yacht."

"He lectured us on that? I thought you were referring to when we were on that research ship in the Arctic."

Diana looked back at Tristan with slight disbelief. The couple slowly took the boat down the coast in search of Charlemagne, but it remained too dark for them to see that far ahead. Charlemagne looked out to the coast as he heard and spotted a moving object in the distance. He then proceeded to wave, but they passed him.

"Damn," Charlemagne remarked, taking his radio. "You've passed me. Turn back around... I'll flash a signal to you."

Diana turned the boat around while Charlemagne took his bodycam and began to flash towards the sea. Tristan pointed out the flashes and they took the boat to the shore. Once Charlemagne could see them approaching he moved towards the beach. The mercenaries had lost track of him from above as he had fallen back further down the beach. The boat came onto the beach while Tristan turned the engine off. Charlemagne brushed against the side of the boat.

"We have to leave quickly," Charlemagne warned. "They're on high alert."

A spotlight shined down on them. Charlemagne pushed the boat back into the water while Tristan reversed. He then climbed into the boat as the bullets started to rain down.

"Get us out of here!" Charlemagne shouted.

Once they were a fair distance from the coast, Tristan took the boat back forward from reverse and Diana steered them out of the way. Luckily, they managed to avoid suffering any bullets to the side of the boat.

"Dad," Charlemagne said, looking to his father. "Is he alright?"

"He's knocked out," Tristan remarked. "It was impossible keeping him awake."

"They must have sedated him," Charlemagne responded. "They've sedated all of their prisoners here."

"You saw the other prisoners?" Tristan asked.

"I saw something much worse, but I can tell you about that later," Charlemagne said. "Right now, we need to focus on escaping because we're not out of the clear yet."

"Do I take us to the yacht?" Diana questioned.

"Yes," Charlemagne responded. "We'll abandon this boat once we return there and then sail away."

Diana and Tristan continued to drive the boat around the mansion island, which was when they met with company on the other side. Charlemagne spotted the boat from earlier as well as two similar black motorboats that had just left the ship.

"Looks like we have company..." Charlemagne remarked, reloading his pistol. "We'll have to lose them. Go past the yacht and continue down the coast of the island. We only need to go as far as they'll chase us..."

"That could be until town," Tristan suggested. "Are you sure?"

"I'm certain," Charlemagne replied, opening fire. "If they'll drive us to town, then so be it. I have a suspicion that you may be right and they may just pursue us until there. Just steer away from deep ocean water – a boat like this can't take it."

"Aye, captain," Diana replied.

The boat went forward and towards the yacht as they began to be chased by the two motor boats from behind. Charlemagne shot back, but at the distance and speed, it was nearly impossible to hit a precise shot, so instead he shot indiscriminately. The boat soon passed the yacht, which took them along the south coast of the main island.

"Steer in random directions! If you steer straight, then they'll shoot us out of the water!" Charlemagne shouted.

Diana began to take them in random directions. Tristan continued to hold the throttle at maximum speed as they zoomed forward at almost forty kilometers per hour. Eventually, Charlemagne landed a random shot on one of the boats, blowing them out of the water, but the other remained ahead almost four-hundred meters behind with another several even further back. Charlemagne reloaded his pistol as Diana took them to the left. Diana quickly turned right as Charlemagne laid down further shots.

Tristan kept his head down as some random gunfire from behind landed in the water beside them. The second boat then ruptured and the mercenaries were left at sea. Charlemagne reloaded and then took a moment to rest.

"Finally..." Charlemagne remarked, taking a deep breath.

"You may want to hold off on that," Tristan remarked, looking back. "They're sending in the big guns..."

Charlemagne turned around and looked behind them. He squinted and sure enough, the patrol boat was gaining on them at a faster speed. There were two of them approaching from either side. Charlemagne returned to prone and aimed his pistol forward, taking some shots.

"Look!" Diana remarked as she looked forward.

Tristan turned his neck and saw what she was looking at. A large grey ship was ahead of them off the south coast. Charlemagne turned around and saw the vessel. He then sat up and looked ahead.

"My goodness," Charlemagne said. "It's a destroyer!"

"That doesn't sound too ominous," Diana sarcastically remarked.

"No," Charlemagne corrected. "it's a U.S. vessel – a warship! Not a destroyer, but a cruiser of the U.S. Navy! Go straight towards it! They'll never open fire on a U.S. warship!"

Diana turned the boat towards the vessel as it was almost a kilometer or two out of reach. Charlemagne took his pistol and held it in both hands. He then took his knife and hid it in the pocket on his lower leg. Charlemagne then looked to Tristan.

"Discard your weapons," Charlemagne said. "We have to present ourselves as peaceful..."

Tristan took his pistol and threw it over the edge. He then took Diana's and did the same. Charlemagne held onto his until they got closer. He then abandoned his favored P99 over the water and sat down as the boat let out a horn. Tristan looked up the side of the beast – the USS Isla Paraiso.

"Tristan, take your knife and stab into the side of the boat as we approach," Charlemagne said. "We'll scuttle our boat and have them rescue us overseas."

Charlemagne moved to grab his father.

"Now!"

Tristan took his knife and stabbed the side of the boat. The boat ruptured and they were soon in the water.

"Help!" Charlemagne shouted as he waved up. "Please, help!"

Tristan looked up and noticed some of the crew members had spotted them. The cruiser moved quickly through the water and by the time an alarm went off, they were far behind. They could hear a P.A. from the ship announce man overboard and the ship also began to blow repeated short horns to signal the same. The four of them simply held on with assurance that they had been heard and they would be rescued. The water in the sea was not too rough for them to hold on, and within minutes, a large speedboat was dropped from the side of the ship and made its way towards them.

Within minutes, they were taken out of the water and back to the cruiser. From there, they met with commanding officers to debrief and identify themselves. They lied about their activities, made no mention to the pursuit, and simply stated that they were tourists. Afterwards, they took them back to the island where Charlemagne quickly found a telephone to make a phone call. He immediately phoned Henry Heavner in Harlech.

"Hello," Heavner greeted. "Who is this?"

Charlemagne didn't waste a moment to spit out the words to him, "Henry, this is Charlemagne. I have evidence that could lead to the arrest of my mother's murderer and the recovery of many missing indigenous children. I need you to leak some information for me as soon as possible."

Epilogue

Charlemagne sat outside his tent on a foldable chair with a drink at his hands. The sun was down and there was a loud banging of drums from nearby and chanting of locals singing songs of joy and celebration with the volunteers. Allodia approached him with another drink in her hand. She offered it to him. Charlemagne looked to her.

"Why do you look so down, Charles? Your man was arrested and the children have been set free," Allodia said. "You should be celebrating with the others."

Charlemagne looked to the bonfire where the indigenous population were dancing around the fire in celebration of Waomoni's arrest.

"There's no reason for me to celebrate," Charlemagne remarked. "The immediate threat against us may be perpetual from now on… We've stirred the hornet's nest and only the doctor and his accomplices were arrested. There remains a world of evil out there, and the sum of the events this past week have not resurrected my mother."

"They've certainly brought out the deep heart and love that she shared with us, and which emanates through you," Allodia responded.

"Of all I've seen in my life, perhaps nothing has been more disturbing than what I witnessed on that mansion, Allodia," Charlemagne vented. "It's like a bad dream, and if I hadn't had that footage… All of those young boys and girls would have been doomed."

"You did good to do what you did," Allodia replied. "I've never been disappointed by you in that regard."

Charlemagne looked aside.

"He's on his own," Charlemagne expressed. "He's lost his life partner. What will happen to him?"

"He'll heal," Allodia said. "He'll manage. I'll be keeping a close eye on him though. I won't let him travel on his own for now. He can help with the Foundation from now on, which is where he belongs."

Charlemagne looked at him with doubt.

"I should go to him," Charlemagne remarked.

"Then go and make your peace with him," Allodia agreed. "He's old and doesn't have much life left in him."

Allodia soon left as she let out a sigh. Charlemagne continued to look towards the sea and over to his father who was by the lips of the water that trickled at his shoes. Everest stared towards the horizon with a gloomier expression than Charlemagne. Charlemagne looked at him for another moment before looking directly forward and down. He then stood up and went to stand next to him.

"I feel like we've spent a great deal of our lives... fighting over her," Charlemagne confessed, "and now she's gone and there's nothing dividing us except ourselves."

"You never understood, Charles," Everest expressed, shaking his head. "I have never actively been in conflict with you – you've always brought the conflict between us yourself."

"You consistently took away a mother from her son," Charlemagne argued. "How could you say that I brought that upon myself? A boy needs his mother..."

"A man needs his wife..." Everest remarked. "Vienna had been my entire world ever since we had met. She was all I ever had. Meanwhile, you were cherished more than my parents had cherished me or even Britannia. Was I wrong to assume that you could have more with them than with us? Perhaps I was wrong to abandon you, but I thought at the time that we could have lived our lives as if we were childfree... However, no matter how much I tried to run, I could never truly escape."

"Nobody can ever escape what awaits them," Charlemagne said, looking at his hand. "Even if we try endlessly to..."

"I'm sorry," Everest expressed. "I'm sorry I was not a better father to you... You deserved better, Charles, and that's all I have ever known. I never wanted you to have what I had, and with Derby, I suppose that was what you received."

Charlemagne nodded to him.

"You have nothing to apologize for," Charlemagne remarked.

Charlemagne sighed.

"What now?" Charlemagne wondered. "If this secret society wanted me dead, they'd have sent someone to finish the job. If I were to assume, they've held their breath and seen that I haven't gone after them, but only Dr. Waomoni. They possibly suspect I have more information that I could release in a second, but they'll surely be keeping a closer eye on me... Whoever these people are that are so foul to prey on the innocent... The thought alone of those that allow children to suffer... it depressed me."

Everest did not respond. Charlemagne let out another sigh.

"What are you going to do?" Charlemagne asked. "The village has been decimated and all of these people are without homes..."

"Only thing that I can do, and that is to help them rebuild their community," Everest expressed. "You're welcome to stay with us and help out."

Charlemagne nodded.

"I'd very much like to," Charlemagne expressed. "Perhaps I can assist in some way that only I can..."

"Financially?" Everest questioned.

"Perhaps," Charlemagne said, "but I've had some ideas run through my mind that I'd like to share with you. Come... I'll show you some designs I've been working on in my tent. I believe I could give these people some form of renewable energy..."

Diana and Tristan watched Everest and Charlemagne from afar. The couple were sat in front of a log on the beach, away from the others. Tristan sat with his knees up, while Diana sat with her legs spread out. Charlemagne and Everest walked back to Charlemagne's tent where they disappeared. Diana let out a deep breath and then placed her head on Tristan's shoulder.

"You did good this month," Diana said to Tristan.

"Huh?"

"All of the work you've done, besides the volunteer work, Tristan," Diana explained. "Beyond the fact you've placed your skills to good use, you've also been really brave and courageous. You're a hero, Tristan. I want you to know that."

Tristan looked to Diana. He then looked back out to the sea.

"I'm not a hero," Tristan modestly remarked. "Really."

"I'm sorry you don't see that," Diana replied, "but maybe it's for the better. God knows though of your exemplary actions on this island. Every woman wants to see their man as a hero..."

Tristan looked back at Diana.

"Alright then, princess," Tristan remarked with a smirk. "If you say so..."

Diana kissed Tristan on the lips. They then parted. Tristan looked at Diana lovingly and continued to kiss her, moving his lips to her cheek and then to her neck. She moaned pleasantly until she gently pushed against Tristan's chest.

"Tristan," Diana cautioned, laughing. "Easy there, you're not a vampire. You're going to leave me bruised..."

"Sorry," Tristan replied, giving a light laugh.

The couple quickly turned their attention to the bonfire as a loud cheer was let out.

"They're really going at it, aren't they?" Tristan remarked.

"They have reason to… they're children have been returned to them," Diana replied. "Wouldn't you feel the same about your own child if he were taken from you?"

"He?"

"Or she," Diana remarked. "Whatever God gives us."

Tristan looked at Diana with slight disbelief, but a minor smile. He then looked out to the sea.

"Who would want to raise a child in this terrible, terrible world," Tristan stated. "Even on this island, which was supposed to be a paradise, we instead found a dystopia. We live in world where creeps like Waomoni exist and secret societies like these 'Children of Moloch…'"

"Evil is not something to fear," Diana earnestly said to Tristan, shaking his arm. "Evil is to be hunted out and destroyed. I hope you're not serious about not wanting to have kids all of the sudden."

Tristan looked to Diana with minor confidence. He nodded as he looked at her eyes.

"No, I'm not," Tristan replied. "I'm just… mad."

"It's okay to be frustrated, but there's no point about being frustrated about that which you can't change. You only harm yourself with that."

"Right…"

Diana took Tristan's arm again and placed her head back on his shoulder. The couple then continued to look out towards the sea whose gentle waves caressed the shore as the two embraced each other from the land known as Isla Paraiso.

"The lies and scams of Marxism present themselves to the suffering and exploited working masses as claims of easy understanding and safe success. Their utopias… seduce the desperate. The little culture of men who work exhaustively, without the time to learn, does not allow them to sense the subtle poison that instills in their brain little by little to plague them."

– Gustavo Barroso